Also available by Holly Danvers

Lakeside Library Mysteries

Long Overdue at the Lakeside Library
Murder at the Lakeside Library

(Writing as Holly Quinn)
Handcrafted Mysteries

A Crafter Quilts a Crime
A Crafter Hooks a Killer
A Crafter Knits a Clue

Read to Death at the Lakeside Library

A LAKESIDE LIBRARY MYSTERY

Holly Danvers

CROOKED LANE

NEW YORK

PUBLISHER'S NOTE: The recipes contained in this book are to be followed exactly as written. The publisher is not responsible for your specific health or allergy needs that may require medical supervision. The publisher is not responsible for any adverse reaction to the recipes contained in this book.

Published in the United States by Crooked Lane Books, an imprint of The Quick Brown Fox & Company LLC.

Crooked Lane Books and its logo are trademarks of The Quick Brown Fox & Company LLC.

Library of Congress Catalog-in-Publication data available upon request.

ISBN (hardcover): 978-1-63910-331-7
ISBN (ebook): 978-1-63910-332-4

Cover design by Jesse Reisch

Printed in the United States.

www.crookedlanebooks.com

Crooked Lane Books
34 West 27th St., 10th Floor
New York, NY 10001

First Edition: August 2023

10 9 8 7 6 5 4 3 2 1

To my lake friends, with love,
for all the fond memories and
laughter I hold dear
and for welcoming me into
your world with such grace.

Chapter One

Rain Wilmot stepped from the log cabin and was immediately met with golden sunshine. In fact, the sun was so bright that she needed to tent her dark eyes before looking beyond the expanse of lawn toward Pine Lake. The body of water was alive with shimmering specks, bouncing and playing across the ripples. Boats sped past, with water-skiers in their wake, and sounds of laughter echoed from nearby swimmers. Rain couldn't have picked a better summer afternoon to host her first book club meeting out on the oversized deck.

Located in the Northwoods of Wisconsin, Lofty Pines in the summertime was Rain's favorite place to be. And now that she was running the Lakeside Library in her great grandfather's original log cabin, on her family's generational compound, she was officially back to being a "Laker." Laker was the term the locals used for those who were fortunate enough to live on or around Pine Lake—something Rain would never *ever* take for granted.

The sound of footsteps, from the staircase leading up to the deck caught Rain's attention, and she turned to see the top of her neighbor's platinum head making the climb.

"Oh, did we luck out, or what? Looks like our weather will hold for the first book club meeting after all!" Julia landed on the top step, and then twirled across the deck, Julie Andrews *Sound of Music* style, as she held her hands to the sky. She then dropped into praying hands as if thanking the weather goddesses for blessing them with remarkable meteorological conditions. The streaks of pink in Julia's hair, which framed her face, shone like cotton candy in the bright sunlight.

"We sure did!" Rain rushed to greet her closest friend with a high five.

"Tomorrow we might be wearing parkas again, but today turned out just about perfect, thank you very much!" Julia sung out with a smile.

"Yeah, I was a little worried when the forecaster mentioned there was a chance of a storm, but thankfully it veered south of us. I really wanted to host our first meeting out here on the deck. The library is just too small to fit a big ole table comfortably, and it sounds like we might have a larger group than I expected this evening."

Julia wagged a finger and smiled knowingly. "Didn't I tell you that the summer book club would turn into a Lofty Pines hotspot! Even when Willow was hosting it, we were growing into a sizable gathering. When is your mother expected to arrive? Is she joining us to discuss our Agatha Christie pick? Your mom always loved a good mystery."

"Mom is leaving all the library duties to me this summer. She said she wants to officially hand over the baton, refrain from the bulk of volunteering, and travel the world with my father. He has enough frequent flier miles to go around the globe and back again. Today, they're en route to Italy; tomorrow, who knows where." Rain shrugged. "I'm sure they'll be back in a few weeks to spend a weekend, but I doubt she'll be helping at the library or staying long enough for book discussions. Unless, of course, I let her in on what we're reading, and she happens to land up here during one of our scheduled meetings."

"And Stuart? What does your father think of all this togetherness? He's so accustomed to traveling for work, alone. Early retirement going well, then?"

"You know, I'm not sure what my father thinks. He sort of keeps a tight lip about stuff like that. But, according to my mother, things have been great between them. She said experiencing new places with my father has enlivened their relationship in a way she never thought possible. I'm happy for them. Seems like they're finally in a good place."

Julia patted Rain on the shoulder encouragingly. "That's so good to hear, Rainy. I know it hasn't always been smooth sailing for them."

The sound of barking caught both their attention as Rex, Marge Duncan's cocker spaniel, came to greet them, with his tail wagging.

"Hey there, Rexy!" Rain knelt to give the dog a pat on the head and scratch under his chin. His fur was so soft to the touch, it instantly lowered her blood pressure. The dog seemed to relish the attention too with a lolling tongue. Marge rounded the corner, lugging a large tote with a bag of potato chips toppling out of it.

"Let me help you with that." Rain rushed to the older woman, removed the tote from her arms, and set it down on a nearby table.

Marge responded with a relieved grunt. "Thank you, my dear."

"You're early, Marge. Book club doesn't start for well over a half hour." Julia said.

"I thought you might need some help setting up, and besides, there's no place I'd rather be than here with my two favorite library ladies." Her sapphire eyes beamed as she adjusted a sun visor over her soft silver waves.

"We're always happy to have your help and see your smiling face." Julia chuckled. "And I can't wait to hear what you thought of *Sparkling Cyanide*. Did Agatha Christie meet your expectations on this one?"

"Oh nooo, my dear. I know you're anxious, but my lips are sealed." Marge warned with a finger to her lips and a lopsided smile. "No discussing the book until all guests have arrived." She lifted her chin in teasing indignation and then took a step closer to the door, leading to the main log cabin. "You mind if I grab Rex a water dish?" She turned to Rain then, waiting for approval. "We've been running errands all afternoon."

"Sure—help yourself. You know where I keep stuff for Rex—you'll find his bowl tucked over by the dog treats."

Marge cocked her head, and her thin brows narrowed in uncertainty.

"In the closet, by the side door," Rain added because she got the impression Marge didn't remember. And then expressed a look of concern to Julia.

Marge seemed to repeatedly forget things lately, and it was mildly concerning to Rain. She hadn't voiced her thoughts about it to Julia yet. But based on their shared look of concern, she noted she wasn't alone in the feeling. And she'd be lying if she said Marge hadn't been on the forefront of her mind lately. Her coworker was always very good about returning books to their proper place on the bookshelves. But Rain had noticed a few books not shelved within the correct genre, and Marge had been the one who had handled the reshelving. It was disconcerting to say the least, especially since Marge was also the library's treasurer.

Rain was about to take the older woman by the arm and show her once again, but then Marge took another moment, and the realization seemed to finally kick in. "Ah, yes, I remember now—the closet by the door. I've got it." she repeated with a snap of her fingers. "I'll go and fill his bowl and be right back."

"Take your time, and grab whatever you need." Rain smiled. "We're good out here." She removed the hairband from her wrist and pulled her straight black hair into a makeshift ponytail atop her head, which instantly cooled the back of her neck. She then carried on with her duties and moved to tuck an Adirondack chair around the oversized table. Julia placed a cheese and summer sausage charcuterie board atop the table and then hurried to aid with chairs.

"Yes, we're going to have to discuss that." Julia nodded her head in the direction of the door where Marge had already disappeared. "But not tonight—it's not the time nor the place. It'll have to wait."

"You mean our forgetful friend in there? I agree." Rain breathed deeply. It wasn't exactly a conversation she was ready to have because it might change things, and change was something she was often trying to control and avoid. Life could be so fleeting. Losing her husband Max in an untimely motorcycle accident had taught her that.

"How many chairs you think we need? I can go snag more fold-ups from my house if we don't have enough?" Julia asked as she lugged another chair closer to the table. "Maybe I should, just in case. So we have backup."

"Or better yet, give Nick a call on your cell. I'm sure he'll resurrect some from storage." Julia's husband was always willing to lend a hand with any handyman projects, lawn care questions, or anything else that Rain needed. Nick Reynolds was a godsend of a neighbor, and she was grateful that Julia outsourced him willingly. Being an only child, he was the closest thing to a brother Rain had experienced in her world.

"Are you kidding? With me not around, Nick was thrilled to escape for the evening. He's out fishing with Seth. But I can go and grab a few if you think we need more."

"Nah, we should have enough. But if Nick's out fishing with Seth, will Kim be able to come tonight? She was so looking forward to book club." Rain frowned. "I'll be bummed if she's a no-show."

"No worries, Kim phoned this morning. Her mom is watching the twins so she can come." Julia confirmed with a tap to the table.

"Oh, that's good. I'd hate for her to miss the first meeting. Especially when it's the time introductions are made, and we'll get to know everyone."

Marge returned, juggling Rex's water bowl, so Rain rushed to open the sliding door.

"Thank you, dear," Marge grunted as she set the dog's bowl aside, out of the way of being a trip hazard. Rex immediately came and lapped up the water.

"You *were* thirsty!" Rain said with a smile as she watched the dog lick the bowl almost dry. "Rex, you're so cute!" The dog looked up at her with a lolled tongue and seemed to smile at her compliment.

"When are you going to finally make the leap and rescue a dog?" Marge asked. "I can see it in your eyes, the love you have for my Rexy. Wouldn't you like a companion here with you at night? Something to consider . . ." She let the comment hang. It wasn't the first time Marge had suggested she get a dog. Rain wondered if she was forgetting that too.

"Yeah, I'd be lying if I said I haven't been thinking about it more and more," Rain admitted. "And I know we've talked about it at length before, but it has to be the right fit. I'm not sold on a specific breed or anything. I just want an emotional connection to happen, you know? I think I'll know when I know, if that makes sense?"

"Hey, ladies!" Kim Rogers rounded the corner of the deck, her hair gleaming like red curled ribbons in the sunshine. Her cinnamon-freckled face was sunburnt, and her green eyes alive with excitement. "I'm so happy for a night out!" She lifted a bottle of red wine from a paper bag and handed it to Rain. "I brought two! Red and white!" she squealed. "Maybe I should've brought more? I might even need a ride home." She giggled. "Or I'll crash at your place, Julia."

Julia smiled. "*Mi casa es su casa!* Whatever you need, Kim. You know Nick and I will always make room for you."

Kim beamed.

"We're so glad you could make it! I was worried you wouldn't get a sitter." Rain accepted the wine bottle from Kim and set it alongside Marge's tote. She reorganized the growing items on the table before confirming, "I think we'll have enough wine. Believe me when I say Julia filled my refrigerator yesterday in preparation." This caused the group of them to send high fives Julia's way. Which she took in stride, as a grin washed over her face.

Rain didn't drink very often—only on occasion. However, starting the new book club, because of her slight introvert jitters, might have her reaching for a glass. Hosting this book club was kind of stepping out of her comfort zone. Stepping out in faith that she could handle herself without her deceased husband, Max, at her side, and become a leader in social situations. Although, with Julia around, for the first time since losing Max she didn't truly feel alone. Her bestie had been right by her side for the last year and a half, through her tears, willing her back to life. Relocating from the high rise in Milwaukee that she had shared with

Max to her family's weekend log cabin had been just what the doctor ordered. Reconnecting with her childhood Laker friends had helped greatly too. It was like boomeranging in time back to people with whom she had a deep history. There had been a pureness about those bygone days, a pureness that seemed to carry into adulthood, as they often seemed to revert to their childlike ways. Especially when Julia and Kim were around.

Before long, the deck was filled with chatter and laughter. Rain wondered how she would corral this lively group for the book discussion. If she waited too much longer, the effects of the wine might hamper the book chat completely and instead lead to summer party mode. She wanted guests to get to know each other—that was important too. But for how long? At times like these, she really missed Max. He knew how to lead a conversation and would know just what to do. She reached for the plate of brownies and held them up in demonstration.

"Ladies! We have brownies courtesy of Brewin Time!" Rain said as she led the plate beneath several noses. The fragrance of chocolate caused the women to follow the scent like a pack of bloodhounds. She set the brownies in the center of the table, and hands reached wildly to snag one before they all disappeared. Rain smiled inwardly. "Now. If we can all take a seat? Our first official book discussion is about to begin."

Little did Rain know, rallying the ladies together for their first book discussion might be the least of her problems.

Chapter Two

Rain swirled her glass of red wine and took a quick sip before interrupting the chatter between the group of women settled around the table. Julia, seated one spot over from her, with Marge sandwiched between them, flashed her an encouraging smile as Rain began.

"Thank you for coming this evening and joining us for our first book club discussion, on *Sparkling Cyanide* by Agatha Christie. How about we introduce ourselves before we begin? Go ahead and share your name and anything else you'd like to add." Rain cleared her throat before continuing. "I'll start. My name is Rain Wilmot, and for those of you who don't know, I run the Lakeside Library here at my family's log cabin. My great-grandfather Lorenzo built the original cabin behind this one and turned it into a library when his son Luis authored a few books. Originally, the library was just a haven for family members, but a few years ago, my mother, Willow, opened it up to the Lofty Pines community. And most of you have visited, as I recognize more than a few faces." She smiled as her eyes traveled to those gathered around the table and then landed on the older woman sitting next to her. Rain patted Marge's hand as a prompt for her to continue the introductions. Then she added, "Marge grew up with my grandfather, Luis, right here on Pine Lake. Isn't that right?"

"Yes, dear." Marge mirrored Rain's smile before turning her attention to the rest of the group. "Hello to old friends and new ones! I'm really looking forward to meeting everyone and learning your story—everyone has a story, yes? I'm Marjorie, but everyone calls me Marge. And that dog over there, basking in the sun, is my baby, Rex." They all turned to see Rex stretching out languidly on the deck, as if he owned the place. "Yes, it's true," she continued. "I've been coming up to Pine Lake for *decades* and grew up with Luis and a few others that have unfortunately passed on. I'm sure I'm the oldest one here tonight." She laughed as she clasped her liver-spotted hands in front of her. "After my husband and I retired to Florida, we typically only returned to Lofty Pines during the summer months. But now that my husband is gone, Rain and Julia have become like my surrogate family." She beamed. "And so I work at the library year-round now. What's down in Florida for a young chicken like me anyhow?" Marge clucked her tongue as she looked to Julia to take over the conversation.

Julia grinned from ear to ear. "Yes, it's true—we love Marge as our own." She tapped the older woman on the arm gently before continuing. "Hi, everyone, I'm Julia Reynolds and I live next door with my husband, Nick. I see a lot of familiar faces around the table, but for those who don't know me, I also work at the library during the summer. So, if there's ever a title you need me to help you find, I'm your gal!" she said enthusiastically. "I substitute teach high school the rest of the year, but I still work at the library on my days off—or whenever I can, really. I actually declined a full-time position and only teach when they really need me now because, between you and me," she said conspiratorially, "I'd rather work here at the library. And I *love* a good mystery!

In fact, mysteries might just be my favorite genre. I'm excited to discuss today's title." Julia turned to the woman sitting next to her, who caught onto the prompt.

"Hi, I'm Lily Redlin." A woman Rain guessed was twenty years her senior introduced herself and then smiled brightly at the rest of the group. Rain didn't recognize Lily from her Laker days and understood why when she continued. "I've lived off-lake in Lofty Pines most of my adult life, but I'm in the process of putting my house on Sycamore Street up for sale. It's a beautiful home, and I worked really hard as an accountant all of my adult life to earn it, but life is short, and I want to simplify and live by the water. I recently purchased a property about ten houses down." She waved a hand in the direction of her new home. "I can't wait to live on the lake so I can kayak every morning and sit on my deck with a cup of coffee and a good book. And I'm excited to be here, as I'm a total book nerd. I love mysteries too. But I'll read just about anything." She sent a crooked smiled to Julia and then adjusted purple-framed glasses on her nose and smoothed her auburn hair.

Clasping her hands in front of her, the woman with the sharp pixie cut and manicured nails continued the conversation going around the table. "Hey, everyone!" She waved shyly. "I'm Shelby Sullivan, and I live a few doors down from Lily's new lake house. Which is funny because we went to high school together, and now we're practically neighbors!" She twirled her hair between her fingers nervously. "I love romance books, but it was okay to read a mystery one too, I guess. I just want to be here with other people who like to read as much as I do. My husband, Dirk, hates reading, or anything romantic for that matter." She frowned. "Anyhow, enough about Dirk." She turned to the sharply dressed woman sitting beside her and said, "You go."

"I'm so thankful that the Lakeside Library is hosting this book club," the woman wearing a fashionable silk blouse and skillfully applied makeup said. Her black hair was perfectly coiffed, and she sent a radiant smile toward Rain, showing gleaming white teeth. "I'm Naomi Mosely, and I'm excited to be here and meet new people." Her smile was contagious, showing deep dimples, and several around the table had no choice but to mirror it back. "I've been coming up to Pine Lake for the last few years since my real estate business took off. In fact, I recently bought a brokerage in the area. I currently rent a condo in town, but I also bought a tiny cottage here on the lake that I'm revamping." She turned to acknowledge the woman with the purple glasses with a nod. "Just like you, Lily." Naomi's gaze returned to regard the rest of the group. "If anyone knows of a property coming up for sale or is looking to sell their own, please make sure and take a card." She removed a stack of business cards from her purse and fanned them out on the table, and Lily rose from her seat and took one. "Oh—and not that it matters—but one more thing: I think I'll probably end up being single for the rest of my life, because I recently turned thirty-nine and still haven't met 'the one.'" She held her manicured fingers in air quotes and continued. "I've pretty much given up on men."

"My dear girl, when you're least expecting it, you'll run into him." Marge said with a twinkle in her eye. "A pretty thing like you won't be single long."

Rain couldn't help but agree with Marge. She couldn't understand why Naomi was single if she didn't want to be, because clearly the woman was stunning and held a solid career. To Rain, she seemed like the perfect catch.

"Hi everyone, I'm Kim." The woman waved both hands enthusiastically, as if she were a participant driving along a parade route.

"I'm a busy stay-at-home mom. I have a set of twin boys—Rory and Ryder—who keep me on my toes." She reached for her wineglass and took a huge gulp. "I don't get out much." She giggled. "Trust me when I say I plan on *never* missing a meeting. I don't care what book we read! I'm just happy to be here." Kim then elbowed the woman to her right.

"Hello, folks, I'm Ruth Thompson," a deep voice bellowed out. Ruth's hair, the color of a squirrel's tail, was cropped short and resembled an old-fashioned swimming cap, tight to her head. She too had a radiant smile as she regarded the group. "I'm probably closest to you in age," she said, looking to Marge with a twinkle in her hazel eyes. "I'm a ferocious reader. I always have a book in my hand or close by in my purse. I even keep one in the car, for doctor appointments and such. So, I'm glad we're planning to meet every other week. I was worried we would only meet once a month." She bestowed a hearty laugh that seemed to fit her voluptuous physique. "And that's just not often enough, in my opinion, especially in the summer." She turned to the woman seated next to her. "That's all I have to say. Your turn."

"Hi everyone, I'm Chelsea McAdams. I manage Brewin' Time, the coffee shop in downtown Lofty Pines. Is this not the perfect spot to host a book club?" Her brown eyes, the color of espresso, traveled to the lake, where the sun was setting and leaving both water and sky a deep lavender. Puffy pink clouds were floating across the sky and reflecting in the placid water. "I'm so happy to be here with y'all. I moved up here from North Carolina about two years ago and never looked back. My parents were born up here, but my father relocated to the south for work, where I was born. Oh, and I seek out books by Wisconsin authors because someday I want to follow in their footsteps. I'm hoping for a chance to publish some of my poetry. Maybe someday, if I'm lucky, I'll get the opportunity. Perhaps after I retire, but I've got ten more years to slave before then!"

She removed eyeglasses from a case, adjusted the brown-framed glasses on her nose, and tucked her dirty blond hair behind one ear. "Anyhow, I'd love to read your grandfather's work, Rain. Especially since he lived here in Lofty Pines. How amazing is that! An author from our little town here," She cooed. "I also host Wisconsin authors at the coffee shop for book signings, so I'll keep you all posted if we have someone pop up on the schedule this summer."

Rumbles of excitement bubbled up from the group at the idea of a meeting with a local author.

Rain briefly interrupted by pointing to the center of the table and saying, "Yes, and we can all thank Chelsea for the brownies we just thoroughly enjoyed, courtesy of Brewin' Time. Aren't they to die for?"

In hindsight, this assessment was, perhaps, a bit too on the nose . . .

Chapter Three

All that remained on the oversized patio table were remnants of brownie crumbs, littered potato chips, and dried-up nuggets of cheese atop paper plates, as the Lakeside Library book club carried on their conversation into the twilight. The strings of patio lights shimmered on the deck while slow-moving boats putted across Pine Lake for one last cruise before dusk. Thanks to Kim and Julia, though, the alcohol supply was still flowing as members continued to sip from their wineglasses and enjoy the soft breeze rolling off the water.

"What did you think of Agatha Christie using cyanide as the murder weapon for the victim?" Rain asked the group.

Julia lifted a hand to share. "I'm not sure about the murder weapon, but I thought it was brilliant the way George gathered the suspects around the table, with each of them having a potential motive for killing his wife, Rosemary. But I wasn't expecting George to be the next victim—not even a little." She moved her fingers together to demonstrate how small. Julia took a sip of her wine and set the glass back down on the table before licking her finger and picking up the remainder of potato chip crumbs off her plate.

"Did you know Agatha Christie worked as a pharmacist in England during the First and Second World Wars, and that's why she used poison in her books? It was familiar to her." Marge said, circling the topic back to the discussion of the murder weapon. Rex sat at her feet, and Marge leaned over to stroke the dog as she carried on the conversation. "Agatha was a fascinating woman. Few women had the opportunity to publish fiction back then, and for her to push through the glass ceiling and write mysteries was quite extraordinary. She really opened the door for so many authors."

"I think I heard that before, that she used her war experience where she acquired a knowledge of the poisons used in military hospital dispensaries," Ruth agreed as she stroked her neck. "Interesting indeed that she would draw on her own life experiences in her novel like that."

"Yeah, and the book was written so long ago. So, I agree, it's interesting, to say the least," Lily said.

"I saw an episode of *Dateline* two weeks ago where a woman killed her husband using a bottle of eye drops. Did you know the same thing that you put in your eyes, if you ingest it, can kill you?" Shelby asked with a grimace. "How does *that* work?"

"I caught that episode too! Sean said it gave him the creeps to know how easy it was to find something over the counter that could actually kill someone!" Kim interjected.

"Not a chance! You can't be serious," Naomi exclaimed, sitting a little higher in her chair. "That can't *possibly* be true. How can eye drops kill you?"

"It's true!" Shelby vigorously nodded her head. "And supposedly it's tasteless too." She covered the top of her wineglass with her hand and giggled nervously. "Watch your glasses, ladies," she teased. And the group erupted in laughter.

"Your husband, Dirk, better watch out for sure, huh? Should I warn him?" Lily chimed in with a lopsided smile. And then Shelby shot her a dirty look.

"I'm glad I don't drink wine!" Ruth bellowed before lifting her water bottle and taking a nice long swig, then wiping her mouth with the back of her hand. "Nothing like spring water to quench your thirst! That stuff will be the death of you, never mind the cyanide. It certainly killed my brother's liver!" she cautioned before holding up crossed fingers as a warning sign.

"I dunno . . . wasn't it Jesus himself who turned water into wine? Who said wine could kill you? Everything in moderation, I say," Kim interjected with a laugh. "In fact, I'm going for a refill before the night is through. Anyone else?" she questioned before lifting the wine bottle to top off her glass.

Naomi lifted a finger in response, so Kim refilled Naomi's glass too before setting the bottle back onto the table.

"Back to the book: I don't think Rosemary loved George. I don't even think she liked him." Lily frowned and then adjusted her purple-framed glasses back on her nose. "Some people just shouldn't be married. Maybe she deserved what she got."

"Are you kidding me? I think that's a bit of a leap." Shelby shook her head. "I mean, how can you judge someone's feelings like that? And you think she deserved to die for it? Who are you to know what goes on behind closed doors in a marriage—and understand the complexities of it? You're not even married, Lily!" Shelby set her wine down on the table a little too hard, causing it to almost spill over.

"Well, Rosemary *cheated* on him, didn't she, with that Farraday character? I can't even remember his name," Lily said defensively. "What was the point of her being married and in love if she was going to cheat!"

"You mean Stephen Farraday?" Ruth replied, looking in her notes.

"Yeah, whatever." Lily waved a hand of dismissal. "And for what? Why'd she cheat on George? She didn't need the money, so she didn't marry him for his wealth. She was decades younger than him. Why was she married to the old guy to begin with? If she wanted a different life?" Lily threw up her hands in frustration. "I didn't like that part. It made me want to close the book. It wasn't realistic why she'd even be married to George in the first place."

"Did the book even say how long they were married?" Naomi asked.

"I don't think so. I think it just alluded to the fact that he was a safe, older man," Ruth replied.

"I think that's the point Agatha Christie was maybe trying to make in the novel. She was creating strong motives for her suspects, don't you think?" Rain piped up. Although she would be lying if she said she didn't also feel the sting of Christie's words about infidelity. Max had cheated on her when, in the aftermath of failed in vitro treatments, their marriage became mechanical and Rain was desperate for a baby. It was like ripping a Band-Aid off her feelings about Max's indiscretions all over again. She and Lily might just have something in common besides the book.

"I couldn't believe George hired an actress to sit at the table to impersonate Rosemary," Kim said matter-of-factly.

Rain wondered if Kim had said that to settle the uptick of tension within the group, but instead it backfired.

"What are you talking about? The actress didn't show up," Lily said sternly.

"What do you mean?" Kim asked.

"The actress . . . the one George hired in the book . . . she never showed up at the table," Lily said, clearly growing frustrated.

Kim's face twisted. "She didn't?"

"Nope. You didn't read the book, did you, Kim?" Lily demanded. She leaned forward and pressed her hands firmly on the table, waiting for an explanation.

Kim didn't answer, but just shrunk back in her chair and spun the wineglass in front of her.

"I think you're completely missing the point." Chelsea shook her head. "This isn't a book about infidelity—or actresses who may or may not have shown up. It's about the motivations of the suspects, just like Rain said. Her books are like a puzzle that you're supposed to try and figure out."

Lily folded her arms across her chest protectively and sat back in the chair, closing her lips in a firm line. She rolled her eyes and slowly shook her head, as if completely offended.

It was evident to Rain that the discussion was getting a little heated, and maybe both Lily and Kim were feeling ganged up on. This was *not* what she had hoped for the first book club meeting, and she looked to Julia with pleading eyes.

"You know, I had to make a chart," Julia said upon seeing Rain's signal for help, and she removed a sheet of paper from her book and held it up for the book club members to see. "I wrote down each suspect and their potential motive so I could keep it all straight. I really felt like I was playing a game of Clue. It was fun for me to try and piece the mystery together, but I admit I wasn't expecting the twist in the end. Were any of you?" Her eyes darted around the table as if hoping others would help pull the conversation back to the riddle aspect of the mystery.

"Yes! That twist surprised me too," Naomi agreed with a nod. "I think it was well written, and I can see why Agatha Christie's books have withstood the test of time and why she's considered the Queen of Mystery—or something to that effect.

Lily's right; Wasn't the original manuscript written a very long time ago?"

Rain removed a notebook from beneath her copy of the book. "I did a little digging, and I wrote this down in case it came up, so I'm glad you asked, Naomi. The original manuscript was published in 1945 under the title *Remembered Death*, and it expands another short story of Agatha Christie's called 'Yellow Iris.'"

"Isn't that interesting!" Ruth said. "I love hearing about the historical record of things. Thank you for sharing that. Maybe it's me, in my old bones, but I find that fascinating." She leaned forward in her chair as if hoping for more history to tumble out of Rain's mouth.

"I couldn't believe Iris was about to be poisoned too, and they caught on to it just in the nick of time," Kim said, throwing her hand over her mouth to cover a hiccup.

"See now we all *know* you didn't read it." Lily stated with an eyeroll.

"What are you talking about?" Kim looked bewildered. "Sure I did."

"No, you didn't. Explain yourself." Lily demanded, her face turning a darker shade of pink.

Kim set down her glass of wine and then 'fessed up. "Fine. I watched *Sparkling Cyanide* on Brit Box, okay?"

"Oh, for Pete's sake," Lily huffed. "I thought this was a serious book club. Not a wine club." She rested her head in her hands and rubbed her temples vigorously, as though she were warding off a migraine.

"Don't be so hard on her. Kim has a set of twins who keep her incredibly busy," Julia defended. "It's hard for her to make time to read." She sent a sympathetic glance Kim's way.

"Yeah, she just wanted a night out. I certainly understand that. All I do is work, work, work! It's fun to get together with y'all," Chelsea piped up, and she downed her wine, causing her to hold back a belch with the back of her fist. Then she smiled sheepishly, seemingly embarrassed by her behavior.

Lily threw out a hand in Kim's direction and said, "But she shouldn't be discussing the book if she didn't actually read it." She stated this as if Kim wasn't even present at the table.

"Back off, Lily. I think you're being too judgy." Ruth said, crushing her water bottle, which set Rex off, barking at the noise.

Marge's eyes widened in surprise—at the comment or the crushing of the water bottle or her dog barking, Rain couldn't determine.

"Forgive me!" Lily threw up her fingers in air quotes. "But I thought this was a book club! Not just a social gathering. If I wanted to hang out and drink, I'd go to the bar!"

A chill came over Rain, and her bare arms erupted in goosebumps. She looked desperately for the sun, which had officially slipped behind the horizon. "Ladies, this has been a lively discussion, and I'm incredibly thankful you all came to discuss *Sparkling Cyanide*. Now, I think it might be time we call it a night."

Groans erupted from those gathered around table.

"Ohh, already? That went fast!" Kim hiccupped before she downed the rest of her wine. And then reached for the bottle for a half glass more.

Julia agreed with a sad face. "That discussion really did go fast. What are we reading next, Rain?"

"Well, Shelby, I think you'll be happy with the next book." Rain looked to Shelby, who was already gathering her things and shouldering her purse as if readying for a quick exit. Rain hoped she'd be back for the next discussion, and tempted her by saying,

"We're leaving mystery behind and heading to romance." She reached to grab a box of books next to her seat and hand them out. She was happy when Shelby leaned over to investigate the cover and then slipped the book into her purse.

Rain hoped a little love and romance was just what the book club needed to solidify their new group.

Chapter Four

Heavy raindrops pelted the windows of the Lakeside Library, making a rather soothing sound within the bookish space. Sometimes a summer storm was the perfect excuse to tuck within the bookshelves and escape into a novel. It was early, though—just before opening time—as Rain walked past the Franklin stove, now shut down until winter.

It wasn't the only thing that had been taking a break, she thought as she touched a hand atop the cold stove in remembrance. Her relationship with the man who had installed it, Ryan Wright, from Wright Installation, had cooled too. Yes, they had gone on a few casual dates and had enjoyed each other's company over a few Friday night fish fries, but something had been missing. Rain hadn't been able to put her finger on it. She wasn't sure if it had just been too soon after Max's death to take the leap back into a serious relationship again. Or if there was more to it than that.

Ryan was devilishly handsome, so it certainly wasn't due to a lack of physical attraction. But she was secretly glad when he'd mentioned that he'd be working a few hours south of Lofty Pines for a while, in preparation for opening a satellite location of his father's business. It would give them the time apart she needed to sort out her feelings. Sometimes Rain missed him, but she realized as time marched on, and phone calls waned, that she hadn't really missed him enough. Although she secretly wondered if he could indeed be "Mr. Right."

The thought that Ryan might relocate to run the second location full time played heavily on her mind as well. She was so deeply connected to the Lakeside Library that the very idea of leaving Lofty Pines left her breathless. Was that the real reason she had chosen to take a step backward in the relationship? she wondered.

And then there was Julia's brother, Jace, who was constantly bringing her flowers from the greenhouse located next to his job at the police station, but wouldn't act any further on his affections. Had it been because of Ryan that he hadn't? Or was it because of her reluctance, which ran deeper than that? Jace was her best friend's brother, and she was fully aware that was why she had stifled her feelings toward him. She wondered if he felt the same. Julia entered the library then, which swayed Rain's thoughts back to the present as they exchanged a friendly wave.

"Morning," Julia said, as she lowered the hood of her yellow raincoat from atop her head and smoothed her hair. "Maybe I should have waited for the storm to blow over before trekking over here." She laughed. "I'm sure I look like a drowned rat."

Rain noticed then that her friend's hair was a bit matted to her head and wet along the edges of her face. "Yeah, I could've handled things over here if you'd wanted to wait."

"Nick offered to drop me off on his way into town, but I didn't realize how hard the rain was coming down until I was halfway here. At least it's a warm summer storm." Julia shrugged, then bent over and shook her hair out before combing through it with her fingers.

"Which could make for an awfully humid day when it finally stops." Rain sighed.

"Yeah, there's that." Julia nodded as she hung her slicker on a coatrack to dry. A crack of loud thunder caused her to nearly jump out of her skin. "Aww, duck water!" she squealed, holding her heart. "Where on earth did that come from!"

Rain laughed. "You crack me up with your expletives."

"Well, just because I'm not teaching at the moment doesn't mean I shouldn't still refrain from using bad language. Cut me some slack—I'm really trying," Julia cajoled. "There's no one in here, right?" She then lifted onto her tiptoes and scanned the bookshelves to verify.

"Nope, you're good. I haven't flipped the 'Open' sign yet."

"Oh, thank goodness." Julia deflated with relief. "How do you think the book club went last night? It was a lively discussion and lots of participation, no? It seems we don't have a quiet one in the group, which is a good thing. Usually, it's hard to get people to open up, so I think it went okay for the first night."

"Yeah, I think the first one went well, but . . ." Rain's voice trailed as she picked up a book that had been left haphazardly aside, and moved to reshelve it.

Julia followed her down the aisle.

"What's wrong?" Julia moved over to Rain's side and leaned a comforting hand on her friend's shoulder. "I know you were nervous about it, but you didn't need to be. I thought you did great leading the discussion. And I'm sure it'll get easier for you in time."

"Thanks. I appreciate that, but it's not what's nagging me at the moment."

"What is it then?"

Rain leaned back against the bookshelf and crossed her arms thoughtfully. "I'm not worried about Kim, because honestly, I think she was too tipsy to even care. However, is it me, or did Lily leave a little bit upset last night? The last thing I want is for someone to leave book club with a bad taste in her mouth. I couldn't get Lily off my mind when I was getting ready for bed. I feel bad. Am I being too sensitive?" Rain chewed at her thumbnail and waited, hoping that she was completely overthinking it.

"No Rain. You're being you." Julia reached out to give her a hug, and Rain willingly accepted and then leaned her head on her friend's shoulder. "And that's why we all love you, my dear." Julia held her at arm's length and met her eyes to confirm Rain had gotten the message loud and clear before finally releasing her.

"Should I call and check on her do you think? Or is that overkill? Maybe I should just let it go."

"Or maybe, if this is really bothering you . . ." Julia lifted a finger as if a brilliant thought had just popped into her head. "I have a better idea."

"What's that."

"How about, when Marge arrives, you and I head over to Lily's new cottage and check it out? Didn't she mention she was spending the night out there? We have the perfect excuse: we just tell her we're being nosy, and we wanted to see her new place. I mean, seriously, she's almost our neighbor. We could even bring a housewarming gift! We'll stop at the greenhouse on the way and pick up a potted geranium or something."

Rain rolled the idea around in her mind.

"Come on—it's actually not far from the truth," Julia confessed. "I really wanna see which house she bought and what kind of shape it's in. Is that bad?"

"No, seems like a plausible excuse."

"Right? So, it's a plan." Julia confirmed with a smile and then moved on with her librarian duties by flipping the sign on the door to "Open" and then returning to the small desk to reboot the computer.

As soon as Julia turned the sign over, patrons rushed in, out of the downpour, and scattered into the library like picnic ants.

Rain loaded a stack of books into her arms and moved to reshelve them, all the while wondering what she should say to win back Lily's trust, in hopes that the disgruntled book club member would give the club a second chance.

A patron interrupted her thoughts and said, "Oh, I was so disappointed to miss the discussion last night. I was excited to dig into an Agatha Christie novel because mysteries are my favorite genre! I'd love to join the book club. Is it too late?"

Rain turned to see a tall woman, which was saying something, as she herself stood five feet nine inches. The woman was wearing pale green hospital scrubs that matched her eyes perfectly.

"Yes, we discussed *Sparkling Cyanide* last night. It was a good first meeting. Hopefully, you can make the next one—though we're exploring all genres. In fact, we have a romance picked for next week's discussion," Rain said. "I lead the book group—I'm Rain." She laughed as she looked up at the tongue-and-groove ceiling, where the rain was still pounding away at the roof, like a drum. "Yep, just like today's storm. I'm sorry, but you don't look familiar. Have we met before?"

"Cool name, Rain. I'm Hannah." The woman in scrubs flung out a hand for a proper introduction.

"Nice to meet you, Hannah. Welcome to the Lakeside Library." Rain smiled.

"This place is really cool." Hannah's eyes traveled the thick pine walls with deep chinking, and then she scanned the stacked bookshelves in awe before returning her attention back to Rain.

"Thank you. The original structure was built by my great-grandfather. I live in the newer log cabin, connected by the catwalk. The one facing the lake," Rain explained.

"Wow. Well, it's absolutely, positively stunning! How nice of you to share it with the community."

"Thanks. Did you grow up in the Northwoods? I'm assuming you live here in Lofty Pines?"

"No. I'm a traveling nurse. I previously handled hospice, and unfortunately my patient recently passed away, so I've been tentatively relocated to the area for work. A friend recommended me. Do you know a man named Alec Shields? I was just reassigned to him, to work as his private nurse while he recovers from a rather intense surgical procedure. He's wheelchair bound at the moment, so I'll be around for the summer, at the very least."

"No, I can't say I've heard of Mr. Shields, but it sounds like he's in good hands," Rain said warmly.

"Anyhow," Hannah continued, "I was really looking forward to the book club discussion last night, but I ended up working later than I'd hoped. I was sad that I had to miss it." She sighed. "Hopefully, next time it will all work in my favor."

"Oh, I'm sorry you missed it too. But, hey, thank you for the work you do. I'm sure it's hard to care for others, knowing their days are numbered. You mentioned that, prior to Alec, you worked in hospice. I can't even imagine—it must be so hard . . ." Rain's voice softened.

"It can be. But it has its rewards too. We all have one thing in common: none of us will live forever. It's true for everyone—right?" Hannah frowned. "All our days are numbered."

"Yes, I suppose you're right. I never really thought about untimely deaths until I lost my husband in a motorcycle accident."

"I'm so sorry."

Rain could sense the genuine concern in her tone. "I appreciate that. Anyhow, enough about death—back to the land of the living." Rain forced a smile and then pointed to Julia, where she remained behind the computer at the checkout desk. "Julia has books over there if you want to grab the next book club pick. We meet every other Tuesday evening at six o'clock. And if you want to bring a snack or drinks to share, you can, but it's certainly not mandatory."

"Thanks! I'll do that. I look forward to joining in with everyone. Nice to meet you, Rain," Hannah said. Then she meandered off, disappearing between the bookshelves.

After discussing the book club with Hannah, Rain's thoughts returned to Lily. She really hated to offend anyone, and the way Lily had left the previous night's meeting weighed heavily on her mind. She couldn't wait to unburden herself once and for all and finally get a chance to clear the air.

*   *   *

Before long, Marge arrived at the library, and Rain and Julia were on their way, with a potted geranium in tow, to pay a visit to the disgruntled book club member. The storm had subsided, and as expected, a heaviness filled the air. Instead of running the air conditioning inside Rain's SUV, though, they had the windows rolled down while the wind whipped at their hair. It was such a short distance to Lily's house anyway that Rain felt it pointless to turn it on.

Julia held her hands over her mouth to cover a sneeze, and then blew her nose once again.

"Allergies bugging you?" Rain asked. "You're not allergic to that are you?" She gestured with a thumb to the back seat, where the geranium was tucked behind her.

"No, I'm not allergic to those, but to everything else, it seems. All the Claritin in the world doesn't seem to help!" Julia said as she reached for more tissues from the box sandwiched between them, and stuffed them into her shorts pocket.

Rain steered with her knees as she attempted to gather her hair, which was whipping across her face, and corral it into a ponytail.

Julia grabbed the wheel. "Jumpin' Jehoshaphat! All you need to do is ask," she said sternly. "Girlfriend, you're gonna land us in the ditch!"

Rain felt very much in control of the wheel and let Julia's comment slide, changing the subject instead. "Which house is it?" she asked as she shooed Julia aside and took back control of the steering wheel.

Julia pointed. "Pull in up there—see the 'Sold' sign? That must be it."

Rain searched the mailbox, and the house, looking for a number to confirm the address, but to no avail. "Why isn't there an address marker anywhere that I can see?"

"Dunno," Julia replied.

Instead of pulling into the narrow driveway, Rain stopped the SUV on the side of the road, just in case they were at the wrong house. The "Sold" sign was hanging crookedly, as if it could fall off at a moment's notice. Rain secretly thought that if it was Naomi's listing, based on the woman's impeccable appearance at book club the previous night, she would never have let that happen; Naomi's sign would be perfect.

They stepped from the vehicle and took in the house. The driveway led in a downward slope toward a small brown cottage with tan trim. Rain couldn't help but think a change in trim color would make for better curb appeal. Overgrown bushes flanked each side of the door and could really use Nick's landscaping touch. The metal railing atop the stoop, circa 1980, needed replacing too. Rain was glad Julia had suggested coming, because they had a chance to view the house before Lily began her renovations, and they could witness the transformation over time. She removed the salmon-colored geranium from the back seat, and the two carefully walked the sloped driveway to the front door, which oddly had been left a few inches ajar. On closer inspection, Rain wondered if it was her imagination or if the lock had been popped open with a screwdriver. Minor splintering in the wood, seemingly freshly scraped, was evident alongside the lock. A few wood shavings even littered the cement slab of the porch, where she set down the potted plant.

Rain finally voiced her observations aloud. "Something doesn't look right. Do you think Lily slept in town and her cottage was broken into?"

Julia removed her cell phone from her shorts pocket. "I dunno, but I think I'm going to call Jace to stop by, just in case. Don't you think? I'll just tell him to come over because there's a cat in a tree, or something like that, so he doesn't come with sirens blazing. I know my brother, and if it's animal related, that'll get him here fast enough," she chuckled.

Rain looked over her shoulder at the driveway they had just walked down, and noticed fresh tire tracks. The skid ran clear out into the road and had kicked up mud as if the car had been in a hurry before exiting. If Lily *had* been at the cottage, she was certainly gone now.

"Yeah, that's probably a good idea," Rain said, turning to face her friend.

Julia's brother worked for the local police department, and he would know exactly how to handle the situation.

After Julia ended her call with Jace, she and Rain exchanged a look of concern.

"What should we do?" Rain asked. "Should I try calling Lily and tell her something might be going on over here?"

"No, let's not set off any alarm bells just yet. How about we wait and let Jace handle that when he arrives. Since we have backup coming though, I'm gonna take a little look-see."

"Julia! You shouldn't!" Rain reached out a hand to stop her.

"Rain, seriously. It's fine—Jace is on his way. I wanna know if her house *was* broken into or if we're just overreacting. I'm not going inside—I'm just gonna take a little peek." Julia removed a tissue from her pocket and used it to push the door open a little wider. Rain knew that her friend was doing this so as not to leave any fingerprints, just in case. They'd read enough mystery novels to know that leaving DNA behind was never a good idea when snooping.

When Julia pushed the door ajar, a gasp escaped from her mouth.

"What?" Rain leaned over her friend's shoulder to observe the horrible situation.

Lily Redlin was lying on the floor, and her hands were as blue as lake water.

Chapter Five

Rain stood motionless, staring down at Lily's lifeless body. It took another half minute for her brain to register the enormity of the situation. The realization came hard then, that Rain would never be able to have the conversation with Lily that she'd so carefully rehearsed in her mind. Nor would poor Lily ever return and participate in the Lakeside Library book club—and not because she was upset. This was so much worse.

"Julia," Rain finally mumbled, "I can't believe this."

Julia blew out a slow methodic breath and then kneaded her forehead. "Me neither, girlfriend. Me *neither*! This was the very last thing I expected to find when I opened the door. I'm kinda sorry I did now, to be honest."

The two exchanged a look of deep concern before their collective gaze returned to Lily.

"There's no possibility she's still alive, right?" Rain asked timidly.

"No." Julia shook her head vehemently. "Not a chance."

"I didn't think so. Her hands are so pale on the top, but blue on the bottom—there's no way she could still be with us. Right?"

"Lividity." Julia agreed, with a decisive click of her tongue. "Her blood is already pooling."

Rain swallowed hard before she forced herself to search for more clues, to try and understand what had happened. "Looks like rigor mortis is already setting in too—see how stiff she is?" Since Lily was lying facedown, it looked as if her hands were reaching out in desperation to clutch the wood floorboards.

Neither of them had crossed the threshold into the cottage. Instead, the two remained as stiff as Lily's hands, atop the stoop.

"We probably shouldn't double-check either—I don't want to contaminate the scene," Julia murmured. "Jace would kill me. Oh, fiddle-farts, that was the wrong thing to say."

"Scene? Hold on a minute. You mean, you think this is a *crime* scene?"

"What would you call it?" Julia flung a hand in the direction of Lily's lifeless body. Which Rain wished, more than ever, would miraculously resurrect itself.

"I dunno. Maybe she passed out and hit her head? Surely, there must be another explanation besides that a crime occurred here!"

Julia rolled her eyes in exasperation. "Come on, Rainy—put your Sherlock hat on. It doesn't take a rocket scientist to put two and two together."

"No . . . noooo . . . it can't be." Rain vigorously shook her head. "Julia, there must be another explanation." Rain refused to believe another crime had taken place in her idyllic "Mayberry" world of Lofty Pines. "Perhaps she fell down a flight of stairs? Is there a staircase behind that door?" Lily's body had blocked Rain's view, but she hoped that could be the case.

"It's a one-story house, Rain."

"Oh, right. I don't know what I was thinking. I guess I'm just grasping at straws here." Rain put her head in her hands to think, because suddenly her mind was spinning wildly out of control. She fought to maintain her equilibrium.

"You're right about one thing, though. It's hard to say a crime took place here when there's no blood or anything. Seizure or something, perhaps? She seems awfully young for a heart attack, doesn't she?" Julia scrubbed her hands over her face and then looked at Lily again with fresh eyes.

Rain, too, scoured the scene once more and noticed that Lily was barefoot, and her feet were a violet purple on the side of them that touched the floor. But she was still wearing the same outfit she had worn to book club: jeans and the red Wisconsin Badgers sweatshirt that she had pulled over her head when the lakeside evening temperatures had dipped.

"Okay. Except, again: How do you explain that?" Julia pointed out the roughed-up lock and then planted her hands firmly on her hips.

"Yes, that could mean something. But let me play the devil's advocate here. What if Lily forgot her keys? And did that damage to the lock herself? It's not outside the realm of possibility, is it?"

"Wouldn't she have just called the realtor to see if there was a second set of keys? Or tried to go through a window or a garage door or something? Why jam her own lock like that? And by the way, how do you explain the recent mud tracks in the driveway? Someone else was here."

So, Julia noticed the tracks in the driveway too, Rain thought.

As they continued to volley these notions, Jace's patrol car arrived and parked on the road directly behind Rain's SUV. The flashing lights were not on, thank goodness. Rain didn't want to attract neighborhood alarm—at least not yet. That would all come with time.

The police officer's winning smile faded as he approached. Jace must've instantly sensed fresh alarm bells after Julia held up her hands in defense. His casual walk morphed into a jog as Jace quickly moved in their direction.

Julia moved to greet him, and Rain followed.

When closer, Rain noticed the officer's blond hair was buzzed short beneath his police cap. He looked like Brad Pitt in the movie *Troy*. The scent of aftershave wafted in her direction as he followed them back to the stoop, making her lose all regard of the scene momentarily. Rain had to catch herself, for with sudden inappropriate timing, butterflies seemed to flutter inside her stomach. She held her tummy with her hands, to calm it, and took a deep breath, filling her lungs with even more aftershave.

"Where's the cat? Is it hurt that bad?" Jace looked to the neighboring trees and then back at his sister.

"Yeah, no cat. Sorry about that." Julia grimaced. "I just didn't want you to come out guns blazing. We have bigger fish to fry . . ." Her extended finger pointed out the issue as she tapped the door with her foot, to crack it open further and reveal their findings.

Jace's eyes darted just inside the door, but he didn't say anything about Lily. He only asked, "Did you touch anything?" The officer then regarded them, one at a time, before removing disposable gloves from his police belt and quickly rolling them on.

"No, we didn't touch a thing," Julia confirmed.

"Why on earth didn't you tell me this over the phone?" Jace grunted.

Rain chimed in, "Not your sister's fault. We found Lily *after* she talked to you."

Jace stepped inside and knelt to check for a pulse. He hung his head before turning to them with sad eyes.

"We kinda figured," Julia said sadly.

"Any blunt force trauma to her head? Or anything like that?" Rain asked.

"Why would you immediately think someone did this to her?" Jace asked.

Rain pointed to the door. "It looks like a possible forced entry."

Jace let out a little chuckle but seemed to consider her words. "Forced entry? Are you no longer the head librarian? You're officially a detective now? I guess I should watch my back; you might steal my job."

Rain shrugged and indicated the damaged lock. "Come see for yourself."

Instead of stepping back outside to look at the lock, Jace examined Lily's body for clues to what might have happened. Moving her sweatshirt aside and regarding her neck, he uttered, "Well, she wasn't strangled." He then continued to search her body with a keen eye. "No bruising that I can see, or defensive marks on her hands. She certainly didn't defend herself, that's for sure."

"Is there any blood in there? On the other side of her, where we can't see?" Julia asked timidly.

"No. None," Jace confirmed. "None that I can see without rolling her over, and I'll let the chief handle that, since we still haven't hired a full-time detective for our jurisdiction yet. I haven't exactly been promoted to the job, but I'm in the running. In any event, it's best I leave her exactly how we found her."

"That doesn't make sense. No blood or anything?" Rain whispered as she scratched the back of her neck. Beads of sweat seemed to instantly pool there and trickle down her back.

"A heart attack, Jace? Maybe the intruder scared the piddle out of her?" Julia suggested.

"Piddle? Really, Julia? That's a new one, even for you. But yeah, maybe someone scared the piss out of her," Jace said with a sarcastic chuckle as he stood up and walked around Lily's body, looking for anything that could explain what had happened.

"Come on, *brother*! You know how hard I try not to curse!"

Jace responded with an eye roll. Then he moved to the other side of Lily's body and looked at her face. "She's been here a while; her face is bloated, pooling lividity, and it looks to me maybe like a dry foam cone."

"What's a foam cone?" Rain asked.

"I've only seen it once, on an overdose victim. It could mean a host of different things." Jace shrugged. "I'll leave that to the medical examiner to determine. I'm not going to jump to any conclusions. That's completely the ME's territory."

"You mind if we step inside for a brief minute?" Julia asked with puppy dog eyes, a look her brother seemed unable to refuse. He held the door open with his gloved hand and his tone was stern. "Don't touch anything. I swear, if you do, I'll lock you up and throw away the key."

Both Rain and Julia held their hands high like they were showing proof that they wouldn't touch a thing.

The officer held a gloved finger in front of his lips as if to silence them. "And don't tell a soul you were here with me. The only reason I'm letting you in here in the first place is so you can fill in the blanks and tell me how you know this woman. I'm not ready either for some neighborhood watchdogs to be eyeing you two standing on the front step with my cruiser sitting out at the curb. So get in here." He hurried them inside and closed the door.

The cottage smelled musty, like it had water damage, or maybe the windows hadn't been open recently. Rain thought that strange, especially because Lily was wearing a sweatshirt. Wouldn't she have been hot? Surely the aged cottage didn't have an air-conditioning unit, and she would've needed to open a window. She added a mental note to walk around the house and check on that.

The three stepped carefully around Lily's body and walked deeper into the residence. A kitchen light was flickering over the sink, so they all moved in that direction. The paneled walls made the kitchen look dingy and small, but the large windows, which overlooked Pine Lake, helped it appear more expansive.

"How do you know this woman?" Jace asked.

"Book club," Rain and Julia blurted in unison, and then they swapped a weak smile.

In the corner of the room, two glasses sat atop a small pub table, and one still had a little red wine in it. The other was empty.

"Looks like Lily had company," Rain said, pointing out the wineglasses.

"Isn't that interesting," Julia said. "Did anyone mention that they were following her home after book club? Perhaps she had plans afterward?"

"I'm not sure—I didn't catch that either. I know she was upset when she left, so I assumed she came back here alone."

"Upset?" Jace turned to Rain for an explanation.

"Not upset, really." Julia dismissed the notion with a casual wave of her hand. "We had a book discussion is all, and Lily seemed frustrated at times. But it was all very vanilla. It wasn't a personal attack or anything like that, just a heated book discussion. Certainly nothing to harm anyone over," she repeated.

"Ah," Jace said, and then looked to Rain as if waiting to see if she had anything to add. Instead, she shrugged. "I don't know what to think at this point. I still can't believe Lily is no longer with us."

"I hear you," Julia agreed quietly. "This is pretty shocking."

"I'm sorry you two have to go through this," Jace said in a tone of deep sympathy. "If this is too upsetting, maybe you guys should be on your way."

Instead, Julia ignored him and stepped deeper into the room. She pointed to an envelope sitting halfway beneath a box of herbed crackers, and they all gathered around. "Hey, check this out." The letter's return address was in view, and it was that of an attorney based in Door County, Wisconsin.

Rain noted *Jonas R. Schulze, Esquire* before Jace tugged at his sister's arm.

"Seriously, I think you two better be on your way. Besides, I don't want the chief to see you inside here. Then I'd have a lot of explaining to do," Jace said sternly. "And the medical examiner needs to get here pronto. Every minute wasted makes the ME's job that much harder to do."

"Wait, seriously? You're not going to open that letter so we can see what Lily and some unknown person were discussing over a glass of wine?" Julia asked. "I can't believe you!"

"None of your business." Jace twirled a long finger in the air as if he wanted them to do an about-face. Which they did. The officer followed them to the entrance and, after one last backward look at Lily, held the door for them.

"Keep us posted," Julia said. "We wanna know what happened to her."

"Yes, please let us know." Rain held Jace's gaze before stepping outside into the hot, humid air that instantly sucked whatever energy she had left out of her. She convinced Julia to take a quick walk around the house to see if any of the windows had been broken into or any other damage was evident. As they left the premises, she looked at the ground and snapped a photo with her cell phone of the tire tread, caked in mud, that had been left next to the driveway. Just in case the clue might come in handy.

Chapter Six

A few days later, Rain and Julia decided to close the library for a glorious hour-long lunch break. The sun danced a glittery golden path across Pine Lake, and a cloudless sky smiled down on them. The humidity had dissipated, leaving a cool breeze to comfort as it rolled off the vivid blue water.

Marge had left them a few hours ago, to take Rex to the vet, but had promised to return for the afternoon shift in case Rain and Julia had an interest in taking a pontoon ride around the lake. Marge was good about covering the library during the heat of the day, as she herself said it bothered her skin to be outside. Until late afternoon, she claimed, when the sun's rays weren't as brilliant and wouldn't bother her rosacea. It worked perfectly to allow the friends time to enjoy all the benefits Pine Lake had to offer, and to avoid being stuck indoors all summer long while still letting them enjoy their work and companionship at the library too.

When her husband died, Rain had gained a rather sizable insurance payout; Max had been so young when he'd passed, and the policy had been expanded just in case the in vitro worked. It was one thing Rain had really been grateful for in her former husband. Despite his indiscretions, he had made sure she and any children (that never came) would be well taken care of in the event of his demise. And she had been. Because unbeknownst to her, during his life Max had also left another IRA account that he'd rolled over from his grandfather's trust. That account had tripled since her husband's death because of smart investments, and the interest was multiplying by the day.

Rain really didn't need to work, but no one knew this; she kept the knowledge close to her chest. And anyway, the library was her lifeline to the community that she loved, and that was ultimately the reason she continued to run it. Because it certainly didn't generate any income. What little the town of Lofty Pines provided to support it went to Marge and Julia and the running of the library itself. But on perfect summer days such as this one, she sometimes questioned her reasoning.

Rain tented her eyes, reached for her sunglasses atop the table between them, and slipped them on. "What a simply gorgeous day!" She took a sip of lemonade before setting her tumbler back on the table. "It's going to be hard to go back to the library after lunch," she finally admitted aloud.

"I know, right?" Julia interjected between bites of her sand-wich. "We really needed this after all the stress lately."

The sound of scratches across the deck caught Rain's attention, and she sat up higher in the chair. She thought it might be Marge, returning with Rex, but it wasn't. Instead, Jace rounded the cor-ner, holding a leash with a gorgeous Siberian husky attached to it. The dog had the palest, bluest eyes, Rain had ever seen, which reminded her of sea glass. The dog's undercoat was pure white. So pure, in fact, it looked almost unreal, or like the dog never had a chance to play outside in the mud.

Rain stood to welcome them. "Oh my! Who is this cutie?" She reached to pat the dog on the head, but instead the dog jumped on her and wagged its tail in greeting.

"Down!" Jace demanded. And the dog obeyed.

Rain stroked the dog's head, and the animal leaned its weight into her, causing her to smile. "Oh, aren't you a charmer," she said. "I'm guessing male?"

"Yes, it's a 'he,'" Jace pointed to the tag dangling from the dog's neck. "According to his collar, his name is Benzo."

"What a sweet boy!" Julia exclaimed, wiping the crumbs from her lips and brushing them off her hands too.

"Hi, Benzo," Rain cooed as she knelt to get a closer look at him. The contrast of his dark silky fur against the white was stunning. He looked at her with sad pale eyes.

"He needs a home," Jace said.

"What do you mean?" Rain couldn't imagine this stunning animal without a home. Benzo, too, seemed to tilt his head and listen perceptively.

"His owner died on the scene of an automobile accident, and his family members can't take the dog because they live in an apartment." Jace shrugged. "It's really sad."

Rain knew what it felt like to lose someone you loved, with the snap of a finger, and her empathy for the dog almost burst from her chest.

Jace continued, "I'm on my way to drop him at the humane society. It's awful—I mean look at this beautiful dog," he said, downcast.

"I'll take him!" Rain burst out.

"Really? Are you sure? It's a big commitment." Jace volleyed a dumbfounded look with Julia before his gaze met Rain's, and then he stared at her intently.

"Yes, I'll take him," Rain said quickly. The thought of the dog being led away to the humane society almost left her breathless.

"It's a big decision," Jace repeated. "One you shouldn't take lightly, although it would make me feel better after all the break-ins happening in Lofty Pines. Especially with so many people who visit the library and know that you live here on this enormous property all alone," he admitted with a frown.

Julia sat up higher in her seat. "Break-ins? Has anyone else we know been victimized? Besides Lily's place?"

"Well, you noticed that Lily's lock was damaged. It should come as no surprise to either of you that break-ins around the lake are on the rise. And as you know, it usually seems to uptick during the summer months."

Rain continued to pet the dog as she spoke. "Are you saying that you've determined definitively that someone broke into Lily's? What led you to believe that? Was she missing valuables or something?"

"No, it didn't seem like anything of value was taken, but it's hard to be sure what someone might have been after. Could be drugs or any of a host of things." Jace rubbed his chin.

"Yeah, but we walked around Lily's house before we left, and not one window was left open," Julia said.

"She's right," Rain confirmed. "And she was wearing a sweatshirt, so whatever happened must've happened soon after the person arrived. Don't you find it odd that, with no air-conditioning unit and all the windows closed, she'd still be wearing one?"

"Interesting." Jace paused. "Which reminds me . . . Julia, when you pushed the door open at Lily's, was it unlocked or in the locked position?"

"The door was ajar, Jace. I only pushed it with a Kleenex to open it farther," Julia replied.

"Oh, so you didn't touch the knob—or play with the lock at all?"

"No, I didn't. Why?" Julia asked.

"Just curious." Jace's gaze wandered out toward Pine Lake, as if he was trying to make sense of something, but he didn't share what exactly.

"Did you ever find out the cause of her death?" Rain asked.

"That's the other reason I stopped by. The medical examiner said preliminary toxicology reports show poisoning of some kind, but the ME hasn't isolated what type of poison yet. You know anybody that might've had it out for Lily Redlin?"

Rain and Julia gasped.

The color in Julia's face drained. "Oh Fudgsicles, that isn't good. That isn't good at all . . ."

"Nooo," Rain shook her head slowly. "That's very bad indeed."

Their collective reaction must've seemed over the top, because Jace asked, "Wait a minute . . . I don't get it. What's up with you two?" Jace handed the leash to Rain, and she wrapped it around the deck post so they could talk momentarily without distraction.

But first Rain asked, "Does Benzo need a dish of fresh water before we continue?"

Jace held up a long finger. "In a minute. Nobody's going anywhere. First tell me why you're both so uneasy to hear that Lily was poisoned." He placed his hands firmly on his hips and regarded them rather seriously.

Rain and Julia shared a look of concern before Rain said, "Not *shocked* really—more a feeling of unease, I guess. Because of . . . well, it's just . . . the book we discussed the night she died was *Sparkling Cyanide*, by Agatha Christie. I mean, is that a coincidence? Or is something more sinister going on?"

"Yeah." Julia gulped, and rose from her seat. "And the victim in the book, Rosemary, ingested the poison in a glass of bubbly . . . if you catch our drift. If I recall, there were two wineglasses on Lily's kitchen table."

Jace's eyes doubled in size. "Cyanide? I'm pretty sure the medical examiner would've mentioned that if he thought that was the cause. Maybe an oversight? That doesn't seem possible—he's usually on point."

Neither Rain nor Julia spoke. It seemed both were overwhelmed by the sudden realization that Lily had died from poison of some kind.

"Did the medical examiner determine a time of death?" Julia asked finally.

Rain said, "Lily wasn't in her pajamas and was still wearing the clothing she had on the night of book club. Like I said before, she had on the same sweatshirt, in what was probably a warm house, if that helps."

"Keen eye, Rain," Jace said proudly. "Her bed was neatly made too, so it was evident to me that she hadn't gone to sleep that night either. To answer your question, yes, the medical examiner did notice those things upon his arrival at the scene, and I'm sure he's taking that into consideration. It's his job to determine the manner and cause of death. My job is to figure out who did it," he said, stroking the slight stubble on his chin.

"We can help!" Julia said eagerly. Whatever you need, bro, just let us know."

"Yes, of course," Rain chorused.

"There is something you can do. Any chance you can watch the dog for a bit, Rain?" Jace asked hurriedly. "I need to go and speak to the medical examiner and confirm if it was cyanide that

Lily ingested. I also need those wineglasses swabbed and rechecked for toxins right away."

"Yes, of course." Rain nodded. "Whatever you need."

"I'm also gonna need to ask that you close the library until further notice," Jace said firmly.

"What? No!" Julia blurted.

"Why?" Rain asked.

The officer in him was unwavering. "Because I think it's wise."

"But won't that set off unnecessary alarm bells? I don't think we should do that," Julia interjected. "It might scare someone off. Then you'll never sift out the person responsible—if indeed Lily was poisoned by cyanide."

"It's my job to keep you both safe. And it seems we potentially have a killer on the loose, and right now . . ." Jace's voice trailed off. He removed his police cap and ran his hand nervously through his short hair.

Rain could see the sweat trickling down the back of his neck. She wanted to soothe him somehow and ease his worry. If only she could reach out and hold him in her arms. She pushed the thought aside and instead said, "How about we compromise? I'll put a sign on the door saying the air conditioning needs to be fixed, or something like that, and we're closed until further notice. That way, we can reopen whenever you think it's safe. Or if you need us to reopen, to search for possible clues that might help with this case. It leaves options open, is all I'm suggesting."

"Yeah!" Julia said excitedly. "Jace, you might need the library to flush out the killer, if it turns out that *someone*, rather than *something*, poisoned Lily. Because clearly, it would have to be someone who knew we were discussing that book at our book club the night of her death! Wouldn't it?"

Jace seemed to ponder Julia's comment carefully, and then he looked to Rain. "Yeah, put a 'Temporarily closed' sign up—because of a broken pipe or something to that effect. You're right, Julia, we may need to use the library as a source moving forward. But first, I need to check on a few things."

"Whatever we can do to help," Rain reiterated. "You just let us know."

"I'll go and grab the dog food and the rest of Benzo's stuff from my cruiser. I'm not asking you to make a permanent decision right now about whether you want to keep him," Jace said, backing away from them. "It's just that I can't take the time to drop him off at the humane society right now. We may have a lead in this case, and you two need to keep this information on the downlow," he continued over his shoulder, and then he disappeared around the corner.

Julia pushed away from the chair and moved over to stand with Rain. She held the back of her hand against her mouth, as if she was holding back a gag reflex.

"Julia, you know what this means if poison is found in Lily's toxicology report," Rain whispered. "And they find that it's not alcohol poisoning or drugs . . ."

Julia put her head in her hands and cowered. "Oh shiplap, I don't want to think about it."

"But we have to! It sounds like Lily was poisoned. But why? Because if the medical examiner finds cyanide in her system, whether we like it or not, it could mean . . . someone in our book club or someone connected to the Lakeside Library . . . might've had something to do with Lily's death."

Chapter Seven

After attaching the "Closed" sign to the library door, Rain and Julia retuned to the outer deck to regroup over another glass of lemonade. Julia tossed a splash of vodka into hers, because of the stress of it all, but Rain wanted to be clear-headed, so she refrained. It wasn't long before Marge arrived and rushed over to them in deep concern.

"The sign on the door says the air conditioning broke? The books aren't going to do well with the high humidity that's expected over the next few days." Marge wrung her hands worriedly. "We might want to open all the windows and get some air circulation going in there. What do you think, ladies?"

"Not exactly what happened," Julia said flatly.

Rain explained everything that had transpired and was met with a shocked expression.

"The authorities think Lily was *poisoned*?" Marge gasped, clutching her chest. "I can't believe that. Especially after our discussion the other night. Oh goodness . . . that's not good." The older woman sank into the patio chair, and Rain rushed to crank up the oversized umbrella to shield her from the sun's hot rays. Next, she poured a glass of lemonade and handed it to Marge, who took it willingly and immediately took a sip. "Thank you, my dear," she said, patting her lovingly on the hand.

Rain smiled weakly.

"We're still trying to make sense of it too," Julia said, breathing deeply. "I'm having a real hard time wrapping my brain around it, to be honest. A senseless act, happening right here *again* in Lofty Pines. What is the world coming to? And it's hitting way too close to home after our book club discussion."

"I guess we have no other choice than to help the authorities figure this out," Marge said with resolve. "We might be their only lead."

"Do you actually think someone from book club followed Lily home that night and is responsible for this?" Rain asked. Even saying it aloud brought bile to her throat. She took a splash of lemonade to flush it back down.

"I'm not sure, dear. But clearly it's someone who knew what book we were discussing, and either they wanted to frame one of us, or it *was* one of us. That's really the only explanation, isn't it? Lily died of poisoning . . . and we discussed poisoning! That can't be coincidental."

"This is awful," Julia said. "I don't like to think that we could've been sitting around the table talking to a murderer the night of Lily's last breath . . ." Her voice trailed off, and she put her head in her hands.

"Can we exclude anyone?" Rain asked. "There were nine of us that night."

"That's a good idea, Rain." Julia looked up eagerly, then leaned forward and drummed her hands on the tabletop. "Let's work this out. Maybe it'll make us feel even just a tad better. If anything, it'll take our mind off the manner of death, and back to the 'why' of it all."

Rain rose from her chair. "I'll need to grab paper and pen for this." As soon as she opened the sliding glass door, Benzo awoke from his nap and rose from the dog bed. Rain had purposely left him inside with the air conditioning, as the dog seemed to pant from the excess heat. She wondered how the previous owner had dealt with that. She snatched a notebook but refrained from allowing the dog outside, because she wasn't sure how Benzo would get along with Rex and refused to allow any interruption to the serious discussion that was about to take place. She would introduce them in time.

After returning to the table, Rain wrote down the names of everyone who had attended the book club discussion. She listed herself, Julia, and Marge first, and then immediately crossed their names from the list and counted the remainder. "Okay, I've excluded us, so we're now down to six. Let's start with Kim."

"There's no way Kim had anything to do with this." Julia shook her head vehemently. "Not a chance."

"I understand you're her good friend, dear, but Lily and Kim *did* argue that night," Marge pointed out. "We need to remain unbiased in our discussions, don't we? Otherwise, we're not giving Lily the proper justice she deserves."

"Or playing fair," Julia conceded. "Okay then"—Julia pointed to the notebook—"write down that they argued." But she quickly held up a finger to make a point. "Hang on a second. I have an alibi for Kim. Nick drove her home that night!" Julia said excitedly, sitting higher in the chair. "She was planning to spend the night at my place, remember? Because she had too much to drink." She turned to Rain then. "But Nick took her home instead, because she wanted to wake up in her own bed. And Seth was there to greet her. For sure he'll corroborate that." She smiled defiantly. "See? I told you Kim had nothing to do with this."

Rain wrote all that down, then skipped to the next name. She thought it a very narrow chance that Kim had anything to do with the murder anyway. "Okay, sadly I'll be removing Lily from the list as she's the victim in this case. That leaves only four people left that were present that night: Shelby Sullivan, Ruth Thompson, Naomi Mosely, and Chelsea McAdams." She ticked the names off on her fingers and then looked up.

"We can't exclude any of them, as we don't have enough information just yet," Marge stated matter-of-factly.

"She's right," Julia said. "The police always start with those closest to the victim and then work outward. We need to dig for connections. We know that Shelby was friends with our victim in high school, so they have history. As far as the rest of them, I don't know if Lily had met any of them prior to book club. Do either of you recall?" Julia's intense stare pinballed between them.

"We have to do some serious investigating," Rain said. "And there's another thing . . ." She massaged her forehead as she felt a headache fast approaching. "Something that Jace mentioned is still nagging at me."

"What's that, dear?" Marge rested a comforting hand on Rain's shoulder and rested it there.

"The doorknob."

"Yeah, she's right. The fact that Jace was even asking about the doorknob makes me think the door was *unlocked*. At least that's what I gathered from his demeanor. You?" Julia asked.

Rain rolled her hand in the air. "Yeah, and that would mean—"

"Lily knew her killer!" Rain and Julia blurted in unison, and then nervous laughter bubbled up from the two of them.

"What you're both saying is that Lily unlocked the door and let her intruder inside willingly," Marge said thoughtfully.

"We're gonna have to get to the bottom of this," Julia said.

"What other choice do we have?" Rain asked.

"None, really," Marge agreed firmly.

Rain pointed to the paper in front of her. "Especially since the killer *could* be one of the four left on our list."

"Oh, cheesy rice!" Julia gulped. "That can't be! One of our book club members can't be a murderer! What does that say about us?"

"Cheesy rice?" Marge laughed.

"I'm runnin' out of words, my friend!" Julia winked, easing the tension momentarily, and they all shared a chuckle.

But Rain corralled them back to the matter at hand. "Hey, like Marge said, Lily willingly opened the door to the person who took her life."

Julia continued, "And whoever jimmied the lock staged it to look like a break-in . . . but we know better."

Julia's cell phone sang out, and they all looked to the table to see a photo of Jace staring back at them. Julia hit the button to take the call and said, "Hey, bro, you're on speaker. Rainy and Marge are here with me too. Go ahead—give us the goods."

The three leaned closer to the phone to listen carefully.

"Oh, okay. Good to know that you're all together because I have some news to share. I'm at the ME's office, and he just showed me the report. No cyanide was found, so I think you can all relax. This may have had nothing to do with the book you read at your meeting. Merely a coincidence."

Nervous looks darted between Rain, Julia, and Marge.

"Accidental overdose or something?" Rain asked.

"No, not that either." Jace said.

"Then what?" Marge asked. "Alcohol poisoning?"

"Nope, not that. Sounds like a different toxin was used. The ME found high levels of tetrahydrozoline hydrochloride in her system. No cyanide," he reiterated. "You should all rest easy."

"I'm not sure we can take that sigh of relief just yet." Marge said as she leaned even closer to the phone so Jace could hear her clearly.

"Whaddya mean?" Jace asked. "I thought hearing that it wasn't cyanide would ease your mind, no?"

Julia cleared her throat and then met Rain and Marge's eyes, before continuing. "You might wanna ask the medical examiner if that tetrahydro-whatever-you-called-it stuff is the main ingredient found in Visine."

"Yeah," Rain cautioned. "Apparently, it does *more* than get the red out."

Chapter Eight

Rain was secretly relieved that the library was temporarily closed, as it afforded her the ability to take her new rescue for a long walk and get to know his habits better. Benzo was leash trained well and seemed only to dart when another dog crossed his path. She talked to the pup as she walked along.

"Who do *you* think did this awful thing, my puppers? What happened to Lily?"

Benzo turned his head and regarded her before returning his attention to the walk.

"Yeah. I don't know either." Rain sighed and slowed her pace, and the dog followed suit. Which surprised her, as he seemed to have boundless energy.

"By the way, sometimes I'm gonna call you my puppers. I hope that's not too confusing, Benzo."

The dog turned to her once again and lolled his tongue like he was smiling back at her.

As she made the turn onto her street, she noticed Nick, standing out by the road with a set of trimmers in his hand and branches littered beneath him. That man was always busy doing something around the yard. There was not a weed to be found or a blade of grass too long.

"Howdy, neighbor," Rain greeted, sharing a casual wave.

"Oh, hey Rain! I've been meaning to stop over and meet your new puppy." Nick set the trimmers down and jogged over to greet them. He knelt to pet the dog, and Benzo jumped all over him, knocking the baseball hat clear off his head. Nick laughed and said, "Easy, boy!"

"Down!" Rain said firmly while she tugged at the leash as a reminder.

"Wow, he's beautiful, Rain," Nick said after regaining his balance. He stroked Benzo down the back and looked him over. "Holy Maloney, check out those eyes! Sometimes with huskies one of the eyes will turn brown, but in this case, looks like he's keeping the blue, eh? I'm not even seeing a hint of brown. What a gorgeous dog."

"I know, right? That's what sold me," Rain confessed with a laugh. "Not only are his eyes the prettiest shade of blue, but he tilts his head sometimes and gives me that puppy-dog face with sad eyes too! He's a charmer, for sure. Aren't you boy?" she cooed as she stroked him on the head.

Just then, Julia moved across the yard, joining them on the road. She was carrying a water bottle and tossed it to Nick, who caught it expertly with one hand.

"Hey! Out for a walk? You should've asked—I can use the exercise too. You're still a skinny little thing, just like when we were kids. It's disgusting," Julia ribbed, tapping her own padded stomach. "Me, not so much. If I could only be fourteen again and have my water-skiing body back." She frowned. "I'd give anything for it. Except of course, my donut addiction." She winked.

"I'll invite you next time if you want. I just needed to clear my head, you know? And this pup here has enough pent-up energy for the two of us; he was pacing the cabin before we left. I'm not sure when he last had a good run of exercise." Rain was surprised to see that Benzo had heeled and was behaving at her side. The walk must've finally tuckered him out.

Nick swiped his ball cap from the ground and shook it out before returning it to his head. "Julia told me what happened to the woman in your book club. I'm so sorry you guys had to find her like that! How crazy is that? I can't *believe* a woman who you guys literally just met ended up dying in her own cottage! And Julia mentioned she didn't think she was that old either. How incredibly sad." He hung his head and shook it slowly.

"Yep, it's nuts alright and simply unfathomable. We're all having a hard time adjusting to it. Speaking of that, any word from Jace today?" Rain asked. "Have anything new to share?" She nudged Julia with a friendly poke of her elbow, hoping there was a recent development that might shed light on the investigation.

"Nah, nothing." Julia shrugged. "You hear from Jace today?" She turned to her husband, who shook his head.

"Not a peep," Nick replied finally, and then removed a bandana from his back pocket and mopped the beads of sweat pouring down his face. "It's getting hot out here," he said with a grimace.

Rain chewed at her cheek and pondered. "I think I have an idea."

"Oh boy." Nick rolled his eyes. "That's code for, 'I'm outta here!'" he said, which caused Rain and Julia to chuckle.

"Before you go, what do you think about a boat ride this afternoon? We could invite Jace to come along?" Rain suggested.

Nick gave her an accusatory glance, "You guys just want to pump the poor guy for information on his off time." He waved his hands as if an umpire calling time out. "I'm not involving myself in official police business, I can promise you that. No way! I keep my distance from the Lofty Pines PD, especially after being wrongfully accused." He started taking backward steps away from them, in the direction of where he'd abandoned his clippers.

Nick wasn't far from wrong. At least concerning the part about pumping Jace for information.

"Does that mean you're not up for a boat ride later?" Julia pushed. "It's a beautiful day."

"I'll go if Jace does, but otherwise probably not," Nick said, jutting a thumb behind him and officially turning on his heel. "Besides, I still have a lot of work left on those bushes."

Julia rolled her eyes. "Come on, Nick! We don't often get free time, but now with the library closed . . . well, we should take full advantage of the time when we get it. Summer goes by way too fast, and then we're back to digging snow."

"We'll see," Nick said over his shoulder. His voice faded as he walked away from them. "If you let me get back to work, I can get my stuff done. Then maybe I'll consider it."

When Nick was out of earshot, Julia immediately tapped Rain on the arm and asked, "So, what's this idea you got, lady?"

Rain lowered her voice so Nick couldn't possibly overhear, and whispered, "Initially, I was planning to cancel our next book club meeting. But I'm reconsidering." She chewed at her bottom lip.

"I dunno if we should talk romance books right now," Julia interrupted, raising her hand. She began ticking off the reasons why on her fingers. "First, I haven't had a chance to read it with everything going on, and second, I'm flat out not in the mood!"

"No, I mean what if one of the book club members had a hand in this? For your own sanity, don't you want to know *for sure*? A lot of things are pointing in an uncomfortable direction, such as the fact that Lily opened her home to someone she trusted; she was still wearing the same clothes that she wore to book club; and she was poisoned. Do I need to continue?"

"Okay. So, you want to host a book club meeting for what? If not to discuss a book? How are you going to get everyone to come to the meeting?"

"Here's my idea. We won't discuss the book. The members will only *think* we're planning to discuss it."

Julia's face reflected her confusion.

"We'll host a reenactment, just like George did in *Sparkling Cyanide*. Remember how he gathered them all around the table where Rosemary died, to see if someone would squirm."

Julia's eyes doubled in size. "Oh! Now I get it!" She grinned devilishly.

"Yeah, and we'll leave Lily's chair open, and we'll require that everyone sit in the exact same seats as they did at the first meeting. Just like Agatha Christie wrote."

"You remember that this backfired for George, and he became the second victim and died in the book, right?" Julia said nervously, twirling the pink streak in her hair into a tight knot.

"Yeah. Let's hope it doesn't come to that."

Chapter Nine

"This is eerie," Ruth bellowed.

"I agree. A bit morbid, to say the least." Naomi nodded and then shifted in her seat. However, her perfectly coiffed hair didn't move when she did so. "I'm not sure I even want to take part in this," she added, her eyes downcast.

At the subsequent meeting, the book club had been reassembled around the table in the exact seating arrangement its members had assumed the first time they'd discussed *Sparkling Cyanide*. Other than Lily, Kim was the only one absent, as she had been unable to find a babysitter, and her husband, Seth, was out of town visiting his brother. However, Hannah, the nurse who'd inquired about the book club, had taken Kim's seat instead. Unbeknownst to Hannah, the chosen romance novel wouldn't be discussed, and she'd find herself, instead, smack dab in the mystery of Lily Redlin's death.

The weather was even cooperating for the reenactment, as it was vaguely similar to what it had been on the night in question. A pinkish tint colored the sky while a low wind caused violet water to lap upon the shore slowly and rhythmically. Meanwhile, off in the distance, boats slowly made their last rounds around Pine Lake.

Rain folded her hands in front of her. "I do apologize if this may seem uncomfortable or even a little unorthodox. The problem is the recent murder seems eerily similar to our last book discussion of *Sparkling Cyanide*, and we all look like suspects when it comes to Lily's untimely death." Her eyes darted to the members seated around the table, to see if she could observe even a hint of squirming, but she saw none. "Though, in my heart, I realize this just couldn't be possible." The lie rolled from her tongue, and a twang of guilt shot through her. She justified the fib in her mind; it was absolutely beyond necessary in order to sift out Lily's killer.

"Maybe I should go grab my Ouija board. Then Lily can tell us something," Shelby suggested with an awkward smile. Her comment, made in bad taste, was met with open mouths and wide-eyed stares.

"What?" Shelby justified. "You guys don't believe in that stuff?"

"Don't be so crass—this isn't something to joke about," Chelsea grimaced.

"I don't think she intended to make jokes. In my experience, people handle stress in a myriad of ways," Hannah said quietly.

"Look," Julia interrupted. "Let's not get sidelined here. I understand everyone's input, but this isn't something we ought to take lightly. Due to the nature of Lily's death, we all look a little suspicious. Fingers are being pointed directly at our book club. And that's not cool." She then shot a look to Rain, which Rain interpreted as *"We're not leaving this table until we have some answers."*

"It's true," Chelsea agreed, wringing her hands. "Julia's correct in that statement. And why wouldn't we be? We all know Lily was poisoned with cyanide." She then held up her hands in a placating gesture. "Right?"

Rain didn't correct Chelsea that cyanide was *not* the poison of choice. Sharing details that she and Julia had learned from Jace, within the group, was off limits. The less information the members were privy to, the better. Julia must've agreed on this point, because she kicked Rain beneath the table. Rain responded with a raised brow.

Chelsea continued, "In fact, rumor has it that the police are gonna haul us all in for questioning real soon. I've been hearing mumblings and gettin' weird looks while I'm pourin' coffee at Brewin' Time. It's gettin' so bad that I'd rather hide under a blanket instead of goin' to work."

"Oh? Do you work there? I love that place! I go there all the time; they have the best coconut cream lattes," Hannah said, turning to Chelsea.

"Yeah, I'm the manager," Chelsea confirmed. "Normally, I love my job, but now, with all this swirlin' around, I'm uncomfortable bein' there. Because let me tell you, the gossip is flyin' in this town!"

"That's not fair!" Ruth interjected loudly. "Because anyone that had access to the library knew what we were reading. There were posters plastered on the shelves and by the checkout area for weeks. Therefore, it shouldn't be only this group of people, those seated around this table." Ruth's face reddened as she stopped talking. She circled her finger high in the air and then cleared her throat before continuing. "I mean, not just us who are considered persons of interest." Ruth pounded a fist on the table, causing it to tremble momentarily. "Sorry, but this is upsetting. And I think I'm having a hot flash," she continued, waving a hand to cool her face and taking a long swig from a water bottle that was dripping with condensation.

"Then it would be in your best interest to share anything that you know about Lily, her background, or anything else you think could be relevant to this case. We need to solve it, to bring justice for Lily. And we also need to reopen the library," Rain said resolutely, and she looked across the table to make eye contact with Shelby.

"Shelby, you grew up with Lily. Anything in her history that might be of interest? Ex-lover or abusive-boyfriend stories? Anything at all you can share with the group? From what I gathered at the last meeting, you probably knew her the longest."

Shelby seemed uncomfortable with the sudden attention drawn to her and scrambled for an answer. "I really don't know. I mean, she only recently moved nearby, and we'd just reconnected. Lily didn't date much and, to my knowledge, didn't have a mean ex-boyfriend or anything like that. I often teased her that she'd become a spinster with a house full of cats." Shelby paused and then seemed to ponder her words and choose carefully before she spoke further. "She did recently bring up something about Patrick's accident. But it happened so long ago that I don't see how that would be relevant now. I mean, seriously, that's just ridiculous." She turned the straw in a can of Diet Coke aimlessly and then took a sip. "In fact, I probably shouldn't even have mentioned it." She shrank back in her chair. "I have no idea why she was poisoned. I can't think of anyone who had a beef with her."

Marge rolled her hand in the air. "Please, continue. Can you explain who Patrick is, and what accident you are referring to? There must've been a reason you brought it up."

"Honestly, I shouldn't have even raised the subject. I really have no idea! Lily was well liked, so I really don't understand how this could've happened," Shelby defended. "But in answer to your question, a friend of ours from high school died out on the lake in a boating accident. Lily always felt that Jimmy should've been held responsible somehow because he was the one driving the boat.

But it didn't happen that way, and Lily would often bring it up in conversation, is all. Honestly, I told her just to drop it, once and for all."

"I'm guessing Patrick didn't survive this accident?" Rain asked.

Shelby shook her head. "No, he did not. But again, I don't see how that's relevant. It was well over a decade ago. And Lily was just making up stories about it, like she liked the drama of us having been part of some seedy past. She loved to embellish; she was weird like that."

"I think I remember that accident." Marge tapped her lips and said, "Patrick, Patrick . . . why is that name so familiar?" She kneaded her forehead as if willing herself to remember.

"I remember!" Ruth shouted out. "It was awful, watching the dive teams searching for that kid's body. And being pulled out of the lake like that." She turned her head as if she didn't want to relive another minute of the memory.

"If you lived up here at the time, I'm sure you heard about it. The accident was big news in Lofty Pines and all over the newspapers back then. Patrick was young. And it was sad to lose a seventeen-year-old kid from our class. His parents never got over it either. Last I heard, they'd moved away and ended up divorcing over it," Shelby said woefully.

Naomi slowly shook her head. "All this death talk is making me uncomfortable. I don't like it." She folded her arms around herself protectively, then rubbed her hands up and down her arms, as if warming herself from a sudden chill.

"I can imagine some of you might be struggling with death, but as a former hospice nurse, I must share with you that death is not the end here. I've watched, firsthand, people's demeanor when they pass. Sometimes they're even smiling at the end of life. I do believe there's another realm out there. I hope that brings you all some peace," Hannah murmured.

"Not in this senseless case," Naomi interjected. "Lily was young and had so much to live for. She'd just learned that she'd inherited a property from a long-lost family member, and the proceeds from selling it were going to give her the funds she needed to be able to fix up her cottage. She was talking about picking out granite countertops, remodeling the kitchen, and buying expensive furnishings. Things were really looking up for her."

Rain's ears perked up. And she wasn't the only one, as all eyes abruptly turned to Naomi. "Inheritance?" Julia asked.

"That's weird. I didn't think Lily had any family around. She told me she grew up in the foster care system. And that's why she didn't really put her trust in anyone—especially men," Shelby said matter-of-factly.

"Maybe that's why she was so surprised to learn that she was going to be the sole heir of an estate. Lily told me that she received a letter, from a lawyer out in Door County, saying she had a long-lost relative named Dennis Richardson, who had recently passed, and he had left her his estate and a sizable insurance policy. She asked if I would look at it, since I'm in real estate, to see if the letter was legit or if I thought someone was trying to mess with her. I looked up the property on the MLS, and it's a stunner, right on Lake Michigan." Naomi let out a slow whistle. "Uh, yeah, it's worth a pretty penny. I talked to the broker up in Door, and it's legit."

"Was she planning to move there?" Marge asked. "To Door County, I mean?"

Naomi shook her head. "No, she said if it was legit, she wanted to use the proceeds to update her new cottage here on Pine Lake. She asked if I could refer her to an agent in Door County to get the ball rolling. That's why this is so awful." She clutched a hand to her heart. "Given how much she was due to receive, it would've enabled her to demolish the cottage and completely rebuild if she wanted to. She had mentioned that possibility, knowing that her bank account was going to swell, big time." Her eyes turned downward. "Now her ideas are just that: worthless ideas . . ."

"Since Lily has no family around, who's next in line to inherit this property?" Julia asked.

"Yeah, theoretically, who would have something to gain?" Rain asked.

Naomi shrugged. "Who knows? Maybe the attorney out in Door County who sent her the letter could answer that question."

Because of the nature and intensity of the conversation around the table, Rain didn't hear the footsteps that had rounded the corner and joined them on the deck.

The group was then interrupted by a familiar man's voice. "Please excuse the intrusion, ladies."

Rain looked up to see Jace, dressed in his police uniform, his official presence towering over them.

"I'm going to need you all to follow me down to the station for questioning," he said resolutely.

"Do I need to go? I wasn't at the first book club meeting, and I never even met the woman," Hannah said quietly.

"No, but the rest of you need to come with me," Jace said, waving them to follow.

Rain met his eyes, looking for answers, but Jace turned on his heel, not giving her any hint of what was to come.

Chapter Ten

Seated on hard plastic chairs, the book club members all waited their turn at the police station. Mumbles reverberated between them despite being told numerous times that they were under somewhat of a gag order and to remain quiet. The Lofty Pines Police Station was not a large building by any means, and the officers had no other choice but to arrange the group against the wall, like books lined on a bookshelf. Each to be taken "off the shelf," one by one, and redirected into the office, for a private interview.

"I told you!" Chelsea wagged a warning finger at the group. "Frankly, I knew this was coming." She slumped in her chair. "I could really use a cup of coffee." Chelsea's lips tightened in a grim line as she turned and leaned her head back against the wall.

Rain was seated next to Julia and whispered in her ear, "Should we be worried? We're not really suspects, are we?"

Julia eyed Rain discreetly, lowered her voice, and said, "Highly unlikely. Because of a conflict of interest, Jace wouldn't be the one interviewing us if that were the case. However, I'm pretty sure they need us here for the show. I mean, look, Marge has already been dismissed and sent home to take care of Rex. It shouldn't be too much longer."

Rain looked to verify her friend's words. She knew Marge had been one of the first ones to be questioned, but had somehow missed her dismissal. She was pretty sure the older woman needed to get back home to her dog. But so did she. She needed to return to Benzo soon and let him out or she'd be greeted with a puddle on the floor. This was a whole new experience of responsibility to which she was totally unaccustomed.

Julia continued, "And I'm guessing we'll be the last ones brought into his office. So, you may as well get comfortable."

"Ahh, that's kinda what I was thinking too. I hate that they confiscated our phones until after we're done here. I feel naked without my phone." Rain patted her pockets with a frown. "Do you think you could maybe ask an officer if you can use a phone to call Nick and have him let Benzo out for me?"

"Already taken care of. I texted Nick before we gave up our phones—no worries."

"Oh, thank you, my friend! I swear, I don't know how I'd survive without your husband."

Julia patted her leg encouragingly and then leaned her head on Rain's shoulder momentarily as if already exhausted before her friend's name was even called.

Rain sat back in the chair and leaned her head against the wall and closed her eyes. All of this was making her very weary too. It had been a long day, and she hadn't slept well ever since she had learned of Lily's death.

"Excuse me, Rain, can you follow me, please?" The sound of her name made her eyes pop open. How long had she been out? She looked at the empty seats beside her and realized she must've dozed off for a bit. She confirmed this when she realized she'd been drooling and that the clock on the wall read eleven PM. Even Julia was missing from view.

Rain rose from her seat and followed Jace into a small office. He closed the door behind her and then held her gaze.

"What were you thinking?" he asked.

Rain dodged his stare, rubbed the sleep from her eyes, and waited for the tongue lashing.

Instead, Jace led her to a wooden chair beside a long metal desk. "Take a seat," he ordered, and Rain obeyed.

Jace stood over her, which seemed like an act of intimidation on his part. "Okay. I'll ask you again. What were you thinking, hosting a reenactment of the book you were reading, which included a poisoning?" He folded his arms across his broad chest. "And don't try and dodge the question because I've already hammered Julia about it. However, I'd like to understand which one of you is the instigator here. Why is it that when you two get together, it seems nothing but trouble occurs. Please, help me understand."

Rain was secretly glad Julia had taken the brunt of it because even though the line of his questioning was a bit harsh by Jace standards, his tone was not. It was more one of frustration. She didn't want to disappoint him in any capacity. Instead, she wished she could jump from the chair and into his arms. But she held back for fear he'd be upset that she didn't take his job seriously. Or she was deflecting. So she refrained and answered meekly, "I'm sorry." Her gaze dropped to the well-worn carpet, where she eyed what looked like a coffee stain beneath her feet. She wondered how long it had been there.

Jace surprised her by dropping to one knee in front of her and reaching for her hands. He held them tight. "Don't scare me like that again, you understand?" His eyes were fervent and compassionate all at once, causing her heart to melt like ice cream on a hot summer day.

"I'm really sorry. I didn't mean to scare you," she whispered again. Her eyes turned away from him, in shame.

Jace brushed his thumb along her cheek and then lifted her chin for their eyes to meet, and he held her gaze. An act so intimate that a thrill ran down her spine, and her heart began to flutter.

"You and my sister are a dangerous combination," he said under his breath. "I need you to be more careful."

Rain held up scout fingers. "I will, I promise."

He was so close that if she leaned in, she would feel his lips on hers.

Jace broke the spell by saying, "Thankfully, we have this under control now." He quickly rose to his feet and distanced himself by taking a seat behind the desk. Leaving her to feel like the desk between them had created an impenetrable chasm.

Rain folded her hands in her lap and inhaled a deep breath to settle the butterflies that had landed in her stomach. "Under control? Are you telling me you have a prime suspect?"

"It's not as cut and dry as you think."

"What do you mean?"

Jace leaned forward in his chair, steepled his long fingers, and said, "Lily has cancer. I'm sorry—let me rephrase that. I mean," he corrected sympathetically, Lily *had* cancer."

"What?" Rain's spine stiffened, and she sat upright in the chair. "She did? But her hair? I mean, Lily didn't look sick. Not at all! On the contrary, she seemed . . . *healthy*."

"Not according to her medical records. And the medical examiner confirmed it, stage four lymphoma."

"Wow, that's a bit of a shocker. I mean, I just met her, but it's the last thing I was expecting you to say. I had no idea she was sick." Rain's eyes darted to the carpet, trying to make sense of this new revelation.

"Yeah, I guess she was recently diagnosed and apparently look-ing for a second opinion. She hadn't started treatments yet. Which is why she hadn't lost her hair." Jace ran his hand through his own short hair, as if thankful for it, then leaned forward on the desk, folding his hands in front of him. "We haven't ruled out suicide. Perhaps she got the idea about the Visine at your book club meeting and decided to take matters into her own hands. We can't ignore that possibility. We need to take all the facts into consideration."

Rain sat back in her chair, dumbfounded. "Are you saying you've cleared everyone in the book club then? None of my fellow book clubbers are suspects, at this point. Correct?"

"I'm not saying that either." Jace drummed his fingers on the desk, an act she often noticed Julia do, and it suddenly made her think of her friend. "Where's Julia?"

"She's out there waiting for you."

"She wasn't out there when I came in?"

"Bathroom or vending machine? Who knows where she went. Maybe she needed a breath of fresh air. Or stepped out to call Nick." Jace shrugged. "Don't worry, you'll get a ride home."

"Would you take me?" Rain blurted. "I mean, can you go and dismiss her, there's no reason she should have to wait for us to fin-ish up. We've all had a long day. And I'm sure Nick is anxious to have her home."

Jace seemed to lighten briefly at the thought. "If you're sure?" he confirmed as he rose from his seat.

"Yeah, I'm sure." Rain wanted more of him. More of what he'd provided earlier when he tenderly touched her face. She had to be respectful at his place of work, but on the ride home she could be herself. She could prod him for more. And she desperately wanted to win back his trust.

Jace left the room, and Rain shivered. The air condition-ing seemed to be cranked full blast. She ran her hands up and down the goose bumps. She must've still been shaking when Jace returned because he asked, "You cold?"

"Yeah. I feel like a popsicle," Rain admitted, wrapping her arms around herself and attempting to warm up, to no avail.

"Okay, I think you've had enough of a tongue-lashing for one night. Let's get you outta here."

"What about Julia?" Rain rose from the chair. "Want me to go and grab a ride with her, then?"

"She just left. I still have a few questions for you." Jace reached for a nylon jacket hanging by the door and tossed it over his shoul-der. "We can finish this conversation in the car. I'll blast the heat, if need be, to warm you back up." He held the door for her, and they moved down a long corridor of pasty concrete walls that led away from his office.

Rain couldn't tell for sure, but it seemed Jace had a bit of skip in his step at the prospect of bringing her home. "I wanted to check in on Benzo anyway. You'll have to stop in at the humane society and fill out the necessary paperwork if you're planning to keep him, because I already alerted them that I was taking him there. Have you made a decision yet?" He attempted to hand her his lightweight police jacket to throw over her shoulders, but she declined with a wave of her hand.

"I'll be warm as soon as we step outside," Rain said. And she was right, as the dank, humid air hit them like a wall as soon as they stepped outdoors.

They drove in silence until they reached the campground, which was a stone's throw from her house.

Jace broke the silence when he asked, "So, you didn't answer me. Have you made a decision yet?"

"Decision?"

"On whether or not you want to keep the dog?"

"Oh, right." Rain smiled. "Yeah, I think Benzo has quickly wormed his way into my heart. I'd like to adopt him, if that's possible. Already I can't imagine what my life would be without him."

Jace loosened his grip on the steering wheel and said, "I can't tell you how happy that makes me."

"Really? Why?"

"I dunno." His eyes left the windshield and regarded her. "I hate thinking of you in that big ole cabin alone. Benzo will keep you company, but more importantly—safe."

"Nick and Julia are right next door, you know. And besides, you should be a little more worried about your sister's safety, not mine. I'm good. I can take care of myself."

"I am, but she has Nick. You have—"

Jace stopped himself from continuing.

"It's okay, Jace. Max is gone. We all know that, and you don't have to tiptoe around my loss anymore, okay?" She reached out and tapped his arm to convince him further. "Trust me, I'm getting used to living alone. I loved Max—I did. And he will always have a special place in my heart, but it's time for me to move on."

"It is?"

Was she imagining it, or was there a hint of excitement in his voice?

"Yes, it is," Rain said resolutely. "I'm ready, I think." She turned away from him and looked out the window at a plume of campfire smoke. Despite the windows being shut, she could still smell a whiff of burnt embers. The thought of s'mores by the fire made her stomach rumble with hunger pangs. It'd been a while since she'd last eaten.

"Does this have anything to do with that heat guy? You still seeing him, or what?"

"You mean Ryan?"

"Yeah, that guy. I haven't seen him around town lately. What hole has he been hiding in?" Jace said with a hint of sarcasm.

"I'm not really sure . . ."

"Not *really sure*? What does that mean?" Jace prodded.

Rain turned to him then. "What's it to you?" she asked teasingly, and then, for fear of coming off too flirty, said, "I thought you wanted to drive me home because you had more questions about Lily's case. Not my personal life. Go ahead—fire away."

Jace blew out a long, ragged breath. "It's been a long shift. I'm tired, Rain."

"I bet," she said as he pulled the cruiser into the driveway. "Then I guess I shouldn't ask you inside for a beer?" Rain's heart pounded in her chest. Part of her wanted him to say yes. She ached to spend more time alone with him. Was she really prepared for that? She felt her face flush, and her hands flew to her cheeks to feel the sudden heat, before she grabbed the door handle for a quick escape.

"I'll check on Benzo, but then I better go. Like I said, it's been a long day." Jace stifled a yawn with the back of his hand. "Too long." He rested his head on the steering wheel as if completely depleted of energy.

Rain hid her disappointment and ran her hand over his back to give a quick rub of encouragement. "You go on home. Benzo will be just fine with me. You can check in on him tomorrow if you'd like. No worries."

Jace responded with a full-out yawn.

"Go! Get outta here!" Rain ordered, and then gave him her best smile. "Thanks for the ride home, my friend. I appreciate it.

And as far as the case goes, tomorrow is another day. Try and get some sleep, okay?"

"Anytime you need me, Rain, you know I'm here for you," Jace said, and he grabbed hold of her wrist to prevent her from exiting the car.

Their eyes met.

"I mean it. Call me *anytime*."

He released her wrist, and she held his gaze a moment longer. "I will."

Chapter Eleven

After donning her sunglasses and readjusting the beach bag onto her shoulder, Rain stepped out onto the pier, causing the crayfish below to scatter and leave paths along the sand. She continued down the pier and met Julia on the pontoon boat. Julia had already lowered the vessel from the boatlift into the water and was lathering up with suntan lotion, leaving several white blotches, quite visible, on her arm. Because of her Mediterranean heritage on her mother's side, Rain didn't typically apply sunscreen after the first initial tan of the season. Julia on the other hand, was so fair she needed to reapply all summer long, or she'd end up like a red lobster.

"I'm so glad we're doing this!" Julia said, rubbing vigorously, as if willing the cream to penetrate her skin. "We need to enjoy this weather because, as you know, weather in Wisconsin . . ."

"Is a fickle itch," they said in unison, and then laughed.

Julia looked beyond her and asked, "Where's Benzo? I thought you were bringing him along?"

"I toyed with the idea but thought I better wait before taking him to an outdoor restaurant without knowing quite how he'll respond, you know? I haven't taken him for a boat ride yet either. It's something I'll need to do soon, because if he's going to live with me here on Pine Lake, that pup had better have his sea legs." Rain chuckled.

"No doubt!" Julia agreed with a smile.

"Unfortunately, we'll have to come back early because I'll need to let him out."

"No worries. I can ask Nick to handle dog duty if we run late. I'll text him. Trust me, he won't mind a bit." Julia reached into her beach bag for her phone and, Rain assumed, shot her husband a forewarning text.

"Thanks, I'd appreciate that because then we wouldn't need to rush back. I'm guessing Marge is meeting us at Portside?" Rain asked.

"Yeah, she said she'll drive over. The sun's too hot for her to join us on the boat today," Julia replied, dropping her phone and the suntan lotion into her bag. She spread out a beach towel, then tucked it beneath her, next to Rain, on the passenger seat.

"That'll work better for her, since we'll probably be seated outdoors at the grill. If she's driving back, she won't have to be out in the sun too long."

Rain tossed her tote down next to her legs so it wouldn't blow away, stepped behind the wheel, and backed the pontoon out onto the water. As soon as the boat was turned in the direction of the restaurant, she hit full throttle. The wind whipped her hair away from her face, and she instantly felt the thrill that came with gliding across the lake. Minor waves sent them bumping along, and they exchanged a knowing smile.

"I love this! Nothing better than being out here on the water!" Julia yelled over the engine noise. She held her hands up to the sky, as if in reverence of the experience.

"Me too!" Rain exclaimed as she felt the sun's heat on her skin slip away, replaced by the natural air conditioning caused by their speed.

Julia leaned over and reached her hand down next to the boat, trying to touch the wave, created from their wake, but it was too far from her hand. Rain tilted the boat playfully in to spray her friend. Julia gasped as she turned to Rain, wet faced.

"Sorry, not sorry," Rain said with a giggle.

Julia held up a joking fist. "I'll get you for that!" She grinned. She pulled the towel out from beneath her and began blotting her face dry, all the while laughing.

Before long, they were mooring alongside Portside Bar and Grill and tying a rope to a cleat to secure the vessel tight to the pier. After the boat was tucked in safe, and they both ran a wide-toothed comb through their hair, Rain stepped from the pontoon, and Julia followed.

A ping rang out from Julia's bag, and she plucked her cell phone from it. "I have a voicemail," she said as they walked along the long wooden dock leading to the eatery. "I didn't even hear it ring."

When they arrived and settled at an outdoor table beneath an oversized umbrella, Julia said, "The voicemail was from Marge. She's not coming. She said she forgot that she had a hair appointment scheduled." Julia frowned, tucking her phone back into her bag.

"Uh-oh," Rain said with a sigh.

"Yeah, we can't put this off any longer. We seriously need to talk about this. Marge's memory seems to be slipping, and I don't know what to do about it."

"I know—it kinda scares me too. Do we mention this to her? How do we go about suggesting she see a doctor for it?"

"I don't know," Julia moped. "I've never dealt with anything like this before. You?"

Rain shook her head. "No, me neither. We might need to seek out some advice on it before we proceed."

"That might be wise."

The waitress came to take their order, then turned on her heel and vanished as quickly as she'd come. They'd already planned to order the fish-and-chips basket, as it was their favorite go-to for lunch at the grill. Rain could hardly wait; she was starving.

"It's busy today." Julia said, looking around at the crowd that surrounded them. Bubbles of laughter and echoes of conversation carried across the oversized deck peppered with colorful umbrella-covered tables.

"Yeah, it's nice to be here, though. I've been craving their food, big time!" Rain turned to adjust the umbrella to shade them fully. "Speaking of busy, I forgot to ask Jace if we could reopen the library. I get the impression that the book club members were all cleared. Did he mention anything to you last night?"

"Oh yeah. He said we could but that we needed to keep him abreast of any murmurs within the bookshelves. Sounds like he doesn't think one of our book club members had anything to do with Lily's death. Did you get that impression too?"

"I did."

"I also wondered if he doesn't want the town of Lofty Pines to suspect anyone from the library, just in case word got out that all the book club members were questioned down at the station. You know how small-town gossip flies," Julia said thoughtfully, resting her hand on a closed fist. "Chelsea mentioned that talk around the coffee shop was running rampant, remember?"

"Yeah, I'm not sure which way Jace is leaning with the investigation." Rain shrugged. "I can't believe Lily was recently diagnosed with cancer. That was unexpected, huh?"

The waitress briefly interrupted their conversation by placing their drinks on the table. Which caused Rain and Julia to reply with a "Thank you!" The waitress already had her back to them and responded with a backward wave of her hand before quickly rushing off to the next table.

"So . . . Lily was sick. But she sure hid that well," Rain said, and then took a sip of her Diet Coke.

"Yeah, that was a real shocker! Wasn't it?" Julia toyed with her straw. "I'm pretty sure Jace only told that information with us on the down-low. No one else in the book club was told that she was ill," Julia zipped her lips and turned an imaginary key.

Rain took another sip of her soda. The warm summer day made her feel like she needed to hydrate, or maybe it was her nerves that were making her mouth grow dry. "Before we talk about Lily any further, I need to discuss something with you. I have something that's weighing kinda heavily on my mind. Can we talk?"

Julia straightened in her chair. Rain's tone must've given off more alarm bells than she'd intended, and it was confirmed when her friend said, "Sounds serious, luv! What is it?"

"I need to be honest with you about something that I've been keeping close to my chest. Something I haven't even said aloud. We can talk openly about anything, right, Julia?"

"Oh gosh, Rain, you're not sick too, are you?" Julia reached out to clasp Rain by the wrist, then gave it a comforting squeeze.

Rain smiled. "No, no. Nothing like that. That's not it at all."

"Oh, phew!" Julia animatedly wiped a hand across her brow and slumped back in her chair. "You scared me there for a second. What is it then?"

Rain wanted to choose her words carefully and wasn't sure quite how to say it. She gnawed on the inside of her cheek as she attempted to form a sentence. But she couldn't seem to find the right words.

"What? Come, on, you're killing me here!" Julia snorted.

"It's Jace," Rain whispered.

Julia sat upright in the chair, spread her fingers on the table, and leaned forward on her hands. "Something's wrong with my brother?"

"No. That's the problem. There's absolutely *nothing* wrong with him."

"Rainy, I'm not following here." Julia sat back in the chair and looked at Rain with a dumbfounded expression, as if trying to read her like a book but failing miserably. "You're going to have to give me a little clarity."

"I'm having trouble being around him lately . . . in the friend zone." Rain's gaze traveled out to the lake. The sun glittered across the water like sequins on a party dress. A pair of neon Jet Skis fled across the lake, as if they were racing. Part of her wanted to jump on one of them and escape this conversation entirely. Instead, her eyes returned to her friend, to see if Julia understood.

"Wait. You mean . . .?" Julia's smile widened.

"Look, this is your brother we're talking about. I would never want to do anything that would jeopardize our friendship. So, if me feeling what I'm feeling is wrong, then slap me upside the head and knock some sense into me. *Please*—and do it soon!" Rain lifted the glass of Diet Coke to her forehead to cool herself and then wiped her forehead of the condensation.

"On the contrary." Julia grinned. "I've been waiting, oh so patiently, to hear these words *finally* come out of your mouth."

Rain's jaw dropped. "You have?"

"Seriously? It's sooo obvious when you two are around one another!" Julia rolled her eyes as if exasperated. "Like we all didn't know," she said while chewing on her straw.

"What do you mean by 'we all'?" Rain threw her fingers up in air quotes. "Who? Who else are you talking about?"

Julia lifted her fingers and ticked them off one by one. "Well, there's me, Nick, Kim, Seth—come on Rainy; we've all seen you two dance around each other. You both light up like a string of patio lights around one another. It's like the rest of us don't even *exist* when you're together. We're all completely dim in comparison. Should I go on?" She laughed and then batted her eyelashes dramatically.

"It is? It's really that obvious?" Rain was surprised her feelings seemed to be so transparent.

"Duh!" Julia mocked good-naturedly, reaching out a hand and swatting her with the back of it.

"And you're okay with it? I mean if I were to choose to pursue your brother. You'd be fine with that?"

"*Rain.*"

"What?"

"You know me, girlfriend. Nothing will ever come between us." Julia reached out a hand again, this time grabbing hers, and gave a tight squeeze. "And that includes my goofy brother." She held up a pinky as if to do a pinky swear.

"But what if . . . well . . . what if things were to go sour? I can't lose you, Julia . . ." Rain murmured. "I can't . . . I can't handle another loss like that. Not in this lifetime. I can't do it." Rain inhaled deep and blew her breath out slowly and methodically. "It's just not worth it."

"Why would you ever think that? You're stuck with me." Julia beamed, taking another sip of her soda.

"But, what if . . ." Rain covered her head with her hands. The memory of Max, suddenly vivid as ever, boomeranged her to the past. The enormity of her loss suddenly bore down on her, like an anchor dragging her to the depths of the lake.

"Don't do that. I've literally been watching you try and push my brother away since the first time you laid eyes on him again. Including during that little stint with that Ryan Wright guy."

Rain looked up.

Julia leaned in closer and lowered her voice. "Which, by the way, I knew was another way to deflect from your true feelings for my brother. Look, I know you suffered a great loss, Rain, and you were both so *young*—too young. Max was only thirty-two years old when he passed. It's not fair that you had to endure that," Julia said sadly, "but you can't protect yourself all the time. Don't you understand that? 'The heart wants what the heart wants,'" she sang out.

Rain slowly shook her head in denial.

"Oh, don't shake your pretty little head at me because apparently," Julia stated, grinning ear to ear, "your heart wants my brother. I can't help but think it'd be kinda fun. I mean, can you imagine? We could actually become related—like legally, officially sisters!"

"Whoa—easy now. Let's not get carried away, Julia." Rain took a sip of her soda and contemplated. "However, it's not only my heart's fault. Why does your brother have to be so darn adorable too?" She smiled timidly.

"Dunno. He got the looks, I got the brains," Julia said with a lopsided grin, as she loaded a French fry with ketchup and popped it into her mouth.

When had their food arrived? Rain had been so filled with turmoil about their conversation, she hadn't even noticed the plate of food that had landed in front of her.

"You're not going to tell him we talked about this, are you?" Rain asked, reaching for her fork. "This conversation stays between us, right?" she stressed with an upraised brow.

Julia zipped her lips. "Not a word, my friend."

Rain sighed heavily. "But what if it doesn't work out between us?"

"And what if it does?"

Chapter Twelve

After lunch, the two enjoyed an afternoon of swimming, tanning, and cruising the pontoon around Pine Lake. When the sun began to slowly slip toward the horizon, and the clouds turned a shade of cotton candy, Rain set the engine to low for one last leisurely trip around the perimeter before finally heading home.

Julia had wrapped herself in a towel and began to shiver from her damp swimsuit. Rain noticed that her friends' lips had turned slightly blue too. She decided maybe their trip around the lake should be cut short, and it was time to turn the boat in the direction of home.

"It was nice of Nick to let Benzo out for me this afternoon, but I probably need to let him out again, and maybe even take him for a quick walk before dark." Rain throttled the engine and took in the remainder of the trip like balm to a weary soul.

"I suppose—if we must," Julia whined. "It was such a great day; I hate to see it come to an end."

"Yeah, back to reality, my friend. I need to do a little work at the library if we plan to reopen tomorrow too. I must admit, it's been kinda nice having it closed. It feels like a mini vacation. But

I'm certain the return box that your husband built for me last year is overflowing at this point."

"I bet it is. We should probably look at that and make sure everything is in order before officially heading in for the night."

Nick had built a wooden return box outside the library. It was a beautifully crafted piece of art, but not large enough to accommodate all the books that Rain surmised had been returned while the library had been closed. She had a feeling some people would be careless, and if the box was full, might leave novels scattered on the ground or stacked on top of the box. She needed to check just in case the humidity was on the rise again or—worst-case scenario—another summer storm was about to hit.

"I hate to leave the boat, though." Julia continued sulking as she wrapped the towel tighter around herself. "Summer always goes by way too fast."

"I know—I hear ya, girlfriend. We need to take advantage more often, especially while Marge is willing to cover for us, too, on warm days like today. Otherwise, we'll completely miss summer and be griping again, come fall, that the season went by too quick." Rain slowed the throttle, then eased the pontoon onto the boat lift and cut the engine.

"Well, thank you again, my dear—it was just what the doctor ordered," Julia said as she gathered her things and hopped off the boat. She then manually cranked the lift wheel to raise the boat completely out of the water.

Rain followed Julia back to the log cabin, and the two climbed wearily up the stairs leading to the upper deck. "Boy, I'm tuckered out!" Rain confessed after reaching the top step.

"Me too! The sun, the breeze—it's exhausting living this life," Julia quipped with a jab of her elbow.

Rain immediately let Benzo out, and he happily greeted her by jumping full body on her and almost knocking her completely over. "Down, Puppers!" she said sternly. "Someone needs a little more training!" she corrected as she leashed the dog and led him to a place where he could do his business.

Meanwhile, Julia waited for her on the upper deck. By the time Rain returned, Julia had donned a sweatshirt, and the color in her lips had returned to normal.

"You don't need to help at the library in your wet swimsuit. Go on home and grab a hot shower—I can handle it by myself," Rain suggested. "It shouldn't take me too long."

"Nah, my suit's almost dry now. I'll help you reshelve and then head home. Not fair to leave you with a mess. Besides, if we do it together, it'll be done lickety-split, and we can both head in and relax for the night. Not to mention, if you wanted to take a quick walk with Benzo before dark. I'd go with you, but I should probably head home and spend some time with Nick. We've been like two ships passing in the night, lately."

"I don't know why you're so good to me," Rain said as she led Benzo back inside the log cabin and grabbed the key for the library door.

As they stepped onto the catwalk leading to the library, Julia stopped short and asked, "You don't think Lily took her own life, do you? Because if that's true, I'll feel awful because then the book club led her to do it? Right? I mean, the suggestion of Visine— well, it's over the counter, easy to find. Lily probably had Visine in her own medicine cabinet. Am I overthinking this? I'm really hoping that's not the case."

"I know—me too. On the other hand, wouldn't she have at least attempted cancer treatments? Especially since Jace mentioned she had an appointment for a second opinion lined up," Rain said thoughtfully.

"Yeah, and Naomi mentioned that Door County estate, worth big bucks. Would that be enough to fight cancer for?"

"Let's go over the facts as we know them. Shall we?"

"Okay."

"First, we found the door to her cottage open," Rain said.

"Yes, but it looked as if someone had jimmied with the lock. So, we immediately called Jace."

"But the door was unlocked, so we determined Lily must've willingly invited someone inside."

"Yes," Julia rolled her hand forward, prompting them to continue. "Someone she knew or, at the very least, felt safe with."

"And two people drank a bottle of wine."

Julia hip-checked her. "And there was that letter from the attorney."

"And Lily was still wearing the clothes she wore to book club, so she hadn't gone to bed or even gotten ready for bed."

Julia lifted a finger to interrupt. "If you were planning to kill yourself, wouldn't you leave a note?"

"You would think so, though it sounded like Lily didn't have much family around. The other question is, would you do it by the front door? Wouldn't you go somewhere else, like maybe a bedroom or a canoe on the lake? Wouldn't you want your last moments to be somewhere you felt safe or that was private or peaceful? Maybe that's just me . . ."

"I suppose we have to determine the effects Visine would have on a person. Maybe it made her feel like running instead of passing out cold. Maybe she went mad and took a screwdriver to her own door!" Julia responded with a shrug. "I realize it's just a lame theory, but poison could have a weird effect on some people. Couldn't it?"

When they reached the library return box, it was just as Rain had suspected. Books were stacked on top of it. She shook her head disapprovingly and immediately got to work removing them.

"What's wrong with people?" Julia huffed as she gathered a large stack of books into her arms, to the point where she could barely be seen behind them.

Rain hurried to put the key inside the lock before Julia dropped a single one. She ripped off the "Closed" sign and carried it in her teeth while she held open the door so her friend could stumble inside with the stack of books. Julia dropped them on the counter with a grunt.

"What's this?" Julia removed the note from Rain's teeth.

"What?"

"Someone stuck a Post-it Note on the closed sign." Julia said, holding the note between them.

The two gasped in unison.

The Post-it Note read:

Refer to the book SPARKLING CYANIDE,
George knew exactly why his wife died,
And just like Lily, it was not by suicide.

Chapter Thirteen

Rain held the Post-it Note between them, stuck to a trembling finger. "Who on earth would write something like that?" she pondered aloud as she studied the handwriting. It didn't look familiar, but it had an impressive slant to it—almost like calligraphy. She wished she could do a script test on everyone who had participated in the first book club meeting, to see if she could find a match. The person who wrote this clearly had identifiable penmanship and had heard the chatter around town about Lily potentially committing suicide. It could've leaked from someone within the Lofty Pines Police Department—but Rain didn't believe that was the case.

Instead . . . she believed the person who wrote it had been copying the clues left behind in the Agatha Christie book they had just read. The protagonist, Rosemary, from *Sparkling Cyanide*, was also accused of taking her own life. Until her husband, George, held the reenactment to prove that wasn't the case. And one by one, each suspect was eliminated.

"Well, that seals the deal that it wasn't Kim," Julia said sarcastically. "Now there's even more to corroborate her alibi, along with her husband and Nick."

"What makes you say that?"

"Because she's the only one in the group who didn't read the book and instead watched the movie. I don't think the anonymous letters that George received about Rosemary's death and her potential for suicide were even in the movie. Remember the arguments that took place over all of that at our book club meeting? It sounds like they took a lot of liberties in the making of the movie."

"Ah." Rain tapped a finger to her lips. "But you make a good point, my dear Watson. Not only regarding Kim but everyone else in the group as well. Because whoever wrote this note clearly must've read *Sparkling Cyanide*. There are no ifs, ands, or buts about it. It's like the person is intentionally leading us by the nose to follow the clues used in the book we just read."

"So, now we're back to square one," Julia said flatly. She twisted the pink streak in her hair and sighed heavily. "Now what?"

"The night of book club, someone mentioned that she had an interest in publishing poetry. Do you recall who it was who said that?"

Julia shrugged and then indicated the note with a pointed finger. "I'm not sure I'd call that poetry. It seems like more of a riddle to me."

"Yeah, I hear you. I realize it's a shot in the dark, but at least it's something. If I remember correctly, I think it was Chelsea who mentioned she wanted to publish a book of poetry. Maybe we should pay a visit to Brewin' Time tomorrow morning and see if she's working."

"I suppose. I'm not opposed to a chocolate donut for breakfast, anyway." Julia's smile widened. "Besides, what other clues do we have to go on?"

"Honestly, not much," Rain admitted, and then blew out a breath of frustration.

"You're not going to like my next thought either." Julia rocked back and forth on her heels and tucked her hands behind her as if pondering their next move.

"What's that?"

"We're not going to tell Jace about this just yet. We'll follow the leads where they go and *then* share our findings." Julia shifted her stance and crossed her arms defiantly. "Unless of course, you want him to shut down the library indefinitely."

"Would he do that, you think?"

"Uh-huh. I'm pretty sure that's exactly what he would do. You ready for that? To be closed up for the entire summer. Can you imagine the outcry from our patrons?" she continued.

Rain wasn't sure about that idea, so she remained quiet.

Julia began to pace the aisle of the library and continued to plead her case. "I know my brother—he'll get all protective and brotherly like, and shut us down." She turned on her heel to face Rain directly, and continued, "But I think we can suss out the killer ourselves." She wagged a finger between them. "You and I know we have a better chance at solving this. We're closer to it. You have to know, the killer was one of us. One of our very own book club members did this deed. There's no other explanation, is there?"

Rain was unsure, but Julia always had a way of talking her into things. She certainly was laying it on thick. Jace was right: one of them was an instigator, but it wasn't Rain. She hesitated before following through with "Maybe we can do this. Of course, we can. Right?"

"Hey, I mean, that's what I'm thinking. We're gonna have a much better chance of making sense of all of this, since we're embedded in the book club. Don't you think the other members will only clam up for the police? Just like they did the first night of questioning." Julia pressed doggedly, "You have to realize, they'll probably ask for legal representation if they feel pressured to talk again. And then the police will have nothing to go on! We can't let that happen."

"I have to agree with you on that. It was my impression that the Lofty Pines Police Department didn't get any further in their investigation after that first night of questioning."

"So, it's up to us," Julia said with deep resolve, lifting her chin. "We'll get to the bottom of it."

"Oh boy, Jace was right," Rain said under her breath.

"Right about what?"

"That you and I are a dangerous combination." Rain laughed.

Julia waved a hand of dismissal. "On the contrary, my brother doesn't know what he's talking about." She tapped a finger to her temple and grinned. "I'll say it again—he might have the looks, but I have the brains."

"I doubt that the person who stuck the Post-it Note to our closed sign left fingerprints behind on it, do you?" Rain asked.

"If it's someone who loves a good mystery and reads the likes of Agatha Christie's work, and left a Post-it Note like that, then they'd be smart enough to wear gloves and not leave DNA behind."

"That's my thought exactly," Rain agreed with a slow nod of her head.

"We can put the riddle in a safe spot, on the rare chance it can be used and tested for prints, down the line. However, it's up to us to find out just whose set of prints *need* to be tested," Julia suggested.

"And we'll start by looking at samples of our book clubbers' handwriting." Rain snapped a photo of the Post-it Note before putting it back on the "Closed" sign and tucking the full sheet of paper away into a tourism book about Wisconsin, for safekeeping.

She then placed the book neatly inside the desk drawer and covered it with another stack of loose-leaf paper.

"I guess we'd better hurry and reshelve these books and call it a night, 'cause it looks like we have a big day tomorrow," Julia said with a grin.

*　*　*

The following morning, after a fitful night's sleep, Rain decided an early walk with Benzo might help clear her mind before she headed over to the library. Upon their return, she noticed Marge's car was already in the parking lot, so Rain hastened her steps to check in on her coworker.

Opening the door to the library, Rain called out, "Mornin', Marge."

Benzo sniffed his way down the aisle, and Rain followed, where she found the older woman fussing over her dog.

"Well, good morning, my dear!" Marge said as she stroked Benzo behind the ears. "Look at this handsome fellow. Oh, I couldn't be happier for you." She beamed. "You finally found a match. And it's a match made in heaven, I'd say!"

"I know." Rain smiled. "Isn't he a love?"

"He most certainly is!" she said, scratching under his chin.

Benzo looked up at Marge with those pale blue eyes and lolled his tongue, as if smiling in response.

"May I ask what brought you in so early today?" Rain asked. "I mean, how'd you know that we'd reopened?"

Marge stared at her with a look of utter confusion.

"Did Julia call you?"

"No. But I'm always here in the morning, unless you two want to go boating. Did you plan to do that this afternoon? I can stay if you need me to."

"Um, no." Rain scratched her head. "It's not that. I was just wondering how you knew we had reopened?"

"Oh." Marge's brows narrowed in a thin line. "We were closed?" she said finally.

It was then Rain realized that Marge didn't remember that the library had been closed. She beckoned her coworker to follow her to the coffee bar and flicked the button on the cordless kettle to make her favorite flavor of ginger-lemon tea.

"Would you like to join me out on the deck before the sun gets too hot? It's early, and the library doesn't open for another hour. How does that sound?" Rain asked.

"Sounds lovely, Rain." Marge smiled. "I was surprised to come to work and find all the books reshelved already this morning."

"Julia and I handled that last night."

"You worked last night?"

"Come on, let's go have a chat." Rain said, carrying their mugs of tea and leading Marge to follow to the outer deck. "Come Benzo," she patted her leg, and the dog obediently trotted at their side.

The two took a seat in the Adirondack chairs overlooking the early morning view of Pine Lake while Benzo curled at Rain's feet. Due to the thick humidity, a cloud of vapor hovered over the water, like a ghost, and the eerie sound of a loon call echoed in the distance.

Marge shivered.

Rain momentarily abandoned her coworker in search of a throw blanket from inside the cabin. She returned and covered Marge's shoulders with it.

"Oh, thank you. This dampness does make it feel a bit chilly."

"I know, right?" Rain said, slipping into the Adirondack next to her. "It's so weird how you can feel hot and cold all at the same time. But that's Wisconsin for ya! I often wonder if it's like that in other places around the world or it's just us that wear sweat-shirts and shorts at the same time. But I love it here, even though we have crazy roller-coaster temperatures and can celebrate both summer and winter all in one day!"

"Indeed," Marge said as she sipped her tea.

"Can I ask you something?"

"Sure, dear. I'm an open book," Marge said with a growing smile.

"Do you remember what Jace asked you? The night he ques-tioned the book club members down at the police department?"

"Certainly, yes. Why do you ask?"

"Would you mind filling me in?"

"Well, thankfully, he didn't keep me long, as I had to get home to Rex. He said I was cleared and never considered a suspect, but that he wanted my take on the situation."

"And did you share your thoughts?"

"Yes, but I didn't share anything that you don't already know. I'm certain he asked us all the same questions."

"Oh."

Rain toyed with her words before she cleared her throat. "Marge?"

"Yes, dear?"

"Have you noticed you've been a little forgetful lately?"

Marge set her tea aside and asked, "What do you mean?"

Rain attempted to keep her tone light. "You haven't noticed? We missed you at Portside, for lunch. Julia mentioned that you'd forgotten about a hair appointment. I don't know. . . you just seem to forget things. And you weren't always like that."

"Oh, that. It's normal to forget things at my age," Marge snapped—her tone a little harsher than normal. "I'm not a young person anymore. I can't keep up with you and Julia and all your goings-on!" Marge mocked with a twinkle in her eye. Rain wondered if the teasing was meant to ease the growing tension between them. "I hope you don't expect me to."

"No, I know," Rain stammered. "And I never meant that you need to. Keep up with us, I mean."

"Just you wait until you're my age—you'll become forgetful too and need to leave notes all over the place. I even found a note in my refrigerator! You're just a young, little kitten! But you wait and see—it catches up with the best of us." She winked.

The problem was, Rain didn't think Marge's current behavior *was* normal. And she didn't know what she should do next to help her dear friend.

Chapter Fourteen

Humid air caused Rain's tank top to stick to her skin like an unwanted hug. She fanned herself with one hand as she held the door with the other so Julia could step ahead of her inside Brewin' Time. The air conditioning hit them like a wall, but Rain took the atmosphere in willingly and plucked at her shirt to dry the sweat-soaked fabric. The smell of chocolate and freshly percolated coffee prompted them deeper into the space. The long glass case was filled with brownies, donuts, scones, and fresh baked cookies, and a line had already formed alongside it as customers were ogling over what to choose.

"What are you gonna order?" Rain asked.

Julia leaned over the glass case, almost touching her nose to it. "There's a sprinkle-covered chocolate donut with my name on it, and I plan to wash it down with an iced coffee. You?" Her eyes doubled in size, and she licked her lips, as if in anticipation of the sugar high she was about to receive.

"That does sound pretty amazing." Rain looked around and noticed Chelsea was not behind the counter. Instead, she spotted her in the corner of the room, vigorously wiping a table. She dug into her shorts pocket and handed Julia a ten-dollar bill. "Would you mind ordering for both of us, and I'll go and talk with Chelsea? I'll just have the iced coffee, though, and skip the donut, for now."

Julia nudged her on the arm. "Go for it! Check and see if she'll take a break with us. I'll just order a half dozen donuts in case you change your mind. I can always bring any extra home to Nick too." She leaned into Rain's ear. "'Cause I'm pretty confident you'll change your mind when you see me take a bite outta mine." She chuckled.

Rain laughed. "Maybe."

"Oh, I know so," Julia said assuredly. "Just send me a wave if Chelsea's able to join us for a few minutes, will ya? That way I can order an iced coffee for her too."

"Will do," Rain said, moving away from the counter.

Although the line was long, the establishment was almost empty of seated customers, as it was already midmorning. She hoped for their sakes it would remain that way, and she could coax the coffee shop manager to visit with them for a bit.

Chelsea looked up and smiled as Rain approached. "Hey, how are you doing this fine, muggy morning?" she asked, tossing a rag into a Rubbermaid bin that was filled with dirty mugs and dishes.

"Great, thanks. And you?"

"Me? I'm just getting past the morning rush, but I'd rather be in here then out in that heat any day of the week." Chelsea groaned before gesturing to the nearby booth. "I just cleaned this table if you're hiding from the muggy weather for a bit."

"Julia and I were hoping you could join us for a coffee break. Sounds like you could use it. Can I tempt you with one of your iced coffees and a donut?"

Chelsea's eyes darted around the room before she consented. "Sure, sounds good to me. I'll be happy to get off my feet for a few minutes. Just give me a second to return these dirty dishes to the kitchen, and I'll be right back," she said, turning on her heel.

Rain sent Julia a wave, and her friend received the message and gave a thumbs-up.

After the three were seated around the table, deep in the corner of the coffee shop and out of earshot, Chelsea whispered, "So how are you two holding up after that night of interrogation? Wasn't that awful? I've never so much as gotten a speeding ticket, and suddenly I felt like I was participating in *America's Most Wanted*! It was intense, to say the least." She plucked a vanilla-glazed donut from the box and immediately took a bite.

"Never mind us—we were wondering how you were doing." Julia leaned in closer, conspiratorially. "You mentioned people have been giving you the hairy eyeball in here lately. Hear any more rumblings at the ole Brewin' hangout? Or has the gossip wheel stopped turning?"

Chelsea shook her head. "Nah, I'm not hearing much here anymore. It seems the more time that passes, the more people are onto the latest gossip. Now, the chatter is that a national chain grocery store is looking at Lofty Pines. Apparently, they want to throw up a building at the old dump site. So, that's now front-and-center news around here."

Rain and Julia exchanged a disappointed glance. And a lull fell between them.

"Was it you, the night of book club, who mentioned you wanted to publish a book of poetry someday?" Julia asked casually.

The question was so out of left field that Chelsea's brows came together, as if she was trying to make sense of it. "Yeah, why?"

"No reason. I just couldn't remember . . . Rain and I were talking about that over at the library earlier, when I was reshelving a book by Robert Frost. If you're willing to share, I'd love to read some of your poems sometime . . ." Julia trailed off.

"Yeah," Rain plucked a small notepad from her purse. And scribbled on the paper. "I like poetry too. I started this one, but I'm a bit confused . . . I mean, does every line have to rhyme? For example," she read aloud: *"Roses, are red, Benzo's eyes are blue, I love my new puppy . . .* Like, what would you write next?" She made eye contact with Chelsea, who looked at her as if she'd just fallen off her rocker.

"I'm not trying to be rude, so please don't take this the wrong way, but 'roses are red'? That's so overused and, quite frankly, not poetic in the least." Chelsea chuckled. "If you want to write a poem about your dog, maybe start with Benzo's eyes, so pouty and blue . . ."

"Oh!" Rain sat up higher in her chair and pushed the notepad in front of Chelsea. "Can you write that down for me! I *love* that. That sounds like a good start, and then I can take it from there. My plan is to write a poem and frame it beside a photo of Benzo, for my fireplace mantel."

Julia's smile widened inadvertently, and then she plastered on a poker face.

Chelsea took the notepad and began to write. Rain and Julia zoned in on her handwriting as if both trying to confirm she'd written the note they'd found tacked on the library door. Instead, Chelsea's handwriting came out in large, friendly loops. Nothing at all like the tight slant of calligraphy Rain had been expecting.

An uncomfortable pause ensued as Chelsea dropped the pen and then toyed with the straw in her iced coffee.

"I'm sorry to bring it up again—I know this is hard for everyone to talk about. But this is all so weird," Rain said. "I just can't imagine anyone wanting to intentionally hurt Lily. I mean, *why*? It just doesn't make sense to me. I'm actually losing sleep over it."

"I agree," Julia said "This is all so crazy! I just keep replaying the *why* in my head too. I guess it's just the mystery reader in me, trying to solve the puzzle." Julia reached for the napkin holder, and after plucking one out, folded it and laid the napkin beneath her iced coffee to catch the condensation.

"Exactly," Rain agreed. "The police must have some idea of a potential motive in this case. I'm guessing *someone* is on their radar if they let us all go without a second glance. Otherwise, wouldn't they have hauled us all back to the station for more questioning?"

Chelsea beckoned them in closer and lowered her voice. "I did share something with the police that I thought could be a potential motive." She held up a slender finger and warned. "But you didn't hear it from me. You got that?"

Rain and Julia shared a look of surprise before they returned their attention to Chelsea and in unison blurted, "Yeah, definitely!"

Chelsea seemed to hold back a little as she hesitated, scanning the room, her lips pressed together, as if maybe she was having second thoughts.

Julia coaxed further. "You can trust us; we'll never tell a soul." She locked her lips with an imaginary key and animatedly tossed it far over her shoulder.

"Yes, I second what she said. Our lips are sealed tighter than a drum." Rain gently tapped Chelsea on the hand as a prompt to continue.

Chelsea glanced around the room again and then looked up at the ceiling before continuing. "Lily claimed that she was in possession of something written by the famous Laura Ingalls Wilder—specifically a manuscript. And that these rare handwritten pages were penned about our great state of Wisconsin. Supposedly, the manuscript was another series that Laura Ingalls Wilder started before her death but never finished. Lily believed it was something of great value."

"Wait. You mean *the* Laura Ingalls Wilder? The one who wrote the *Little House on the Prairie* series?" Rain sat back in her chair, stunned.

Chelsea nodded her head vigorously. "The very one."

"Did she show the manuscript to you?" Julia asked eagerly.

"No. And that's the thing. We were supposed to meet up, and she was planning to show it to me. When we were walking to the parking lot after book club, she asked me if I would be interested in seeing something like that. She said she only brought it up to me because I had mentioned I was interested in Wisconsin-based authors. And who better than the famous Laura Ingalls Wilder! I sort of got the impression that she was attempting to downplay the confrontational banter she'd had with some of the members in the group that night, and wanted to leave with a few people in her corner to reconnect with at the next meeting. She basically told me that books were her life, since she wasn't married—no kids or anything."

"Wow," Rain said.

Chelsea continued, "Yeah, I know. That's kinda how I felt about it too. Lily said that Laura Ingalls Wilder wrote *Little House on the Prairie* based on her time growing up in rural Wisconsin. But she said she also began to write a story that was *about* Wisconsin. You knew the author grew up in Pepin, right?"

"Yeah, I've heard that," Rain said. "But how did Lily end up with these manuscripts in her possession? I mean, where did they come from?"

"Beats me," Chelsea said, picking up a tiny piece of donut with her fingers and popping it into her mouth. "The last thing I expected was for Lily to die and never get the opportunity to show me. Now I'll never know." She shuddered and then took a sip of iced coffee.

"Lily didn't tell you anything else? Like where she kept these manuscripts? Or any proof of their origin, anything like that?" Rain pressed.

"Nope. Nada on the origin. However, she did tell me to come over to the cottage on Pine Lake to see it, so I'm assuming that's where she kept it. So, y'all, what if Lily told someone besides me, and the person killed her for it. And what if that person went and stole those priceless artifacts?" Her eyes darted to theirs for confirmation. "Hey, I've heard people kill for less. Sounds like a potential motive to me."

"I agree, that could be a motive. Money can certainly be a driving factor," Julia said, twirling the pink streak of her hair between her fingers thoughtfully.

"What about Shelby? Have either of you talked to her?" Chelsea asked. "Wasn't she the one who knew Lily the best out of all of us? I thought Shelby said they grew up together. If Lily had something as priceless as a Laura Ingalls Wilder manuscript, wouldn't she have told her friend about it?"

"That's a very good question," Rain said.

"Are you suggesting Shelby is a suspect?" Julia asked.

Chelsea waved her hands defensively. "No, no. That's not at all what I'm implying. I'm just saying maybe Lily didn't tell that many people about the manuscript, but there's a chance she could've confided in Shelby too. Hopefully not, because being linked to this might put us both in danger," Chelsea said, her eyes growing wide as if the realization had just hit her.

"How so?" Julia asked.

"If the person who stole the manuscripts finds out that I know about them, won't they come after me too? Because clearly, if these phantom Laura Ingalls Wilder pages are found or end up at auction, we'll find Lily's killer!"

"She's kinda got a point," Rain said.

"And you told the police this?" Julia asked.

"Did someone say police?" a familiar male voice asked.

Rain's eyes rose to see Jace standing over the table, his hands planted firmly on his hips. The three had been so deep in conversation that none of them had seen him approach the table. And he didn't look happy.

Chapter Fifteen

Julia pushed the box of donuts in Jace's direction. "Care for a treat, brother?" she asked in her honey-dipped voice. A tone Rain had often heard when they were kids and their hands had been caught in the cookie jar, so-to-speak.

It didn't deter her brother, though. Jace peeked in the box, removed a jelly-filled donut, and took a huge bite, causing the sugary red liquid to ooze out the side of his mouth before he caught it with his finger.

Rain handed him a napkin, and he mumbled a "thank you."

Chelsea rose from her seat. "I'd better get back to work. Thanks for the coffee, Julia. I should've met you at the register—I could've bought you one on the house." She dug into her pocket for payment, but Julia shook her head adamantly.

"Nope, the coffee is on me this round," Julia said warmly. "It was great chatting with you, Chelsea."

Jace wolfed down the rest of his donut, wiped his mouth with the napkin, and asked, "Chelsea, may I have a word?"

Chelsea's eyes darted to Rain and then to Julia, nervously, before her tentative voice squeaked out, "Sure, of course."

"You can have this table—we were just leaving, right, Rain?" Julia rose from her seat and scurried out of the booth. She closed the lid on the donuts and tucked the box under her arm before reaching for Rain with the other hand and dragging her out of the booth behind her.

Rain wanted to linger in Jace's company. She also understood he wanted to talk to Chelsea, alone, she assumed about the case. But was it? A tinge of something akin to jealousy came over her, surprising her. She tapped Jace on the arm before walking away.

"Can I see you later? Stop by after work," Rain said boldly as she backed away from him. She had never asked Jace to stop by her cabin unless it was for a barbeque or campfire, or something planned for a large group of friends. And this time, nothing was in the works.

Jace's expression was one of surprise. "Yeah, sure. I can do that."

Her eyes met his directly. "Great. Looking forward to it." Rain gave him her most winning smile.

Julia then tugged her arm once again, and the two headed out the door.

"Oh, I love it!" Julia squealed as soon as they were back outdoors, smack dab in the center of the unbearable heat wave. "You're planning to use your charms on my brother to hear what they're talking about back there. Good work, Rainy!"

"I am not," Rain said, stopping in her tracks. The words flew out of her mouth so fast and so stern, she surprised even herself.

And it was obvious Julia was taken aback. "You're not?"

"No. I genuinely want to spend time with him. Just because . . . I want to," Rain corrected. "Plus, he mentioned he wanted to check in on Benzo. So, there's that too."

"Oh." Julia seemed at a loss for words, which was completely unnatural for her friend.

"I'm sorry. Is this all too uncomfortable?" Rain asked, returning to her quick stride to keep up with Julia's pace.

"No. You're fine." Julia recovered with a wave of dismissal. "But please. Do promise me you'll press him even a wee little bit about Chelsea if you get an opportunity?" She dropped the donuts on the center console before settling herself behind the wheel of Nick's truck. "We need to figure this out. Can you do that for me?"

Rain squeaked open the door to the passenger side and hopped in. "I guess."

"Don't you wonder what he's talking to her about? You think she's a suspect?" Julia asked as she put the key in the ignition and pulled away from the curb.

"If she is, she's not the one who wrote the note and left it on the library door," Rain said.

"Yeah, I caught that too," Julia said with a sigh before checking out the rearview mirror to see if it was safe to pull onto Main Street.

"I suppose the person who left that note wouldn't want to bring that kind of extra attention on the book club, or would they?" Rain asked thoughtfully.

"Yeah, there's that. Unless it's someone who participated at the book club meeting that's trying to pin the crime on someone else within the group. There's always that possibility."

The two remained in their own thoughts until Julia pulled into the library's parking area. Marge's car was parked in the lot along with only one other car.

"I need to run home and drop off the rest of these donuts to Nick," Julia said as she parked for Rain to exit.

"Sounds good. I'll let Benzo out and then meet you back at the library."

The two parted ways, and as soon as Rain leashed Benzo, the dog gave her a hard tug. Despite the unbearable heat, she knew, at the very least, she'd have to take him to the end of the road, to rid him of some of his excess energy. As the two rambled along, Rain's mind returned to Lily.

"What do you think, my puppers. How are we gonna solve Lily's murder? Huh? I don't know about you, but this crime has my head spinning!"

Benzo turned his head to her, lolled his tongue, and kept his pace.

"I know—you don't have the answer either. And right now, you're panting. You must be so hot under that coat of fur." She patted him on the back, but the dog kept trotting along. "We'll get you some water just as soon as we get back. I promise."

Suddenly a car pulled alongside them and rolled down its window. "Hey ya, Rain! What a beautiful dog you have there!"

Rain wiped away the sweat that was dripping into her eyes and encouraged Benzo to heel, then held tight to the leash. "Oh hi, Shelby. Thanks—I just adopted him."

"Wow. A purebred Siberian was up for adoption? Look at those eyes! I'm guessing you must know someone in the humane society who pulled a favor. He's bea-u-tiful!"

"Not exactly. Benzo's owner was in an automobile accident and didn't survive. It's a set of unfortunate circumstances that sort of led him to me." It was as if Benzo understood the conversation, and suddenly the dog hung his head. Rain reached out to pet and comfort the animal.

"Aww, that's so sad. You know, speaking of loss, how you holding up? Personally, I can't seem to get Lily off my mind."

"Me neither," Rain admitted. "It's been rough, hasn't it?"

"Yeah, especially when she and I were sort of combative with each other that night of book club. I just feel awful about it. We used to be so close back in the day. I hate that my last memory of my classmate is one of us pecking at each other like hens," Shelby confessed sadly.

Rain wasn't quite sure what to say. She wanted to ask Shelby about the Laura Ingalls Wilder manuscripts but didn't want to tip her hand in case Lily hadn't shared the news of the rare pages with her. Instead, she asked, "You don't think Lily killed herself, do you?"

"Suicide? Why would Lily do that, with so much going for her? Not a chance!"

Rain wondered then if Shelby knew about Lily's cancer. "I don't know, it's a theory, I guess." She shrugged.

"It is? Is that really what people are saying? That she took her own life?"

"No. I don't think so. I guess I'm just grasping at straws." Rain readjusted the leash in her hand and wiped her sweaty palm on her shorts. "None of this makes sense, and I'd hate to think that someone in Lofty Pines is responsible. I guess it's just easier for me to think Lily could be responsible for her own death, instead of one of our neighbors."

"And poison herself? That's an awful way to go," Shelby said. "I can't imagine she'd do that."

"Yeah, I suppose you're right."

"The police will find the person responsible for Lily's death. After all the grilling the other night, I'm sure they now have a few leads," Shelby said, and then closed her lips tight.

The way she held back led Rain to believe it was Shelby who had provided something of value to the police department. "A lead? Would this have anything to do with the boating accident that happened years ago? Did you happen to share something with the police that you didn't share with the group the other night?"

Shelby looked in her rearview mirror as if hoping for an escape, but the road was devoid of cars.

"Please. You can tell me," Rain pressed. "I really want to understand what happened to Lily. I feel a little responsible since I was the one who picked a mystery book about a poisoning the first night of book club. And now a woman is seemingly dead because of it. I need to get to the bottom of this."

Shelby reached a hand outside the car window to comfort her. "This is not your fault, Rain. If some deranged lunatic chose to do this, that's not on you. Don't do that to yourself."

"I appreciate you saying that, but honestly it doesn't lessen the blow. I can't help but feel somewhat responsible."

"I'm sorry. I guess I can understand why you might feel that way, but try not to take it to heart, okay?" Shelby regarded the rearview mirror again before continuing. "I told the police officer that Lily was looking into Patrick's death again. We were all drunk the night Patrick drowned, and honestly I don't remember much. In fact, I didn't even get on the boat that night. I was sick and couldn't go along. However, according to Jimmy, who was driving the boat, Patrick fell over and drowned because he was drunk. Lily said that wasn't true. She claimed that Jimmy hit the throttle and then gave Patrick a final *push* into the water, and she was going to prove it."

"Why didn't anyone rescue him?"

"No one went after him because everyone was drunk that night and didn't want to meet the same fate."

"How could she possibly prove that he was pushed off a boat after all these years?"

"I didn't think it would be possible either, but she said that Jimmy's dad still owned the boat from the accident. And that, believe it or not, it's still located in his boathouse. Lily said with the DNA advancements, she thought she would be able to find evidence of foul play. She said, *in her words*, that there was definitely evidence left behind."

"Jimmy's dad still owns the boat from the accident. Seriously?" Rain tried but failed to understand how that would be possible. "Why would he keep it after all these years? And hasn't it been used? The water would destroy any DNA evidence, wouldn't it?"

"No, that's the thing. Jimmy's dad took years to meticulously refurbish the boat; it was his pride and joy. But after a teenager died on it, he never took the boat out on the lake again. He refused to. But because of all the hours he had taken to restore it, apparently he couldn't part with it either. The man is in his early seventies, and he still won't sell it! Honestly, I think he's a little cuckoo."

Benzo suddenly tugged hard on the leash, almost pulling Rain's arm from the socket. A nearby chipmunk darted into a hole, and suddenly she understood. Luckily, she had a tight hold of the leash.

"Whoa! Good you had him tight!" Shelby exclaimed. "Or that little rodent would've gone bye-bye."

"I know, right?" Rain said as she realized she'd held Benzo at heel long enough. "I'd better get moving. He's going to need water soon. Poor thing—it's too hot for him out here."

"Yeah, I hear you. In this heat it's almost too hot for any of us. Take care, Rain," Shelby said before slowly pulling away from them and rolling down the road.

Rain waved goodbye, all the while wondering if digging into Patrick's accident had possibly led Lily to join him in the grave.

Chapter Sixteen

The soft breeze off Pine Lake, along with the slight dip in humidity and the sound of rhythmic waves methodically lapping to shore, felt like a cosmic gift. Rain had just set the book she had been reading aside, to rest her eyes, when she heard footsteps joining her atop the outer deck. Benzo, who'd been sprawled at her feet, jumped up to greet the visitor.

After regarding the dog with a pat on the head, Jace collapsed into the Adirondack chair beside her. "Hey, you," he said with a weary smile. He was still dressed in his uniform, and he removed his police cap and set it on his lap before vigorously brushing his hands through sweat-soaked hair.

Rain gave a look of deep empathy. "You look beat."

"Yeah, I kinda am," he confessed, wearily wiping his hand over his face and then tapping his cheeks, as if to revive himself.

"Sorry you had a rough day. Do you wanna talk about it?"

"No, not yet." He sighed. "Man, it's still hot out here." Jace looked to the lake longingly, as if he wanted to strip off his clothes and jump headfirst into the water.

"It sure is. I shouldn't have asked you to come over after a long shift at work—that wasn't fair of me."

Jace surprised her by saying, "You up for a skinny-dip?" And then quickly recovered by correcting, "Just kidding. I have gym clothes in the cruiser. You mind if I borrow your shower before we visit? I literally had a guy vomit on me today."

Part of Rain wanted to see him choose the skinny-dip option, but she refrained. "Go for it. If you don't mind, use the one in the master bedroom, since there's soap and shampoo in there," she replied. "Towels are in the closet. You hungry? I can throw in a frozen pizza while you clean up."

"Seriously, that sounds great. I'm starving. I'd eat a cardboard box if you've got it."

"Meet you back here in about twenty minutes," Rain said, rising from the chair, causing Benzo to leap up with excitement. She leaned down to pet her dog before coaxing him to join her inside.

While Rain doctored up a frozen pizza to make it a little more palatable, Jace went to retrieve his gym bag. She wished now that she had planned a better meal for the hard-working guy and inwardly chastised herself for asking him to stop by on a work night when he was quite obviously hungry and exhausted.

When they finally met back out on the deck, Rain had the pizza, presliced and arranged on a plate, and a cold beer waiting. She did a double take when Jace walked through the door. He was wearing a muscle shirt, which clung to his broad chest, and long, silky shorts that hung to his knees. His feet were bare. He ran a hand self-consciously through his wet hair, as if he was unpresentable. But to Rain, he was far more than presentable. His boyish, unabashed grin only made her want him more. Especially when she caught wind of the scent of her shampoo. She had to physically stop herself from reaching for him.

"Is this okay?" he asked, leaning back on his feet, as if he were introducing himself to the grand jury. "This is my typical Laker uniform. I'm probably in need of an upgrade. I think these shorts are at least ten years old." He chuckled. "I'm not much of a shopper. But hey, at least I no longer smell like puke."

"You're fine." Rain recovered and quickly reached for the beer and handed it to him.

He took the amber bottle, cracked it open, tossed the cap on the table, and immediately took a long swig.

"There's more where that came from. You can ease up a bit," Rain joked.

"Yikes, I'm sorry," he said, wiping his mouth with the back of his hand. "Am I being rude? Something about a cold beer when it's hot outside just makes it go down like water. Maybe I should've had an old-fashioned instead. Now, *that* I would sip on."

"I've never had one," Rain confessed.

"*What?* You can't be serious?" Jace's jaw dropped, and his eyes doubled in size. "You can't tell me that you were born in Wisconsin, and you've *never* had a brandy old-fashioned? That's impossible!"

"Hard to believe, but it's true." Rain shrugged.

"Oh, we're gonna have to change that." He grinned as he slipped into the Adirondack chair facing the lake. He made himself comfortable, holding his beer in his lap, and every once in a while tipping the cold bottle to his forehead to cool himself.

The two sat companionably side by side, and in no time they'd devoured the pizza between them.

"That hit the spot—thank you," Jace said, finally coming up for air.

"I'm sorry—this isn't the most nutritious meal on the planet. I owe you something a little better than frozen pizza," Rain replied after wiping her mouth with a napkin and brushing the crumbs from her lap. "That crust tasted like cardboard, in my opinion."

"I have no problem with it. It's going down mighty fine on my end. I hesitate to say that, though, if it means I'm going to miss out on another meal with you," Jace said, then looked away bashfully, like he'd shared too much.

Rain thought it adorable when the color crawled up the back of his neck and behind his ears. It seemed he was hesitant to show his true feelings toward her, but she knew he would open up in time when they both felt safe to do so.

Jace recovered quickly by changing the subject. "Would you mind if I gave Benzo a crust?"

"Thanks for asking, and to be honest, I *do* mind. I don't want my dog to get used to people food. I refuse to train a beggar." She laughed.

"Ah, I see your point. Sorry, fella," Jace said to the dog as he popped the full piece of crust into his own mouth and brushed his hands free of the crumbs.

Rain rose from her seat. "That being said, thanks for the reminder. I bet he's hungry. I should probably bring him inside to eat—I'll be right back. You need anything?" Rain tapped at her leg for Benzo to follow, and the dog leaped to his feet excitedly and made a beeline for the door.

"I'll take another beer, if you've got it."

"Sure."

When Rain returned, Jace was leaning over the railing, looking out over Pine Lake. The wind had eased, causing the water to turn unusually calm. Barely a ripple could be seen except for a fish jumping in the distance. The sky was violet with streaks of fuchsia clouds splattered across it, where gulls flew past in tandem. She abandoned the beer on the table and joined him at the railing to watch the beauty of it all unfold.

"The view up here is stunning." Jace breathed in deeply and slowly exhaled, finally unwinding. "It's good to be here and take this in."

"You had a rough day." Rain leaned her hip on the railing and faced him.

Jace turned to her and moved a string of hair away from her eyes. An act so intimate, and pure, that it gave her goose bumps.

"You're cold," he said with a frown. "How can that be, as hot as it is out here?"

"Nah, I'm okay."

Jace stepped behind Rain and engulfed her into him and held her there momentarily. He softly stroked her arms to rid of her goose bumps, but it only caused more to erupt. Meanwhile, the two looked out at the picturesque scene before them, which could only be described as a gallery painting. Rain felt so safe and warm tucked into him. The smell of soap still lingered on his skin, and she was sorry when he pulled away.

"Tell me the truth. Did you ask me here to learn more about Lily's case or because you wanted to see me?" he asked tentatively, lifting her chin to face him fully. He searched her eyes deeply, like he was hopeful of the answer.

Instead of answering with words, Rain leaned toward him and kissed him gently on the lips. "Does that answer your question?" she asked with a shy smile as soon as they'd parted.

They didn't part long, though, because Jace reached to brush his fingers through her hair, stroked her face, and then kissed her again, this time lingering. Then he wrapped her in his arms as if he never wanted to let her go.

When they finally parted again, he said with a large grin, "Okay. I'll take that as your answer."

Rain leaned her head on his shoulder and said cautiously, "Though I wouldn't be opposed to you sharing anything new that you felt might be relevant to Lily's case. I'm pretty good at keeping secrets."

"Ahh, I see," he said, searching her eyes, as though he wanted to see where her heart lay. Which at that moment was fully with him.

Chapter Seventeen

The stars were twinkling like gems in the night sky. With the drop in humidity, and the moon glow, which caused a sparkling path across Pine Lake, Rain thought it had turned into the perfect summer evening for their first official date.

"Now that you know where my heart is, will you tell me about your day?" Rain asked tentatively.

"I dunno. I'm having too much fun to go there right now." Jace poked at her side playfully, causing her to jump closer to him. He then thew an arm over her shoulder and drew her in completely.

Rain's cell phone, which had been abandoned on a side table, interrupted with a text. "I should get that," she said, pulling away from him.

"Nooo, you don't have to," Jace whined, reaching for her. But even in his complaint, he was way too cute to correct.

Rain opened the text from Julia, which read: *May I approach?*

"I think your sister is spying on us." Rain laughed. "Julia wants to come over—is that okay?" She looked at Jace to verify and allow him to be the one to make the decision.

Jace grunted. "I suppose. Who am I to monopolize all your time? Honestly, I should probably go . . ." He turned away from her, and she reached for his hand and pulled him back.

"*Stay.*"

His answer was a lopsided grin.

Before long, the two were joined by Nick and Julia on the deck. Jace and Nick were nursing beers at the railing while Julia scooted Rain out of earshot.

"Did you get anything out of him?" she asked bluntly.

"You mean about Lily?"

Julia rolled her eyes. "Yes, I mean about Lily! Anything else you and my brother do or talk about, moving forward, is now on the DL. I don't need to hear it."

"Really? You want me to keep it on the down-low?" Rain was surprised at her lack of transparency. Typically, her friend wanted to know everything.

"I don't need to know the gushy stuff that goes on with my brother," Julia said with a shy smile. "But I really was hoping you got something that might move this investigation in a direction. 'Cause it seems we're all over the place right now."

"Well, then, let's ask him right now." Rain turned away from Julia and moved in Jace's direction, which caused the officer to grin ear to ear as he watched her approach.

Julia followed. "Listen, bro," she said abruptly when she reached Jace's side, "we need updates on Lily's case. Whatcha got for us? We'll promise to share with you if you share with us."

"Are you threatening an officer of the law?" Jace asked with a curl of his lip, then took a sip of his beer, nonplussed.

"No." Julia slapped her brother playfully with the back of her hand. "However, you know, deep down in your stubborn heart, that Rain and I are amazing when it comes to getting to the bottom of things. There's really no avoiding it. We're planning to investigate Lily's death whether you like it or not, so you may as well just share."

"Is that so? Maybe you both should join the police academy and make it official," Jace taunted, which caused Nick to spit out a little of his beer in laughter.

"Can you imagine! *My wife* at the academy?" Nick slapped his leg so hard in jest that they all heard a crack.

Rain interjected, "In all seriousness, you boys need to understand: the fact that Lily died from poisoning, and the connection her murder had to the book I chose for book club, isn't exactly sitting well. It's no laughing matter."

"No, she's right. It's not." Jace exchanged an empathetic look with Rain and added, "Okay, what have you two uncovered so far?"

Julia reported their findings and ended with saying, "We know that Lily didn't commit suicide because we have reason to believe that her death was either linked to Patrick's drowning or these phantom Laura Ingalls Wilder manuscript pages. Or the letter from the attorney about a potential inheritance. Those motives are strong in our opinion."

"She's right," Rain nodded assent. "Is that why you paid a visit to Chelsea at Brewin' Time? To question her further about the manuscript? Did you search Lily's cottage?"

"Keep in mind, anything discussed here tonight stays in the vault. We can't tip our hand," Jace said firmly. "I'm attaching imaginary badges to you all at this point. Don't disappoint me."

The group nodded their heads vigorously in response and compiled a four-way pinky swear. Jace continued, "You're correct. Lily did not die at her own hand. My fellow colleagues down at the station and I are quite convinced of that. The ME agrees too, as he has officially ruled Lily's death a homicide. But again, our job is to follow the evidence and rule things out based on the facts of this case, and not just our own intuition. We're not sharing our findings with the public either. We don't want to scare the perp into hiding."

"So, we were right." Rain shot a knowing look at Julia. "Did you find the manuscript then? You think that's the motive?"

"We did a thorough search of the cottage and didn't find anything that fit that description," Jace stated evenly. "Which makes it hard, because no one has seen the documents Chelsea told us about. How do you prove they were stolen in the first place if that's just based on hearsay?"

"Did you search Lily's other house in Lofty Pines? The one she has on the market?" Rain asked.

"Not thoroughly," Jace conceded. "Chief and I did a walk-through, and it's staged for sale. Looked to us like most of her personal items had already been removed from the residence."

"Lily told us it was in town somewhere. Where is it? Off Main Street?" Julia asked.

"Yeah, it's on Sycamore Road," Jace replied. "Chief and I are under the impression she wouldn't leave priceless artifacts in a house that people were traipsing through day after day, anyway. Would you?"

"Yeah, I suppose not," Julia tapped a finger to her lips. "But you agree the cottage was not broken into, right? That whoever jimmied that lock only wanted it to look that way. Correct?"

Jace landed his hands firmly on his hips. "How'd you figure that out?"

"She warned you we're good at this," Rain teased with an elbow bump, which caused Jace to respond with a boyish, lopsided smile and a disillusioned shake of his head.

"Look, this ain't our first rodeo, bro." Julia stuck her tongue out at her brother, like they were only five years old, and he responded with an eye roll.

Nick interrupted the banter, when an unexpected gust of wind took his baseball cap clear off his head, "Whoa!" He reached out and grabbed it seconds before it flew off the deck, and then replaced it on his head with a grin. "That was a close one! Looks like the wind is shifting."

"Good catch, honeybun," Julia said with a chuckle. "I wonder if a storm is brewing. Feel that sudden rush of cold air?" She ran her hands up and down her arms as if attempting to warm herself.

"Yeah, I should probably get home and close the windows in case it rains." Nick said, kissing his wife goodbye on the cheek.

"That's a smart idea. Thank you, honey!" Julia swatted her husband on the backside to encourage him in that direction.

"I'll leave the sleuthing to you guys. This is totally outta my field of expertise anyhow. But if I hear any rumblings around Lofty Pines, I'll be sure to clue you in." Nick turned on his heel and, with a backward wave of his hand, disappeared into the darkness.

"Well, and then there were three." Julia assembled the group together like the Green Bay Packers head coach bringing the team in for a huddle. "Yeah, it'll be up to us three to find out what happened to our dear friend Lily . . . See my rhyme there?" Julia chuckled.

Rain cringed because she knew there was a chance it might implicate someone in the book club. "Forgot to mention to you, Jace, there's something we need to tell you about a rhyme . . . but promise us you won't force us to close the library this time."

Chapter Eighteen

The next day, Rain was on alert for even the littlest smidgen of gossip between the bookshelves at the Lakeside Library. She couldn't help but believe that the person who'd left the Post-it Note, was someone who frequented the library, which made everyone who walked through the door a suspect. As she rounded the corner to reshelve a book, she walked smack dab into Ruth, who let out a startled sound and dropped a John Grisham novel to the floor.

"My dear girl!" Ruth boomed out. "You scared the life out of me!" The older woman held her hand to her heart with one hand while she fanned her face with the other.

"I'm so sorry!" Rain exclaimed, scooping the book up off the floor and attempting to hand it back to her.

However, Ruth continued to frantically wave at her face. "Give me a minute. I'm having a doozy of a hot flash right now! Either that or I'm having a heart attack," she said cynically.

Rain waited for Ruth to collect herself and then apologized again. "I'm so sorry for crashing into you. I should be paying more attention, but unfortunately my mind is elsewhere," she explained. "I'll try and be more careful."

Ruth accepted the book from Rain's hands, along with the apology, and lowered her standard loud voice to a mere whisper. "Is your mind still on Lily too? I normally have no problem concentrating on my 'to be read' pile, and zip through several books a week. But ever since Lily's unfortunate demise, I haven't been able to concentrate. I can barely get through a chapter before my mind is back on that poor girl and what she must've went through. It's horrible."

"I can't agree more," Rain admitted easily.

Ruth searched her face eagerly. "Have you heard? Do the police have any leads? It's my understanding that a burglary took place. At least, that's what the rumor mill has been spreading. But that doesn't make sense to me one bit. Because if her death was the result of a burglary, then the perpetrator certainly wouldn't use poison as a method of taking her out. Now would they?" Her eyebrows furrowed in deep concern. "Don't thieves usually carry a gun or something like that?"

Rain let the older woman's musings percolate. She and Julia had already determined that Lily had known her killer, or at the very least hadn't felt threatened, and had willingly invited the person inside her cottage. And they didn't think it was a burglary that had caused the crime either. So then, would the early manuscripts of Laura Ingalls Wilder still be considered a motive?

"Are you listening to me?" Ruth roared.

"Oh yes. I'm sorry. See what I mean?" Rain managed a smile.

"Do you think Lily died because of a burglary," Ruth pressed. "Or something else?"

"Honestly, I wish I knew. But the more I study the motivation behind the crime, the more confused I seem to get." Rain folded her arms across her chest, leaned her weight into the bookshelves, and pondered.

Just then, Julia skipped down the aisle, interrupting them. "Hiya Ruth, how ya doing? Anything I can help you find?"

Ruth held up the Grisham book in one hand. "Doing just fine. I think I found something to hold my interest, but thank you."

"Excellent." Julia smiled. "Hey, I hate to interrupt, Rain, but Marge said she needs a second of our time over at the checkout area, when you get a minute."

"Well, don't let me be the one to keep you." Ruth started to walk away from them, and Rain stopped her with an outstretched hand.

"Ruth, wait. Do you happen to know the year that boating accident took place? The one that Shelby was referring to the other night at our meeting?"

Ruth turned to face Rain fully and then said thoughtfully, "I'm not a hundred percent sure, but if my memory serves me right, I think it was the year my husband was redoing our deck, and that's why the accident was so significant to me. Because the rescue squad was retrieving that poor fellow out of the lake. And I remember standing on a heap of dirt instead of watching from my patio chair, which normally I would do. That was the summer of ninety-nine, if I remember correctly," she trumpeted proudly. "As a matter of fact, I'm desperately in need of a new deck. Mine is again rotting to the core," she said under her breath in a tone of frustration.

"Hold that thought," Julia said, and darted away from them. In no time, she returned with a pad of paper and a pen. "Can you write that down—and anything else you remember about the boating accident? Nothing is insignificant. Was it early summer perhaps? That sort of thing. That would really be helpful to determine whether this might've been the motive behind Lily's murder."

"Sure, no problem." Ruth handed the novel to Julia to hold while she took the pad of paper and leaned it against the bookshelf.

As Ruth began to write, Julia looked to Rain before they both zeroed in on the woman's handwriting. Ruth printed everything she wrote neatly and didn't use cursive to put her notes to paper.

Rain deflated and mentally took Ruth off the suspect list—at least, she couldn't have written the Post-it Note. And then Rain traded a look of defeat with Julia.

Ruth handed the sheet of paper back to Julia, who then stuffed it deep within her pocket. "Do you really think this will lead to Lily's killer?" she whispered conspiratorially.

"Maybe, maybe not," Rain said. "Thanks, Ruth—take care of yourself. We need to go and talk with Marge, but you have yourself a good day."

Ruth moseyed down the aisle while Rain and Julia went in search of their coworker. They found her scurrying around the checkout desk, her face in a fluster and her hands waving frantically.

"What's wrong?" Rain asked.

"I can't find my glasses!" Marge exclaimed. "They were right there." She pressed a pointed finger atop the desk and glared, as if they should reappear at a moment's notice.

"Marge?" Julia asked tentatively.

"What?" Marge scowled.

"They're on your head," Julia said, holding back giggles with the back of her hand.

Marge absently put her hands onto her head and then her eyes doubled in size. This caused the three of them to bubble up in laughter, to the point that patrons were giving them odd looks.

"Well, now." Marge said, slipping on her glasses and adjusting them on her nose. "That's better." She beamed a crooked smile.

Rain chuckled. "Now that we got that straight, Julia mentioned you needed to talk with us?"

"Oh yes. Julia mentioned that Benzo is with Nick today, on one of his landscape jobs. Is that right? I haven't seen him yet today, so I just assumed you left him home for a bit."

"Yes, why?" Rain asked. "I thought it would be good for him to spend time outdoors for the day. Also, because Nick's always bugging Julia about getting a dog, she wanted him to see firsthand the responsibility that comes with it." She elbowed her friend, who then joined the conversation.

"That is correct!" Julia said with an agreeable nod. "I have no problem getting a dog, but I want him to be all in before we commit. I'm not taking all the responsibility if he's not sold on the idea. He's always said, 'Baby first, dog second,' so . . ."

"Perfect. I'm glad Benzo is taken care of because I have something in mind for you two to work on today."

Rain and Julia studied Marge, waiting for an explanation.

"I've been wracking my brain about that young man's drowning back in the day. And I couldn't help but overhear you two talking about it with Ruth just now as well. Anyway, I reached out to my friend Pearl—she's the reference librarian up in Waters Edge. She's expecting you."

"Waters Edge? That's like almost an hour away." Julia groaned.

"Would you rather I go?" Marge asked, removing her eyeglasses and popping the arm of the frame into her mouth.

"No, I suppose it's a good day for it, since Benzo and Nick are gone for the day," Julia agreed. "You think she'll be able to shed light on the boat accident, eh?"

"Yes, I do. They keep all the newspaper archives from Forest County up there. You should be able to find something of value. More details into all of this might shed light in a direction for us." She nodded. "I'll hold down the fort here until you both return." Marge shifted her attention to wave to a patron who had just walked through the door.

"Sounds like we're going on a road trip," Rain said, nudging her friend.

Julia lifted a brow. "Only if we can stop for snacks along the way."

Rain grinned. "Fine, let's go."

Chapter Nineteen

The Waters Edge Public Library was located on the far side of Forest County, on a country road not far from a walking trail. For a split second, Rain wished she had brought Benzo along, and mentally added to her checklist to return with him sometime soon for a stroll through the deep woods. A few years ago, the library had been moved from downtown Waters Edge to its new location, a stone's throw from the high school. Rain's immediate thought was that it seemed as if the library was in the middle of nowhere, as the only two buildings were the school and the library, and then what seemed to be miles of ginseng farmland, abutting the trail. However, the newer red brick building was expansive, along with its parking lot, and it was the largest library in the Northwoods. And the only one, to Rain's knowledge, that held both the archives and a vibrant historical society.

They stepped through the large double doors, which led to an atrium filled with natural light, where a hushed silence reigned. As they moved deeper into the space, reasonably priced oil paintings from local artists lined the walls. One such, depicting a Wisconsin sunset over a lake, drew Rain in. She stopped to look at it until

Julia pulled her by the arm toward the expansive rows of endless bookshelves. Rain wished they had more time, and she could linger deep within the shelves of books. They seemed endless in comparison to those at the Lakeside Library.

The two made their way to the reference desk, where a rather snappy-looking woman with cropped white hair greeted them with a welcoming smile.

"What can I do for you?" she asked warmly.

"We're here to see Pearl," Julia said. "Is she around?"

"Today's your lucky day!" the older woman beamed. "I'm Pearl. How can I help you."

"It's nice to meet you, Pearl. I'm Rain," Rain said, then gestured to her friend and continued, "and this is my coworker Julia. We run the small log cabin library in Lofty Pines."

Pearl's face lit with animated enthusiasm, and she clasped her hands in delight. "Oh yes! How wonderful! It's on my bucket list to come and pay your lakeside library a visit. My dear friend Marge sent you. How is she? We haven't seen each other in quite a while, it's been far too long. We chat on the phone, but that's just not the same," she sighed.

Initially, Rain wasn't sure quite how to answer that question. Except for Marge's memory, their coworker seemed vibrant and healthy, but Rain was still concerned.

She was glad when Julia responded for them: "Marge is doing well; we love having her work with us. She's holding down the fort so we could come and peek through your archives. This is a stunning library, by the way. I haven't had a chance to visit yet." Julia's eyes traveled the space and then back again.

"This place is amazing," Rain said, nodding assent. "Years ago, when I was a child, my mother brought me to the original Waters

Edge Library, but I barely remember it now. I only remember that it was tiny. And that she took me out for ice cream after," she added with a smile.

"Yes, I agree, the new building is quite grand, isn't it? Especially compared to that little old building we used to occupy downtown. We rather outgrew that many, many years ago, and now we're a bit spoiled." Pearl put her hand to her cheek and smiled coyly.

"Yeah, it's lovely," Julia interjected, and then elbowed Rain as if to hurry them along. "Marge mentioned you could share a newspaper article or two with us. We were hoping to get some information on something."

"Why yes, of course! Follow me," Pearl said, beckoning them to a separate room with a sign over the door that read "Forest County Historical Society."

"This is the historical society's room," she explained. "But for now, they share it with archives."

"Wow, this is cool." Julia eyed the space as they passed various Forest County artifacts on display, such as fossils, farm tools, and the like. They even had rare out-of-print books on display. "Pearl?"

"Yes?" Pearl turned to face them.

"Have you ever heard whether Laura Ingalls Wilder wrote other books besides the famous ones we're all familiar with? I mean, you've never heard rumblings of lost, unfinished manuscripts or anything of that nature. Have you?"

Pearl shook her head slowly and tapped a finger to her lips, as if thinking through her answer carefully. "No. Not that I've heard of. However, there's a gal who works here at the library—her name is Irene. She's part of the Historical Society and might be someone you can connect with on that question. Irene has studied Ms. Wilder's work extensively and has traveled to the Laura Ingalls Wilder Museum, located in Pepin, on multiple occasions. Before you leave, remind me, and I'll give you her phone number. She isn't bothered if you call her at home—she's not like that at all. Irene loves to talk history and, quite frankly, might talk your ear off if you let her." She chuckled.

"That would be great—thanks!" Julia said, giving Rain a discreet high five behind Pearl's back.

"Now then. Marge mentioned you were looking for a particular article about an incident that occurred on Pine Lake, in Lofty Pines. Is that correct? I've already loaded the microfilm into the system. Unfortunately, I don't know the exact date, so you'll have to flip through. Marge did share the year, though; she phoned me again about a half hour ago. And to her knowledge, she believed it to be around the time of the Fourth of July celebrations. Hopefully, that will narrow it down some for you."

Rain took a seat at the small desk while Julia stood over her shoulder.

"Let me know if there's anything else I can help you with," Pearl said before turning on her heel.

"Thanks, Pearl. We've got it from here," Julia said, as Rain had already begun rolling through the microfiche.

"I'll be back at the Reference desk, if you need anything further," Pearl added over her shoulder before disappearing from the room.

Rain flipped the microfiche pages until she came across a photo of members of a dive rescue team, on a boat, searching a body of water, with a headline splashed across the front page:

TEEN MISSING ON PINE LAKE

—Lofty Pines—

Lofty Pines Police Department is investigating a boating acci-dent that left a local teen missing. At approximately 9:15 p.m. on July 4, Lofty Pines authorities received a distress call from a witness on the shore of Pine Lake, who claimed screams were heard from a boat that had been parked out on the water to watch the fireworks display. Witnesses report that it was hard to witness exactly what had happened, as the fire-works had not yet started, and it was past dusk. At this time, 17-year-old Patrick Gleason still remains missing.

Rain scanned subsequent microfiche pages for more informa-tion on the incident.

TEEN DIES IN BOATING ACCIDENT

The town of Lofty Pines mourns the life of Patrick Gleason, who was taken way too soon. The 17-year-old teen and pro-nounced drowning victim died after falling from a boat the night of the Fourth of July fireworks. The driver of the boat, Jimmy Callaway, has not been charged. The Lofty Pines Police Department claims underage drinking was the cause. The victim in this case was recently pulled from the water by a rescue team, who have been searching since early this morn-ing. The official investigation has now been closed.

Rain sat back in the chair and breathed deeply. Reading about the accident firsthand sent a wave of empathy for Patrick's friends and family coursing through her. How awful not to fully understand what had happened that night. Had Patrick's parents immediately accepted the authorities' findings? And the stress of what Lily might have been going through, having kept an awful secret all those years if she did indeed believe the accident was the result of foul play.

Julia interrupted her thoughts by pointing to the screen. "If the boat was parked that night, how did Patrick fall off? It's not like Pine Lake typically has rough seas—unless there was a storm brewing. In that case, wouldn't the fireworks display have been postponed?"

"Yeah, unless Patrick was so intoxicated that he was swaying. It's not out of the realm of possibility, is it? The thing that bothers me, though, is how the authorities were initially informed. The article claims people on the shore heard screaming." Rain chewed at her cheek. "Unless those who were still on the boat started screaming because they realized Patrick was no longer with them. But wouldn't they just talk among themselves and not resort to screaming right away? Or better still, wouldn't they dive in and try to save him? Or was everyone on the boat that night really that drunk that it wasn't a possibility? That's something I don't think we'll ever know. Especially with Lily gone. There's a lot of unanswered questions here."

"Yeah." Julia nodded. "You and I know that after dark, when the lake is calm, you can hear conversations clear across the water." Julia wagged a finger between them. "Remember how we used to spy on people when we were kids? Even when the water isn't super calm, you can hear laughing and carrying on. I still here chatter to this day, just sitting on the pier. Something feels off there. Because someone on shore must've heard something."

"You think Lily might've been on to something?" Rain asked.

"Yeah. I'm guessing Lily might not have been the only one who remembered exactly what happened the night Patrick drowned. Someone heard something. And I'm thinking it wasn't only alcohol that was to blame."

Chapter Twenty

By the time Rain and Julia rolled into Lofty Pines after their journey to Waters Edge library, it was twilight. Julia had spoken extensively to Irene on the ride home regarding the Laura Ingalls Wilder manuscripts, and true to Pearl's word, the woman had the gift of gab. Rain wondered if it had depleted her friend of words completely, which would have been a momentous occasion, to say the least. They both remained quiet, each lost in her own thoughts, until finally Julia asked, "Hey, can you do me a favor? Swing by Sycamore Road on the way home, would you?"

"Sure, why?"

"Because Jace mentioned that Lily's other house, the one she had up for sale, is on that road. I just want to drive by and get a feel for it. After talking to Irene, I'm wondering if Lily's prior residence was one that might have some historical value. Irene mentioned that at one time Laura Ingalls Wilder had some close friends who lived in the area. Perhaps someone the author knew owned Lily's house years ago, and that's how she came into ownership of it. If it's a newer house, then probably not. But it's worth a drive-by, for a look-see, don't you think?"

"Did Irene think that there were undiscovered manuscripts lying around?"

"She didn't think so, but couldn't say for sure. If anything, they would have to be authenticated by a handwriting expert to determine if they were actually written by Laura Ingalls Wilder."

"Here we go again with handwriting expertise." Rain chuckled.

"Right?" Julia grinned. "Maybe we should be the ones to authenticate them if they actually exist.

Rain made a right onto Main Street and then a left onto Sycamore, then slowed the speed of her SUV to a crawl as the two searched eagerly for a "For Sale" sign. It was more than a half mile down the road before Julia pointed out a white garrison colonial with black shutters and exclaimed, "Hey, look! That could be it. Pull in here."

A shadowy figure in the distance caught Rain's eye. "Wait— who's that at the door?" she asked.

"Dunno," Julia replied, squinting. "That's a very good question."

Rain struggled to get a visual too, but then a realization hit when she noticed the coiffed hair. "Hang on a second. That looks like Naomi. And she's playing around with the lockbox. It sure doesn't look as if she has a showing, does it? She's all alone, and she's looking over her shoulder a lot. Wonder what she's up to." Rain rolled the SUV along the curb and turned off the headlights.

Naomi stopped what she was doing and looked in their direction, as if straining to see whether she was being watched. This caused Rain to tap Julia frantically on the arm. "Duck! duck!" she exclaimed as she sank deep into the seat to hide from view.

Naomi looked furtively in both directions before slipping inside Lily's house and closing the door behind her.

Meanwhile, Rain and Julia peered covertly over the dashboard.

"Now what?" Julia whispered.

"I really hope Naomi didn't recognize my SUV. I'm not sure why she would unless she's seen it in the library parking lot. In any event, I don't want her to catch us watching her from the car. Let's go and sneak along the side of the house. Maybe we can peek inside the windows and see what she's doing in there," Rain suggested.

"Oh, I like the way you think, Rainy." Julia grinned. "Yeah, I agree she's up to something. Naomi didn't turn any lights on, a sure sign she doesn't have someone coming to look at the house. Otherwise, she'd have the place lit up like a fireworks display. Wouldn't she? Besides, what happens when a person passes away? I thought Lily didn't have any family to speak of. I mean, are realtors able to continue to show the house after a death? Or does the property end up in probate? Not to mention, have the police cleared it yet? Or is it considered part of a crime scene? Especially since the investigation into Lily's murder is still ongoing."

"All very good questions. Let's go and see what Naomi's up to," Rain murmured. Then she quietly opened the driver's side door, and crouched down next to the SUV before making a run for it.

Julia followed.

They passed what Rain assumed was Naomi's car, as she noted vanity plates that read: "HM SOLD," and the logo of a real estate company stamped on the side of the expensive-looking SUV.

They hurried across the front lawn until Julia diverted, running instead to the front steps.

Rain gritted her teeth.

What is she doing?

Rain waved a hand frantically to beckon her friend to return to the task at hand and follow, but to no avail. Per usual, Julia had her own ideas.

Within moments, Julia met up with Rain next to the house, where she was already leaning against the siding, panting heavily and holding her chest. "Where did you go?" Rain whispered when she finally caught her breath. "Are you *trying* to get us caught?"

Julia held the lockbox in her hand and dangled it like a pendulum in front of Rain.

"Oh nooo. What did you do?" Rain hissed.

Julia shrugged sheepishly. "I borrowed it."

Rain shook her head disapprovingly.

"What? She didn't lock it shut. She only closed the door," Julia said defensively, as if that was a perfectly good explanation. "Now Naomi can't lock us out. We'll take a quick peek inside Lily's when she's finished, then close it up tight. Easy peasy, lemon squeezy!"

"Yeah, except your fingerprints are all over that," Rain pointed out.

"I highly doubt Naomi is going to confess that the lockbox was stolen and then returned on her watch. I'm guessing she'll go back to the office to find another one, and by the time she comes back, I'll have this one back and locked into place. No worries."

"No worries? Are you serious, Julia? You'd better hope that your brother doesn't catch wind of any of this. He'll have our hides for sure! We'll never be able to sit down again with the butt kicking he'll give us!"

Julia nudged her with an elbow and grinned. "That's what you're here for, buttercup: to butter him back up."

Rain hated that idea. Not when she could still taste Jace's lips on hers and wished for more. She wondered if he'd completely change his mind about pursuing her after a stunt like this.

"Besides," Julia persisted, "Jace is going to thank his lucky stars when we help the Lofty Pines PD solve this case. You know that's true," she added cheekily.

Rain crossed her arms defiantly across her chest.

"Come on—you know I'm right." Julia stood on her tiptoes to see through the window but couldn't reach. "Give me a boost," she said, laying a hand on Rain's shoulder.

Rain interlaced her fingers, and Julia stepped a foot inside while Rain boosted her up. Julia peeked inside and then returned to the ground. "She's not in that room," she whispered, pointing a finger toward the backyard. "Let's try the back of the house."

Rain was thankful that a wall of overgrown arborvitae trees blocked the view of the neighboring property as they crept inconspicuously alongside the house. Otherwise, the authorities would've been alerted already, and they'd be in the back seat of a cruiser, on their way to the Lofty Pines Police Department, in handcuffs. She really hoped Jace would be merciful if he caught on to what they were doing. Would he be so upset that he'd never kiss her again? Her mind lingered on their last embrace, and she shook her head to remove the memory. She needed to halt this train of thought—it was terrible timing for notions of romance! Her focus needed to remain steadfast, or they would most certainly get caught.

When they reached the back patio door, Julia remained hidden with her back up against the siding. This time, Rain chanced a peek inside. Naomi was wearing what looked like a pair of leather gloves and was frantically sifting through closets and drawers. Rain attempted to see more, but it was dark and shadowy, so she came up empty. Finally, she ducked away from the glass door and stood out of sight, like a statue, at Julia's side. "Well, I hate to admit that we're right. No question she's looking for something, and it's not real estate related. Do you think Lily told her about the manuscripts?"

Julia shrugged but remained quiet, her finger held to her lips.

Unexpectedly, the doorbell rang, alerting them both. Rain sucked in a breath, and held a hand to her heart, before a beam of light shot out the door, in their direction. Naomi had flipped a light switch, and suddenly the room was flooded with light.

"Coming!" Naomi's voice trailed away from them as she traveled to the front of the house.

"Who the heck is here? You think Naomi has a showing? And just used this opportunity to dig into Lily's demise? Sort of like we are?" Julia whispered. "Is that a possibility?"

"Not sure. Let's go back to the front of the house to see if we can get a better view."

"Okay." Julia nodded.

The two tiptoed along the side of the house until they reached the front. Julia chanced a quick glimpse and then covered her mouth with her hands. "It's that girl in the scrubs, the nurse—what's-her-name. What's she doing here?"

"Hannah?" Rain asked.

"Yeah, Hannah," Julia replied. "Now what?"

Rain bit at her thumbnail, then scratched her head. "I think we should move the car. So, they don't catch us. We'll come back after they're gone, but maybe we should park down the road a bit."

"Yeah, let's do that."

After Hannah entered the house, the two darted to the SUV. They hurried inside the vehicle and, with the headlights off, rolled slowly down the road. Rain eased the car far enough out of view so they wouldn't be caught, yet still close enough to keep a watchful eye on it.

It seemed like an eternity passed before Hannah stepped out the front door. The nurse spun around to look at the house one last time just as what looked like an unmarked police car rolled by, causing Rain to forcefully shove Julia down and out of sight.

When Rain finally chanced a peek, the cruiser was gone, and so was Hannah.

"That was a close one!" Julia squealed.

"Just a drive-by to check on the place, you think?" Rain asked.

"Hope so."

Not long after that, Naomi returned outside and frantically searched for the missing lockbox that was at that time in Julia's possession.

Julia caught on to Naomi's agitation too, as she sheepishly grinned and said, "What?" before sinking back down into the seat like a turtle, as if to hide again.

Rain shoved a packet of antiseptic wipes in Julia's direction. "Before you attach that back on the door, you may want to consider wiping your prints off. These have alcohol in them, so hopefully that'll work. Otherwise, you're gonna have some explaining to do."

"Yeah," Julia agreed, stuffing them into her shorts pocket. "I'll wipe it down, I promise. But not until after we take a peek inside." She grinned devilishly.

Chapter
Twenty-One

"How much time do you think we have?" Julia asked as the two rushed up Lily's front steps.

"If Naomi is as good a realtor as I think she is, she'll be back with a lockbox, or the police will be informed in no time. We need to hurry." Rain encouraged Julia to snap the lockbox in place, making sure the key was tucked safely inside. She gestured at it with a pointed finger, to remind Julia to wipe the box down for a second time.

As soon as she completed the task, Rain tugged Julia by the arm and rushed them inside. "Come on—hurry! Before someone sees us!" It took a few minutes for her eyes to adjust in the darkened space.

"Where do we even start?" Julia asked.

"Not sure." Rain flicked on her cell phone's flashlight app, keeping the beam of light low to the ground, away from windows, and led the way. "Well, my friend. Where would you hide rare manuscripts that you thought had great significance and might be worth something?" she whispered.

"Probably in a safe deposit down at the bank," Julia replied mockingly. "But that's not exactly helpful at the moment, is it?"

The two tiptoed away from the narrow hallway and steep oak staircase that had greeted them upon entering. To the right, they passed a formal dining room, which displayed an ornate, over-sized, mahogany dining table, which, along with tufted chairs, filled the room. And to the left, a formal sitting room with stiff-looking furniture, overlooked an enormous wood fireplace. The fireplace had been updated with an expensive-looking mosaic tile surround that didn't fit the period of the house, making it not an ideal choice. Jace had been right; other than that, the house looked perfectly staged, as there were very few personal items or knickknacks scattered about. It almost felt to Rain as if they were touring a hotel instead of Lily's personal residence. Or maybe that's just what she was allowing herself to believe, to make the fact that they were breaking and entering seem like a logical move and acceptable.

A carpet runner, covering a hardwood floor, led them like a path to the back of the house, where they had earlier witnessed Naomi sifting through drawers.

When they reached the kitchen, Julia exclaimed, "Ooh! My dream kitchen right here. I love the white, don't you? It's so fresh and inviting. I've told Nick so many times we should consider this when we redo our kitchen, but he's more into the wood paneled look, which, in my opinion, is hideous." She chuckled. "I should walk him through this house so he can see for himself. Maybe then he'd reconsider."

The kitchen looked like it had been recently remodeled, as everything was gleamingly clean and stark white. Rain couldn't help but concur with her friend that the choices made here were stunning.

Julia reached for a door and swung it open wide. "Just look at this butler's pantry," she cooed, and then chatted on merrily, even as her voice disappeared, about the pros and cons of having a walk-in pantry.

"We really shouldn't be touching anything. We don't want to leave fingerprints." Rain pointed out when her friend made a reappearance.

"Oh, I wouldn't worry about that. If this house has been shown to potential buyers, I'm guessing fingerprints are everywhere. Plus, now that I think of it, I'm ninety-nine percent sure that the police have already cleared the house. Otherwise, I'm guessing the lockbox would've been confiscated, and it wouldn't be open to showings at all," she said with a wink and then a raised brow.

"Maybe." Rain shrugged, then took a step in the opposite direction, to rummage through a few drawers, in search of the manuscript, but came up empty.

Julia opened another door and shrieked with delight.

"What?" Rain turned to find Julia holding the door ajar and excitedly summoning her. Her friend's face was lit up like Fourth of July fireworks.

"Rainy, you gotta see this! There's a hidden staircase!" Julia beamed. "Most likely for the servants back in the day. This house must have been built in the mid 1800s," she added over her shoulder.

"That would certainly fit the time line. Then it's quite possible that Laura Ingalls Wilder might have been friends with the original owners of this house," Rain said as she followed Julia upward.

The stair treads were painted a dark brown, and the risers had been scuffed white. It looked as if the staircase had been repainted on multiple occasions, as paint chips and the obvious wear and tear from over the years was evident. The paneled walls had been covered by many layers of white paint, and Rain was thankful for that. It made the space far less claustrophobic, because the stair-case was remarkably narrow.

When they arrived on the top step, they were greeted by a hallway and a row of closed white doors, all with matching brass doorknobs. Rain assumed they were all bedrooms.

"This place is really cool," Julia said as she reached for the first doorknob. "I feel like Nancy Drew!" she exclaimed with delight.

To their surprise, the two didn't walk into a bedroom, but stepped into an expansive library with wall-to-wall shelves of books.

Rain's eyes doubled in size. "I think Lily has more books than we do at the Lakeside Library!" she said in awe. "I can't believe she was willing to let this go. These books certainly wouldn't fit inside the new cottage she just bought on Pine Lake. What a collection!"

"No kidding," Julia whispered. "This is an impressive room. If only we had more time to peruse these shelves, eh? Oh, I could easily get lost here." She took a slow spin around the room, trying to take everything in.

Rain couldn't help but wonder what would happen to all these beautiful books after Lily's house was sold. She'd love the oppor-tunity to share a fraction of them with their library.

"Look, I think Naomi was searching here too." Julia pointed out a spot where a line of dust had obviously been disturbed, and a book had been reshelved. Coincidently, it was a copy of Laura Ingalls Wilder's *On the Banks of Plum Creek* that had left the track.

"So, do you think Naomi knew about the manuscripts too?" Rain asked. "How many people did Lily tell? This isn't going to help our cause at all."

"I know, right? I was just wondering the same thing. Perhaps Naomi found the missing manuscripts. Or do you think she was in cahoots with Hannah?"

"Hannah wasn't at the first book club meeting, so I don't even think she met Lily."

"Oh, right. I forgot about that. So, you think Naomi was seriously just showing Hannah the house because she has interest in purchasing it?" Julia asked thoughtfully.

"That's a great question, Hannah did mention relocating here. But we're going to have to find that out definitively so we can confirm what both are up to."

"You know what Jace would say: the absence of evidence is evidence," Julia said with a raised brow. "Maybe one of them found the manuscripts and took them."

"My head is spinning."

"Mine too," Julia said with a deep sigh. She leaned back against a bookshelf and must've shifted something, because she shot up like a cannon. "Fudgesicles! Did you feel that?!"

"Feel what?"

"Okay, I'm officially losing my mind. It felt like the ground moved. All this sneaking around must have me a little freaked. Maybe we should hurry up and get outta here." Julia slouched and leaned her weight against the bookshelf again. This time, the entire wall of books creaked open, revealing another hidden room.

Rain gasped.

"Snickerdoodles!" Julia gasped. And then covered her mouth with her hand. "I'm seeing stars! That scare just about took the pink right outta my hair!"

The two shared a wide-eyed look before hesitantly stepping into the hidden room.

"Okay, I take that back," Julia whispered. "I wouldn't keep my valuables in a safe deposit at the bank. I'd keep them right in here! This room is amaze-a-balls."

"I'm with you there. I can't believe Lily would sell this place. I don't think I could let go of a library with a hidden space. It's way too Nancy Drew to give all of this up!" Rain said in astonishment.

Although the concealed space was a neat find, spiders seemed to like it too, as cobwebs were everywhere. On the door jambs and on the dusty shelves, webs were spun, including lining the inside walls. Rain flicked her hands around her head so nothing would land on her. She was thankful neither of them suffered arachnophobia, as Julia didn't even seem to notice. Her friend was too enamored with the hidden room.

"What *is* this place?" Julia reached onto the shelf and blew the dust off an antique mason jar, causing a cloud to rise in the air. She coughed and waved it away with her hand.

"It can't be a root cellar—it's too warm having it upstairs. Though with those old jars, something was kept in here. It's definitely weird, to say the least," Rain mused.

"Well, in any event, if Lily claimed there were priceless manuscripts by Laura Ingalls Wilder, I would think this would be the place she'd hide them. Don't you agree? Or maybe when the author came to visit, she'd hide in this room for a little anonymity." Julia giggled. "Maybe it was their panic room."

"Perhaps."

Rain found an antique wooden box with a skeleton key jammed in the lock. She was just about to turn it when she heard a familiar voice yell, "All clear!"

Chapter
Twenty-Two

Both Rain and Julia's mouths dropped, and a look of alarm passed between them.

"Jace!" they uttered in unison.

Rain wrung her hands frantically until Julia said, "We need to close the bookcase; he'll never find us back here."

"He won't?" Rain asked, her heart beginning the uptick of panic. "Are you sure?"

"My brother is a lot of things, Rainy. A reader he is *not*. He won't linger in Lily's library; I promise you that. Once he sees that no one is in the room, he'll split."

"He's not? What about all those times he stopped by the library and checked out books?"

Julia's grin widened.

"You mean, he never read them?"

Julia slowly shook her head.

"Really?"

"Duh."

"Oh." Rain could feel the heat flush from her neck to her cheeks. She couldn't believe all Jace's visits to the Lakeside Library had been strictly to see her. She recalled all the times he had stopped in to drop off flowers for the library's checkout desk. He said it wasn't out of his way, as he went right past the greenhouse, and he hoped others (in his words) could enjoy them too. Secretly, Rain wanted to return to the library to verify exactly how many times Jace had paid a visit and checked out books.

"Yeah, he's not much of a reader," Julia repeated bluntly. "Which we can discuss, at length, another time. Right now, we have to hurry," she flustered, her tone growing borderline hysterical. "Otherwise we're toast, Rainy."

"How do we close the door from the inside?" Rain whispered.

Julia's hands were grasping at everything within a one-foot radius of herself, in a growing panic. "I don't know. I don't know! Oh, shooties!" she hissed.

The two searched desperately for a knob or a lever to close themselves inside, but continued to come up empty. The only thing Rain seemed to find was more cobwebs, and one very big daddy long legs, which she flicked from her shoulder.

"Poppycock! I think I hear him coming up the steps—we need to hurry!" Julia squealed.

Pure anxiety overcame Rain at the thought of Jace catching them there. Would he ever forgive her? She didn't want to disappoint him or do anything to jeopardize his growing feelings for her. Not now when she was finally open to pursuing him.

Rain touched what looked like a brass novel, and the room sucked them in and pushed them backward, causing both to land on their backsides with a thud. Julia covered her mouth to hide her cackles. Rain couldn't help but catch on to the giggles too, as they both held tight to their squeals and doubled over in laughter. The laughing stopped abruptly, though, at the sound of heavy footsteps coming uncomfortably closer. Rain straightened her back and held herself eerily still. Only her eyes darted from side to side, waiting.

Meanwhile Julia scrunched her face and held back a sneeze.

Rain reached out and held her hand over her friend's mouth in case it should happen again. Julia always seemed to sneeze in multiples, and the timing couldn't have been worse for her allergies to kick in.

Julia mouthed the word *sorry*, causing Rain to break out in suppressed giggles once again.

Julia swatted Rain teasingly with the back of her hand, to stop her from joining Rain in laughter.

The two held their breath until they heard Jace yell, "All clear!" and footsteps moving quickly away from them.

Finally, Rain gulped a deep breath and held a protective hand to her chest.

Julia followed suit.

"That was way too close," Julia whispered. "We're gonna have to be more careful."

"By 'more careful,' you mean, avoid any more breaking and entering?" Rain scolded, tapping Julia on the nose. "And not stealing lockboxes?"

"I wouldn't take it that far." Julia mused. "We just need to be a little more careful that we don't get caught by my brother or anyone else from the Lofty Pines PD," She stood and wiped the soot from her backside, then held out a hand to help Rain up off the dusty wooden floor.

Rain remembered the skeleton key hanging from the antique lockbox and moved back over to investigate. She clicked the key, and the box opened with a creak. Inside the black velvet interior lay an unmarked cassette tape still in its case.

Julia joined her side and asked, "Whatcha find?"

"Not sure." Rain flipped the tape over in her hand. "Looks like an old cassette. A mixed tape perhaps?" She removed the cassette from the case and flipped it over once again, but there was no writing to be found.

"Oh my goodness, do you remember the mixed tapes your mom used to share with us when we had nothing to listen to 'cause the radio station was so spotty up here?" Julia asked. "Do you still have any of those? It would be fun to listen to one. Remember our obsession with George Michael back in the day?" She grinned.

"So true. It's utterly amazing how a song can catapult you back in time, isn't it?"

"Hey, you gotta have Faith! Faith! Faith," Julia sang out, and did a wiggle dance. "Which is exactly what we need right now. *Faith* that we will solve the mystery of Lily's killer."

"I couldn't agree more," Rain replied. "I think we're going to take this and give it a listen. Do you still have a boom box at home that will play it? I think Mom gave hers away to Goodwill a few years ago."

"Yeah, there's one in the garage. Nick turns the radio on when he's working out there. Why? Do you think this could provide something of value?"

"It certainly seems like Lily went to great lengths to hide it—inside a secret room, in an antique box with a lock on it. Seems to me it must've been important. What do you think?"

Julia raised a brow. "Yeah, but the key was left in the lock. If it was that important, or a secret, why would she do that? Maybe the tape just held sentimental value. Like an old mixed tape made by an ex-boyfriend. I think those tapes were considered love letters back in the day. Didn't your mom tell you that?" Julia's brows came together as she tried to make sense of their find.

"Yeah, I'm not sure. Shelby made it sound like Lily didn't date much. Perhaps she was interrupted by someone at her door, just like we were and accidentally left the key inside."

"Maybe." Julia shrugged. "We'll never know, will we?"

"Either way, don't you think we should give it a listen?"

"It can't hurt to take it. I'm just not sure we'll be able to return it when we're done."

Rain dismissed the concern with a wave of her hand. "I'm not worried about that. Clearly, Lily isn't coming back. If it's an old tape from a boyfriend, like you say, then we just toss it. No big deal."

"True. I see your point."

"It might lead us to something."

"Yeah, I agree. Let's take it and give a listen."

"I know Jace was just saying we should join the police academy as a joke, but maybe we should. I love the way we volley to try and solve crime."

"Me too, girlfriend." Julia grinned. "Me too."

Chapter
Twenty-Three

Rain and Julia discovered Nick whistling a happy tune inside the garage while rearranging gardening tools on top of his workbench. He turned to welcome them with a friendly wave as soon as Julia caught her husband's attention with a flirty whistle.

"Hello, miladies," he said with a wide smile, mopping the sweat from his brow with the back of his arm. "I'm about ready to call it a day. How about you? What are you two up to?"

Benzo pulled on the leash, and Rain released it a bit so that the dog could go and greet Nick.

"We just took Benzo for a walk," Rain said. "Didn't we puppers?" She looked to her dog, who responded with a smiling, lolled tongue.

"Yeah, and we recently came across an old mixed tape that we want to listen to. You mind if we borrow your radio? It's not marked, and we can't remember what songs are on it," Julia piped in and then shot Rain a look as if to say, *"Let's keep where we found this cassette, on the downlow."* Rain replied with a conspiratorial zip of the lips.

Nick gestured to the dusty radio on top of his workbench. "Help yourselves—it's all yours," he said, and then leaned in to ruffle the top of the dog's head. "I bought Benzo a bone from the hardware store, but I left it back in my truck. Is it okay if I give it to him?"

"Aww, that's so sweet of you, Nick," Rain said, and handed him the leash. "Go for it. I'm sure he'll love it."

"Yeah, your dog is quickly winning over my heart. Aren't ya, buddy," he said, and he crouched down to give Benzo his full attention.

"I can't agree more." Rain smiled. "It was love at first sight for me too."

"He's a cutie—there's no doubt about it," Julia pipped in with a grin.

"Does that mean we're getting a dog soon?" Nick looked up at his wife with pleading eyes as he continued to stroke Benzo down the back. "I think he needs a friend, don't you, buddy?" He regarded the dog.

"Hey, you were the one who suggested baby first, dog second. That's on you." Julia's tone was not the least bit hostile, only one of gentle reminder.

"Guess we need to get busy making babies then, don't we?" Nick rose and swatted Julia on the backside, and she playfully pushed him away, but her smile widened.

"Do I need to leave?" Rain asked playfully.

"No, it's all good. Plenty of time for that later, right, Julia?" Nick winked.

"You betcha!" Julia returned the wink before kissing her husband on the cheek and snuggling into his shoulder.

"Seriously, I can head for home if you two need some alone time." Rain smiled and jutted a thumb toward the door.

Nick reached out a hand to stop her. "No, no, Rain, we're just messing with ya. I'll get outta you guys' hair now." Nick gave

Benzo's leash a tug. "Come on, buddy. I've got something special for you. Just wait until you see what I bought for you."

Benzo seemed to understand and abruptly bolted toward the garage door, which made Nick almost lose his grip on the leash. "Whoa buddy!" he said with a smile as the two trotted out of sight.

Julia reached into her shorts pocket and plucked out the cassette and held it in her hand like an Academy Award. "Alright, Rainy, let's see what we got here." She removed the cassette from its case and popped it into the boom box before hitting "Play."

At first, nothing but static could be heard. There was no Wham! singing out, or any other singer from the late 1980s for that matter. Rain was just about to call it quits and remove the cassette from the boom box when Julia stopped her with a tap on the arm.

"Wait."

"What?"

"Did you hear that?"

"Nope, didn't hear a thing." As soon as Rain uttered the words, she thought she heard talking, but it was barely audible.

Julia reached to turn up the volume to full capacity and the two strained to listen.

"Happy Fourth of July! Wooo-hoo!" a male voice said.

"Fireworks should be starting soon," a female voice. *"Cut the engine!"*

Someone uttered, *"The fireworks are between those two. Tell 'em to go get a room."*

"Jimmy, stop! Cut it out! You're hurting me!" a female voice.

"That voice is familiar. Younger, but still familiar," Julia said. "Did you catch that?"

"Shelby?"

"It could be." Julia frowned. "Yes, that's exactly what I was thinking. It sounds like Shelby."

Rain held a finger to her lips so they both wouldn't miss a beat.

"I said, stop it!"

"Leave her alone, Jimmy!"

Julia pointed to the boom box. "That sounded like Lily, didn't it? The one who said leave her alone?"

Rain agreed but remained quiet.

Suddenly they heard what sounded like glass shattering, and then someone said, *"Put the bottle down, Jimmy!"*

Julia mouthed, *Shelby*, and pointed again to the radio.

"Leave her alone," a gruff voice said.

"Or what? What are you gonna do about it, Patrick?" The male voice was patronizing and then the sounds of a scuffle took over.

"Stop playing around, Jimmy! You're gonna cut Patrick with that broken bottle!" Lily said. *"It's not funny! Drop it!"*

More scuffling, as if two boys were wrestling. Grunts and possibly the hammering of fists landing could be heard, and then a screech followed by an epithet.

"Nooo!"

A gigantic splash and gasps and more swear words before the tape unexpectedly cut short.

Rain and Julia mirrored a look of horror.

"That's awful . . ." Rain whispered. "Lily definitely remembered more to the story."

"Yeah, I think this is the evidence Lily was talking about. Not just blood or DNA found on the boat. It's almost like hearing a firsthand account of what happened, that night." Julia murmured.

"But didn't Shelby say she wasn't there? That she'd skipped going out because she wasn't feeling well?" Rain asked. "She made it seem like only Lily had been on the boat the night Patrick died."

"Clearly, Shelby was lying. That's her voice. Right?"

"Yeah, I'm ninety-nine-point-nine percent positive she was there," Rain mused, and then a pondering pause ensued between them.

Suddenly Nick reappeared, and his smile faded as soon as he noticed the looks on their collective faces. "What's wrong?" he asked.

"I'm not sure this is something you're gonna wanna hear," Julia stated matter-of-factly, "but we think we just found a motive for Lily's murder."

Chapter Twenty-Four

"We need to take a look at that boat," Rain said determinedly as she reshelved the last returned book before closing time at the Lakeside Library. "That's the only way we're going to know if there's enough evidence that would hold for a conviction against Jimmy, besides just the cassette tape. And if it was indeed the motive for Lily's murder. Seems to me someone wanted to keep her from bringing up the past."

"Yeah, no sense bringing my brother into the loop yet either if all we have is a tape and hearsay, right? Especially hearsay that no one wants to talk about. With Lily gone, this might be tougher than we think. You know?"

"That's what I'm thinking." Rain sighed heavily. "Especially since Shelby is refusing to admit that she was even on the boat that night."

"Goodnight, ladies!" Marge rounded the corner with Rex close at her heels. "I need to run; I was invited to my neighbor's Pampered Chef party this evening, and I'm already running late. And I still need to stop at the supermarket to pick up a bag of tortilla chips and salsa, as promised."

"Are you working the morning shift tomorrow? Julia and I might need to run a few errands," Rain asked as she knelt to scratch Rex on the head.

Marge lowered her voice, even though it was only the three of them left inside of the library. "If this is about Lily and helping sort out some clues and identifying the perpetrator of this crime, I'll be here. You can count on me."

Rain nodded assent. "Thanks."

"Of course. See you girls in the morning then. I'll even bring donuts from Brewin' Time!"

"Yay, thanks, Marge! I'm already calling dibs on a chocolate one, then," Julia said, licking her lips. "Have I told you recently how much I love you?"

Marge chuckled. "You bet. Have a good night, you two!" She turned on her heel and patted her leg for Rex to follow, which the dog did, obediently, with a skip to his step.

"Well, that settles that," Julia said. "I guess we're covered then."

"Do you want to wait until morning to go over and see about that boat?"

"I'd prefer to go now. I need to know, don't you? I'm not sure I'll sleep otherwise, with this rattling around in my brain," Julia said expectantly. "You?"

"Yeah, I'm okay to go now. And Nick's okay with that idea?"

"Are you kidding? I phoned him and told him we were going to Portside Bar and Grill for dinner. We'll have to pick him up an order of perch and fries before I go home, even if we don't eat there." Julia chuckled.

"Oh, boy, I'm sorry I asked. I don't want Nick thinking it's my fault we're sneaking around." Rain rolled her eyes.

Julia waved a hand of dismissal and grinned. "I'll ask forgiveness over permission. I promise you he'll be fine once this is solved. Won't we all?"

Rain wasn't sure Nick would see it that way, but she didn't want to have another restless night of sleep either—not definitively knowing the motive behind Lily's murder. "If you say so. I guess we're boating over to Jimmy's dad's house then. Is that the plan?"

"Yeah, I printed a map of all the Lakers that live on Pine Lake, along with their addresses, which I received from the last Lake Association meeting. I already highlighted the house on the map, so I'll grab it when I go home and change into my swimsuit. It isn't far from us—not too far from Lily's cottage, to be honest."

"I'll meet you out on the dock," Rain confirmed with a nod, before moving over to the computer to power it down and officially close the library for the evening.

* * *

The water was unusually choppy as Rain carefully navigated the pontoon across Pine Lake. The wind whipped, causing the boat to rock and Julia to grab hold of the railing so as not to fall off the seat.

"Whoa!" Julia squealed after the boat crashed into a forward wave and sprayed her.

"Sorry! I'm not trying to splash you today!" Rain yelled. "I really tried to avoid it this time."

"No worries!" Julia gave a thumbs-up. "But are you going to be able to tie this thing up at Jimmy's dad's house? Maybe we should abort this mission and take a car over there."

Rain looked to the western sky. Dark clouds loomed, and off in the distance she thought she heard a roll of thunder, but she chose to ignore it. Besides, the sky ahead of them looked sunny and clear. Wisconsin could be completely unpredictable like that. "We won't be long over there. If anything, the storm might provide a good getaway excuse, if need be. We're okay, I think."

"True," Julia hollered back over the wind as she wrapped a beach towel around her legs and tucked it tightly beneath her. "Not sure why I wore a swimsuit under my clothes. I guess I was hoping for a jump in the lake after our visit, but I don't think that's in the cards."

Rain lowered the throttle and slowly maneuvered the pontoon closer to shore, but not so close that they would hit any rocks along the shoreline.

Julia looked at the map, then at the scene before them, and pointed at an upcoming pier. "I think it's that one," she said, rising from her seat and stumbling to the bow. "If you can get us close enough, I can hop off and tie us on."

Rain finessed the pontoon alongside the pier and cut the engine while Julia leaped from the boat and secured the rope to a cleat on the deck.

An older gentleman, with a full head of wiry white hair stuffed beneath a sunhat, walked toward them on the pier and greeted them with a friendly wave. "Having boat trouble? Something I can do to help you gals out?"

Julia held out a hand to shake the man's. "Hi, I'm Julia, and this is my friend Rain."

"Nice to meet you ladies. The name's Mickey, but my friends call me Mick." He tipped his hat and then placed it securely back on his head and clamped his hand down on it before it had a chance to blow into the lake. "Rough day to be out on the pontoon, eh? What brings you by?"

"We heard a rumor that you might have an antique boat for sale. I'm looking to surprise my husband for his birthday," Julia inquired, and then shot a look to Rain.

Mick lifted his cap to scratch his head. "I'm not sure who it is in Lofty Pines that keeps spreading that rumor, but there seems to be a sudden interest in my boat. You're the second person to ask about it. I wonder if my wife is pushing for the sale behind my back," he muttered, more to himself than to them, "Could that be it? Was it my wife?" His eyes narrowed in on them as he looked to confirm what he seemed to think was the answer.

Second person?

A look of knowing was expressed between Rain and Julia before Rain said, "No, we didn't hear it from your wife. But you mentioned someone else beat us to the punch? Who was it that stopped by and showed interest in it?" Rain asked to confirm.

"Yeah, a woman with purple glasses inquired about it. And then I heard she was dead."

Chapter
Twenty-Five

"Lily Redlin was here?" Julia asked.

"Yeah, I believe she mentioned her name was Lily. That sounds about right," Mick confirmed with a fixed gaze.

"And she was interested in buying your boat? Did she happen to take a look at it?" Rain asked.

"She never got the chance," he said sadly, his eyes downcast.

Rain and Julia exchanged a look of confusion before Mick continued, "She stopped by the house and asked about my boat, but I needed to take my wife to her cataract surgery appointment. I asked her to come back later in the week, when it would be more convenient, but she died before that happened. And after talking with my son, Jimmy, about it, I can't understand why that woman would've wanted to purchase the boat anyway." His thick white brows came together in a frown. "Can you?"

"What do you mean?" Rain asked.

"Clearly you've heard. You'd have to live under a rock to not have heard about the accident . . . everyone in Lofty Pines knows what happened on that boat, which, by the way, I meticulously restored with my own two hands." He held up his hands in front of them as to demonstrate his labor and then dropped them to his sides with a heaviness. "I was shocked to learn from my son, that girl was the only girl aboard the night Patrick died. And she shows up at my doorstep now? After all these years, why would she be interested in buying my boat? It seemed rather odd to me. To Jimmy too." The older man lifted his cap and scratched his head again before returning it to his head. "That doesn't seem odd to you?" he asked pointedly.

Rain remained quiet about Shelby also being aboard his boat that night. She wondered if Jimmy and Shelby were in cahoots about her purported absence. Because without Shelby's testimony, it would be difficult to prove there was ever any foul play.

"Maybe the accident haunted Lily all these years, and she was looking for closure. Honestly, I'm a little more confused as to why you wanted to keep the boat in the first place?" Julia asked cautiously.

"Do you know the hours and money I invested in it?" Mick's fists clenched at his sides. "More than you can count on the pink hairs of your head!" he said, his tone quickly rising and his face transforming to the color of beet juice. "I'm sorry, but restoring that boat meant everything to me back then. That boat was my *life*! I never should've let Jimmy take it out on the water. That was my mistake," he added grimly. "And let me tell you, my family has paid dearly for it."

Julia shifted on her feet and then leaned toward Mick and laid a comforting hand on his shoulder. "The accident wasn't your fault. But isn't the boat a burden that you no longer want to hold onto as well? I'm sure it hasn't been easy for you either," she said gently. Then, seemingly realizing that she might've stepped over the line by physically comforting a complete stranger, she took a few steps backward.

"That vessel, and everything that came with it, just about destroyed my family." Mick's gaze darted between Julia and Rain.

"Tell me." He paused dramatically. "Were either of you supposed to join the boys on the boat the night Patrick died? Is that why you're here too?" He studied them carefully before leaning back on his heels and crossing his arms across his chest. "Nah, you look quite a bit younger than my Jimmy. Though the accident has taken its toll and aged my son. He's been in and out of rehab most of his adult life."

"I'm sorry to hear that," Rain said compassionately.

Julia murmured her condolences as well, and then said, "Yes, we heard about the accident, but it was a few years before our time. I do hope your son can find some closure and someday put this all behind him." She looked to Rain then, and they mirrored a sympathetic look, as they knew Jimmy's fate might not be what Mick had planned for his son.

"The wife and I are hopeful that maybe his life will finally turn around. In fact, I just sent Jimmy back to Door County to see about getting clean again. There's a facility over there that seems to have made some headway. He's even met a nice girl over there . . . says they're in love. His future seems promising . . ." His voice trailed off as he rubbed the back of his neck absently.

"Would you consider selling the boat? Or at least letting us look at it?" Rain asked timidly.

Mick took a deep breath and let out a long whistle. "I don't know. I'm not really sure."

"We'd love to see it," Julia pressed. "My husband is into rebuilding boats too, and even if you don't want to sell it to us, I'd love to take a look, even if only for restoration ideas." Julia held crossed fingers behind her back that only Rain could see. "I was hoping that maybe . . . I could surprise him," Julia pushed.

Mick beckoned them to follow. "Sure, if you want to look at it, I suppose there's no harm in it. I guess one of these days I should consider letting it go. If I sold it now, I might be able to help my son with all the rehab bills he's racking up too. Maybe some good could finally come of it."

"I couldn't agree more," Julia said.

As soon as Mick's back was turned and they were following him, Julia grasped Rain's hand and gave a squeeze. Then they shared a grin.

They followed Mick away from the dock, over his over-grown lawn, and then across the street, to where an enormous storage building was hidden within a copse of towering pines. Rain couldn't help but think Nick would salivate at the size of the garage. Mick removed a keyring with a host of keys from the pocket of his denim overalls and slipped one of them into a large padlock. He grabbed the handle and lifted the spring-assisted door, making a grunting sound. The three took a step inside the dark, damp space. Rain blinked her eyes momentarily to get her bearings in the room, which held no natural light.

Various objects were covered in massive tarps, coated in dust and scattered with dead bugs, as if in a time warp. It was regret-tably obvious none of these protected toys had been touched in decades. They walked to the back of the storage building until they came upon a large blue tarp, which Mick began to roll sys-tematically off the boat.

Julia raced to the starboard side and grabbed the other side of the tarp. "Here let me help you with that," she encouraged.

Rain could only stand in awe of the vessel after its reveal. The hull was a deep rich mahogany, and she could only imagine how, if dusted and shined, the boat would gleam in the sunshine.

"Wow," Rain finally said aloud. "What year is it?"

"Meet *Second Chance*—she's a twenty-seven-foot 1953 Shepard Express Cruiser," Mick said proudly, rubbing his hand along the hull.

"Can we have a look inside? You have a ladder handy?" Julia asked.

The boat was sitting on a trailer, and it was clear that neither of them would be able to manage to climb inside without assistance.

"You bet," Mick said, and disappeared momentarily before reappearing with a stepladder in hand. He set it up on the starboard side and gave a little shake to verify that it was stable before gesturing for them to come aboard. "Have a look."

Julia was making the climb when they heard,

"Mick! Mick! Are you in here? Where the devil are you?"

Mick's face turned ashen, and he held a finger to his lips. "Don't let my wife see you back here. I'm not sure she'd be happy if she knew I was showing the boat without talking to Jimmy first. I'll be right back. Or better yet, meet me by the dock when you're finished," he said before rushing away from them.

"Well, I guess we know who wears the pants in the family," Julia said, smirking as she clambered onto the deck. "Clearly, I don't have that kind of effect on my own husband."

"Oh, I don't know about that," Rain bantered before hurrying up the ladder after Julia, in hopes they could have a few extra private moments to investigate the vessel.

"Man, what a shame. This is gorgeous," Julia whispered in awe. "What a beautiful boat."

"I know, right? Just look at the teak floor," Rain whispered. "I've never seen anything like it."

As they both eyed the gorgeous wooden floorboards, Rain noticed the broken glass scattered beneath their feet. "Check it out!" she indicated the shards with a pointed finger.

Just as they'd heard on the old cassette tape, the glass from a broken beer bottle was littered accusingly across the floor.

Julia moved toward the stern of the boat and leaned over the side to examine the motor. "That's not all," she exclaimed. "There's blood!"

Neither Rain nor Julia wanted to get caught talking to Mick about what they had discovered on his antique boat. They had decided it was time to get Jace involved. The two scurried down the stepladder and rushed for the exit, in hopes of avoiding the owner.

As they raced across the street, Rain noticed Mick out of the corner of her eye, heading in their direction. She gazed up at the darkening sky, pointing it out to him, and yelled, "Sorry, Mick, we need to hurry before the storm strikes. We'll be in touch!" And then, not waiting for an answer, she looped Julia by the arm and picked up speed across the lawn. As the two moved toward the pier, the wind swirled around them violently. A crack of thunder shook Rain to the core before she dashed to untie the rope from the cleats. "On second thought, is it too late to tell you that you were right? We should've taken the car!"

"Hurry!" Julia screamed as she boarded the pontoon and detached the Bimini top. "I'm taking this down so that the wind doesn't rip it. We might get wet, okay?"

"Yeah, do it," Rain said as she started the engine and pulled away from the dock. A gust of wind whipped from the west, making big waves splash along the portside of the boat.

"Whoa!" was the last thing Rain heard before a ginormous wave came over the bow and completely soaked Julia.

Chapter
Twenty-Six

"Are you okay?" Rain yelled, as the wind tossed the pontoon around like a child's play toy inside a jetted hot tub. She did her best to navigate despite the growing uncertainty in the western sky and the cooler temperatures that followed.

Julia tripped from the bow to the passenger seat, and then wiped her face with a beach towel that had been left out in the elements. Her friend gave a thumbs-up. "I'm okay! Just get us flippin' home!" she exclaimed with a weak smile.

Momentarily, the wind grew eerily calm. The calm that happens when the world is about to fall apart. The feeling was heightened when Rain noted the sky morph into a weird greenish hue. She looked at the clouds building and churning and wondered if they would make it home safely, if at all. She also thought they should turn back to Mick's, but after catching her bearings, she realized they were closer to the cabin than the house they had just visited. There was no turning back now.

It wasn't long before her fears came to fruition, and the hail came. Pellets pinged off them like unwanted confetti.

"Ow-ie, ka-zow-eee!" Julia squealed.

"I'm so sorry! We're almost there!" Rain shouted as the pontoon bounced over yet another large wave, catapulting Julia like a rubber ball from her seat onto the floor.

"Oh no! Are you hurt?" Rain reached out a hand while clutching the wheel with the other, to help get her friend back onto her feet and steady. She watched as Julia crawled back to the passenger seat, and inwardly scolded herself for not listening to her friend and taking the car over to Mick's instead. As usual, it was too late for regret.

"Yeah, that one's gonna bruise later." Julia looked down at her leg, gave it a hard rub, and grimaced.

"I'm so sorry!"

Beyond the hail, streams of water began to pelt at them sideways, as if the heavens had suddenly opened or a hose had been turned on full blast.

Rain caught a glimpse of the log cabin between the raindrops that were blocking her vision. She blinked her eyes to clear them and noticed Nick and Jace frantically waving them in, from the edge of the pier. Relief overcame her when the men finally appeared in full view.

Nick cupped his hands around his mouth and yelled, "You'll never get in without hitting the dock! Let us help you!"

"Yeah, we're tossing around too much to come in full throttle!" Julia shouted over her shoulder as she stumbled her way back to the bow to toss the guys a rope.

"Cut the engine!" Jace yelled. Nick caught the rope miraculously on the first swing. Rain had no idea how he pulled off the long catch and secretly wondered if Max was looking on from the heavens and had somehow lent a hand. It had been a few days since her former husband had crossed her mind. And she wondered now, if it was due to their perilous predicament that he was suddenly catapulted to the forefront of her mind.

Grief was so like that. In the oddest times, when least expected, she would feel his presence, almost as if he were still alive, somehow. She still vacillated between her great love for him and the hurt she'd felt over his transgressions. Would he be okay with her pursuing Jace? Was *she* even okay with it? Or was she just trying to fill the void Max's death had left behind?

A sudden jolt from the pontoon caused Rain to catapult back to the present. She gripped the railing momentarily before losing her balance and falling to one knee as the two men manually hauled them toward the boat lift. Julia reached out a hand to help Rain back on her feet, and they looked at each other with relief. When they'd navigated close enough, Nick tossed the rope back onto the deck while the pontoon glided below the overhead cover to safety. "We gotcha . . . You're in now," he said cranking the lift wheel to secure them.

"Phew!" Rain released a breath and held a hand to her heart. "That was a close one! Thanks, guys!"

"No kidding, girlfriend!" Julia said. "I thought you were gonna dump me in the lake!" She giggled. "Glad I wore my suit, eh?"

"You mad at me?" Rain stared at Julia, who looked like a wet dog after a full-on jump in the water. Her pink hair was matted to her face like it had been glued there. "Sorry for the rough ride. I thought at one point you might toss your cookies." She grimaced. "Your face turned as green as the sky!"

Instead, Julia doubled over in laughter under the safety of the canopy. Hail returned and bounced above them, on top of the pontoon lift, which was now keeping them somewhat dry. The two men jumped aboard too, to avoid the piercing hail. "It's all good," she said between hiccups of laughter. "Glad we made it in."

"Not funny!" Jace's nose crinkled, and he play-slapped his sister on the side of her matted head with the back of his hand. "What the heck are you two doing playing around in those massive waves! Are you nuts or what? You're lucky you weren't seriously hurt out there!"

"Yeah, didn't you see the storm blowing in from the restaurant? I thought you two normally sat outside. Why didn't you leave Portside when you saw it coming? You know how quickly the weather can turn here in the Northwoods!" Nick said, reaching for his wife and gathering her into a wet embrace.

A look of shame passed between Rain and Julia before Julia responded. "Sorry, hon. I didn't get your order of fish and chips for supper. In fact, neither of us ate, and to be honest, I'm starving. Mind if we take this up inside?"

"If you're willing to run through the hail, I have summer sausage and cheese back at the cabin," Rain suggested. "You're all welcome to come inside, dry off, and warm up a bit."

"I'll run through a storm for food!" Julia grinned as she tossed her beach bag over her shoulder, leaped from the boat, and began a sprint toward the cabin.

Rain dodged the hail that looked like bits of Styrofoam, and yelled over her shoulder, "Last one in is a rotten egg!" as she followed closely on Julia's heels.

The four rushed up the steps toward the deck in single file, like a train of cars. Benzo met them at the door and jumped excitedly as soon as Rain stepped in out of the storm.

"Down, Puppers!" Rain exclaimed as the dog followed her around the oversized quartz island, deeper into the kitchen. She went to fill his food dish and regarded Julia over her shoulder. "Can you grab everyone some towels in case anyone needs to dry off?"

"I'm on it!" Julia said, heading in the direction of the bathroom.

When they were all finally dried off and were seated around the long wooden table, Rain brought over a charcuterie board filled with summer sausage; cubes of Colby, cheddar, and pepper jack; crackers; grapes; and tortilla chips. Meanwhile, Julia followed close at her heels with a six-pack of beer for the guys and a chilled bottle of pinot grigio for the girls.

Jace uncorked the wine for his sister and went in search of wineglasses while Rain set out paper plates and napkins in front of them. "It's not fancy, but it'll have to do on short notice," she explained.

"It's perfect, Rainy." Julia smiled. "We appreciate your hospitality. Don't we, guys?"

"We sure do!" Nick said as he popped the cap on the amber bottle and tossed it on the paper plate in front of him. He took a long swig and sighed. "Ahh, now that's better."

Jace poured a glass of wine and handed it to Rain. "Looks like you could use one too," he said with a wink.

"I must look like a hot mess, hey?" Rain chuckled, as she self-consciously ran her fingers through her long dark hair.

"On the contrary, you look amazing." Jace met her eyes directly and held her gaze until Rain shyly looked away. She wasn't accustomed to his change in demeanor, and it was a little unnerving in front of his sister. Rain quickly looked up to see if Julia was taking notice, but instead her friend was fist deep in stacking summer sausages with cheese and popping them, double fisted, into her mouth.

"What are you guys doing over here anyway, besides rescuing two damsels in distress?" Julia asked between bites.

Nick rose from his chair and set his hands firmly on Jace's shoulders. "The officer came with some great news. Hopefully, news that will help you two rest easy." He then turned his attention to Rain. "You have any more of that black bean salsa to go with those chips?"

Rain gestured a hand to the pantry. "Yeah, go ahead and grab yourself a brand-new jar from the cupboard. And a bowl to dump it in if you wouldn't mind grabbing that too."

Nick spun on his heel in search of the salsa while Julia shot up from her seat to retrieve a large ceramic bowl and then set it on the table.

"You two must be beyond 'hangry' to not be all over me about the Lily Redlin case." Jace chuckled. "You're not berating me for not telling you right away, I'm speechless."

Rain and Julia exchanged a look of confusion.

Rain scratched her head and asked, "Wait. Huh? You're right, I totally missed something."

"Yea, what'd we miss?" Julia popped a nugget of cheese into her mouth before continuing, "Come on, spill it . . . what news you got for us, bro?"

"We're close to making an arrest in Lily's murder. I thought you would both be happy to know that," Jace said proudly.

"An arrest?" Rain asked.

"Yup." Jace's grin grew wide.

"Who?" Rain and Julia said in unison, and then shared a smile.

"Naomi Mosely."

Chapter
Twenty-Seven

With a thud, Julia dropped the chunk of summer sausage she was holding in her fingers to the paper plate. "Wait. What? Naomi? You can't be serious."

"On what grounds?" Rain asked. "That's a pretty serious accusation."

"Oh, for Pete's sake. When are you two gonna quit playing around with our number-one Lofty Pines police officer? Stop acting as if you weren't there and don't have a clue about what's going on. Give my bro some credit: the man's not stupid." Nick removed his wet Milwaukee Brewers baseball cap, ran his fingers though his thick hair, and then set the cap beside him on the floor, where Benzo came to take a sniff. Nick then proceeded to give the dog his full attention.

Rain and Julia mirrored a look of uncertainty before Julia uttered, "I have no idea what you're talking about. I haven't seen Naomi in days. Have you, Rain?" Julia pleaded to Rain with her eyes.

Rain followed along and held up scout fingers. "No, honestly, I haven't."

"You two are so busted." Jace rolled his eyes in contempt. "Rain, I saw your SUV there that night. Don't even try to deny it."

"Where? What night?" Rain asked.

Julia leaned toward her brother and clasped her fingers in front of her as if ready to plead their case. "Yeah, where? And what are you talking about?"

Jace's response was an exasperated look.

"Enough dancing around, Jace. If you have something to say, please just say it. What are you talking about?" Rain asked squarely.

Jace seemed irritated at Rain's sudden straightforwardness, as the vein on his neck began to bulge and twitch. But she didn't care. Rain was tired of silly games and wanted answers. It had been a long day, and she was quickly growing weary. She silently wondered if he knew about everything they had learned about Shelby and the accident. And if so, how.

"At Lily's house . . . the one she had up for sale. I saw your SUV parked not far from it the evening Naomi called our department to report that the lockbox was missing from the property. Do you have any idea how the lockbox magically reappeared when myself and a few of my fellow officers from Lofty Pines arrived? Huh? Do you?" Jace drummed his fingers on the table and waited for an answer, with an upraised brow and a continued twitch in his neck.

Rain's face immediately flushed hot, and her eyes turned down toward the table.

"Exactly. That's what I thought," Jace said, sitting higher in the chair. "So don't play me a fool and act all innocent. I would hope you two would tell me the truth. In fact, I was patiently waiting for it."

"It's not her fault . . . it was mine," Julia said, reaching out a hand to her brother. "Don't take it out on Rainy."

"Whatever." Jace waved a hand of dismissal. "You two together are a dangerous mix," he huffed. "I'm not sure you should be egging each other on as much as you do. One of these days . . ."

"One of these days?" Julia pressed.

"Never mind," Jace said, obviously annoyed.

"Will you tell us? What you have on Naomi?" Rain asked hesitantly in an attempt to change the subject back to the case, and not the part they had played in it.

"Why should I?" Jace rose from the chair and then tucked it beneath the table, as if he was done with the conversation.

Rain moved over to Jace's side of the table and touched him gently on the arm, trying to stop him from leaving. "Please? Don't go. This is getting out of hand. We need to talk this through."

Her touch seemed to melt him like butter in a hot pan.

"Will you at least admit to me you were there that night?" Jace asked, searching her face for the truth. "Otherwise, I'm going home."

Julia blurted, "Wait, Rainy! Don't tell!"

Rain interrupted her friend with a halt of her hand. "Yes, we were there that night."

Julia let out a puff of frustration. "But Jace . . . we didn't . . ."

"No, you didn't. But we did," Jace regarded his sister and then returned his attention to Rain. "We found the alleged Laura Ingalls Wilder manuscript in Naomi's car the night the lockbox went missing off Lily's house in town. We're having a handwriting expert compare it with the manuscripts in the Laura Ingalls Wilder archives at the museum in Pepin, to see if it's a match and if indeed the famous author wrote it. Or to figure out if this was some sort of hoax that Lily was caught up in. Either way, we believe Naomi had plans to sell the manuscript for big bucks. We have our motive."

Both Rain's and Julia's faces registered a look of shock.

"You didn't know?" Jace asked. "I thought for sure that's why you were there. To verify that Naomi had stolen it?"

Rain was afraid to speak so she decided to let her friend take the lead, which Julia did by blurting, "Yes, for sure, we thought that the manuscript could be a potential motive. However, we weren't aware of Naomi's involvement. I promise you that. Otherwise, we would've told you. Have you arrested her yet?" She darted a look to Rain as if to say, *"Keep quiet on the rest of our intel."*

"No, we're trying to get our ducks in a row before proposing the case to the district attorney," Jace said. "We need to be able to prove criminal intent, and we have that with Naomi. Evidence doesn't lie—people do. Which is why I'm here. I was hoping both of you could provide some testimony regarding the book club and Naomi having taken part in it. A little corroboration might help our case."

"Ahh," Rain said finally. "Is that all?"

"For now." Jace looked at the oversized clock in the living room, and his eyes grew large. "Shoot! I didn't realize how late it was. I'm taking the night shift for Bentley tonight, so I need to get home and change into my uniform."

"Wait!" Julia held out a hand to stop her brother from leaving. "How did Naomi explain to the Lofty Pines PD why she had the Laura Ingalls Wilder manuscripts in her possession in the first place? Have you asked her?"

"She said that she has no idea how they ended up in her car, and we have no way of proving otherwise," Jace replied. "But we don't believe that, not after talking with Chelsea. If Lily told Chelsea about the manuscripts, what would stop her from sharing it with Naomi?" Jace looked at the clock again. "Look, I know it's a weak case at this point. Which is the reason we need more to seal it shut, and we'll get there. But for now, I gotta run."

"You mind if I walk you to the door?" Rain asked hesitantly. She had the impression he was still not happy with her *or* his sister. And the last thing she wanted was for them to part on bad terms.

"Not at all," Jace said as he leaned over and patted Benzo on the head and then shook Nick's hand in a bro-shoulder handshake. His sister said goodbye, but he barely gave Julia the time of day.

Rain knew for sure then that Jace was still ticked. She followed him to the door, where she hoped they could share a private moment. "Dinner tomorrow? Something better than frozen pizza, or cheese and sausage. A truce?" she whispered, and then took his hand in hers and rubbed circles along it with her thumb.

Jace wrapped his arms around her waist and brought her in close. "I'll eat whatever you want to cook. But don't ever lie to me again. Do you understand?" He lifted her chin so their eyes would meet. "Can you promise me that?"

She let their kiss wash away any guilt that she held inside for not telling him more. Jace's lips transported Rain to a place she wanted to linger and forget that the world around them even existed.

Chapter
Twenty-Eight

The continued rain overnight caused the library to bustle with patrons the following day. Storms were expected on and off throughout the week as well, and those stuck indoors seemed desperate to fill the void with something fun to do. Or, at the very least, a plan to entertain their bored children. Rain noticed this especially in the children's book section, where it looked as if a bomb had gone off among the bookshelves.

Most who traveled to the Northwoods during the summer months were spoiled with countless outdoor lakeside activities. So consecutive rainy days sometimes caused visitors to quickly lose their patience when the fickle Wisconsin weather didn't exactly cooperate with their plans. However, Rain didn't mind, as the busyness made the day move swiftly. Rain and Julia took care of reshelving books that had been abandoned on a chair or misplaced on the shelves, and Marge handled the checkout area. It was all hands on deck, to make the day go smoothly. And it wasn't until late afternoon, just before closing time, that there was finally a lull, and Rain had a chance to take a breath. She headed to the coffee bar for a much-needed break.

Instead of only offering warm drinks at the coffee bar during the summer months, Rain had decided to try something new. Homemade strawberry lemonade and cucumber lemon water were also offered. It was the first week of attempting the addition of cold drinks, and so far, Rain couldn't keep up with demand. Since they were at the end of the workday, though, she decided not to refill either of the glass beverage dispensers, and just to add a little more ice from the ice bucket, for her coworkers to enjoy at the end of their shift. She was just adding ice cubes to a disposable cup when Julia rounded the corner and joined her.

"Wow. Crazy, huh?" Julia said with a dramatic sigh. "I can't remember a day that was so busy without so much as a break."

Rain agreed with a chuckle as she handed Julia a cup of lemonade. "I hear you. I'm ready to head outside and sit out on the deck and relax. Maybe we should grill out tonight. I wonder if Jace and Nick could join us?"

"I'm sure Nick would be up for that. Speaking of Jace, though . . . It's been so busy today, that I haven't even been able to reach out to my brother yet, to see if they made the arrest," Julia said. "I'm sure he's still mad at me."

"Arrest?"

Rain and Julia had their backs turned to the person who'd come up on their heels. But the sound of the familiar voice sent a shiver down Rain's back. She turned to see Naomi standing behind them with a bewildered expression and a book in her hand.

"Did I hear you say they're close to making an arrest in the Lily Redlin case?" Naomi repeated.

Julia squeezed the cup she was holding, so tightly that lemonade began to spill over from her overactive grip. Rain doubted it would be able to contain the liquid inside at this point, as she heard it crack open. She hoped Naomi hadn't noticed Julia's reaction. Julia quickly drank it down before it had a chance to spill more.

Rain's attempt to compose herself and not seem as rattled was a little less obvious. She pasted on a friendly smile and said lightly, "Hey, Naomi, we didn't see you there."

"Well, are they close?" Naomi pressed, ignoring Rain's greeting completely.

"Yeah—I mean, no." Julia shook her head. "I was just saying, I *hope* that my brother helps with the case, and the Lofty Pines PD will be able to bring a resolution soon."

Rain knew her friend so well, and the slight twitch in Julia's eye was a big tell that she hoped only she herself would recognize.

Naomi shifted her weight and looked at Julia with an accusatory glance. "Oh? Your brother works for the police department? I guess I didn't put the two together when we were questioned. You never mentioned anything that night. How come?"

"Oh? I didn't? Yeah, my married name is Reynolds, so I can see the confusion," Julia said quietly. "Officer Jace Lowe is my brother. He's been a police officer for Lofty Pines for a couple years now. In fact, I think he'll be promoted to detective soon. Lofty Pines doesn't currently have one. A detective that is," Julia said hesitantly, and then frowned as if she might've overshared.

"Ahh. How nice to have a brother working in law enforcement. Well, I do hope they bring justice for Lily soon. Do they have any leads? Do you know?" Naomi's perfectly manicured brows came together in a slight frown, and she clicked her polished nails along the book she held in her hand.

"Nah, not that I'm aware of . . ." Julia coughed. "My brother is pretty tight-lipped about his work. I try my best not to pry. He gets upset at me otherwise," she added with a dramatic eye roll to drive the point home.

Rain stood motionless, unable to think of something logical to add.

"Well, I sure hope they wrap this up soon. I have a few interested buyers who want to walk through Lily's house—the one she had listed for sale in town, and until this is resolved . . ." Naomi trailed off.

"Oh? Are you not able to bring potential buyers though the house until her case is resolved?" Julia asked pointedly.

Naomi responded with a curt nod and then said, "At the moment. We're kinda locked out." She grew silent then, and her eyes studied the floor.

Rain inconspicuously winked at Julia before asking, "Do you remember Hannah from book club? I heard she might be looking for a house. Have you reached out to her yet?"

Naomi studied Rain before answering. "No. Is that so? I didn't know she was in the market for a house. I don't even think she took one of my business cards."

Clearly, it wasn't only Julia who was hiding things in this conversation.

"Maybe we can help!" Julia said a little too excitedly. "Here." She ripped off a piece of notepaper from the list she was holding and handed it to Naomi. "Write this down," she ordered with a pointed finger.

Naomi rested the paper on the book she was holding and waited with a curious expression.

"Write down 'Hannah,' and I'll give you her phone number." Julia scrolled through her phone in search of the number, and she and Rain watched carefully as Naomi wrote down Hannah's name. The penmanship was small and tight, and Naomi didn't use cursive. It didn't resemble the Post-it Note where the cursive script had been flawless.

"The number?" Naomi asked with an upraised brow.

"Oh yeah—that." Julia stopped scrolling and said apologetically, "I thought I had it, but I guess she didn't give it to me after all. Sorry." She shrugged.

"Oh."

To thwart the awkwardness Rain asked, "Would you like a lemonade? We're about to close up for the day, but you can take one to go, if you're thirsty."

Naomi tucked the note with Hannah's name inside the book she was holding and held it upright. "No, but I better go and check this book out before your staff takes off. You both have a good rest of your day."

"You too!" Rain and Julia said in unison. They waited until Naomi was far out of earshot before either spoke again.

"I wonder if we'll ever see that book again. If Naomi's behind bars, who will return it?" Rain said under her breath.

"Did we really just talk with Lily's killer?" Julia whispered.

"I don't know. There's a lot of holes to the story!" Rain declared.

"I agree. I wanted so badly to ask about the manuscripts, but I thought better of it. I was afraid if I mentioned it, I'd tip her off, and we're already in enough hot water with my brother. Now, I wish I'd asked, though." Julia sulked. "How could she act like she wasn't even on the suspect list when she knows that the police are verifying the legitimacy of Laura Ingalls Wilder's handwriting at this very moment? And that they found those documents in her own car. Doesn't she realize they're building a case against *her*?"

"Yeah. And why didn't she admit that she took Hannah through Lily's house? What's the connection there?"

"Huh. I don't know. I didn't even think of that. I was too busy trying to match her handwriting to the note found on the library door. Good question, though," Julia said thoughtfully. "Anyway, I'm sure my brother will fill us in when all is said and done. We're gonna need to talk to Shelby, though, to see if she's going to follow through with Lily's findings on Jimmy and share them with the police so that Patrick finally gets his justice too."

Rain replayed the conversation with Shelby in her mind and then said, "Shelby and I talked about the accident, but never once did she acknowledge she was there or admit anything about the cassette tape. My best guess is that she doesn't realize that Lily had concrete evidence in her possession of Shelby being there that night, or anything that can prove foul play."

"Do you think we should wait a little longer to see how this all plays out? Or should we tell Jace now? I know he has a lot on his plate right now, and muddying his case might not be in his best interest."

"Yeah, I still feel like we need more information, but we can't keep our findings about the cassette hidden for too long. I don't want him mad at me either. I'll be the one to bring it up once Naomi's brought in. Anyhow, one thing at a time—my head can't handle all this brainwork. Let's skip the lemonade, close shop, and head out onto the deck for something a little stronger. How about a glass of wine before you head home? Believe it or not, there's another bottle left over from book club the other night, if you want to share. It's still in my refrigerator. I'll clean up this mess and meet you out there. What do you think?"

"Sounds good to me. Jace seems to forgive you a lot faster than his sister, so I'll let you fill him in when you get a chance!" Julia groaned. "And I could use something stronger than this lemonade!"

Marge met them in the aisle and said, "I just checked out our last patron, and I need to run. Rex needs to be let out, and I didn't take him at noon, like usual. I feel horrible!"

Suddenly the three heard Rex whining by the door.

"Oh dear!" Marge said, turning on her heel. "I'll see you both tomorrow," she said over her shoulder.

"Wanna join us for a drink out on the deck?" Julia asked.

"Not tonight. I'm late for dinner with my friend Judy. I need to run," Marge replied before they heard the door close behind her.

"All good?" Julia asked. She was just about to follow in Marge's wake when Rain let out a gasp.

"What?" Julia turned to face her.

A chill ran down Rain's spine when she noted a copy of *Sparkling Cyanide* on the desk. The problem was, it wasn't a Lakeside Library copy, as the cover art was different from the ones she had ordered for book club to read. It was an older version, potentially a first edition. Rain held the book up for Julia to see.

Julia's eyes widened. "Where did you get that?"

Rain pointed to the corner of the desk. "It was right here; I don't know how Marge could've missed it."

"Unless someone slipped in here while we were all working? Is that possible? It was so busy today, I'm not at all surprised, to be honest."

"Or Marge was so consumed with ordering the new books that she didn't notice someone place it there?" Rain suggested. "Because she's the only one that handled the checkout desk today. Or worse, she just plain forgot again."

"Huh. That could be."

"Do you get the same eerie feeling as I do, seeing this?" Rain's hand trembled as she set the book back down on the desk.

"Yeah, absolutely." Julia picked it up and fanned it in her hands. A loose-leaf paper was stuck between the pages. She removed the paper and opened it to see handwritten notes taken on the story. Julia held the paper between them. And the handwriting looked oddly familiar.

Rain opened the desk to reveal the Post-it Note that had been left on the door. The handwriting was a match.

Chapter
Twenty-Nine

The next morning, Rain could hardly wait to return to the library and meet with Marge to show her what she and Julia had discovered. After a few too many glasses of wine the previous night, Rain wasn't sure if Julia would make an early appearance, as originally planned. So, she was surprised to see her friend crossing the parking area and heading up the catwalk. Meanwhile, Marge stood in front of the library, her purse flung over her shoulder and a tote full of books in her arms, while Rain hurried to unlock the door.

"What a gorgeous morning! The humidity finally dropped," Marge said enthusiastically when Julia joined them by the door. "If it's slow today because of the turn in the weather, you girls can certainly take off on the boat. I'm sure the tourists will be out in full force now that the sun is shining again."

Julia kneaded her forehead and squinted her eyes. "I'm glad one of us is chipper this morning. I, on the other hand, am nursing a headache. Thanks, Marge, but at the moment, the thought of a boat ride makes me wanna throw up!"

"A headache or a hangover?" Rain teased.

"Same thing. Let's not pick nits." Julia chuckled while she rubbed at her temples and then forced a smile.

"Sorry I missed the party last night. You girls have a little too much fun without me?" Marge asked, as she shifted the weight of the books in her arms. Julia caught on to her predicament and reached to unburden her.

"It was nice to spend some time with my friend, Judy, though. I haven't seen her in ages," Marge continued. "Oh, did we laugh! So much so that my stomach still hurts." She handed off the tote full of books to Julia and then reaching for her side as if still hurting from the laughter.

"Sounds like a wonderful reunion. Glad to hear that, Marge. It's so nice to catch up with old friends you haven't seen in a while, isn't it?" Rain said over her shoulder before throwing open the door.

"By the way, where's Rex?" Julia asked, looking to the ground in search of him.

"Out with my neighbor's dog until noon. The weather's been so nasty the last few days, she offered to let him play outside in her fenced yard with her dog, Bugle, for a change. I'll pick him up later. Not to worry. A little fresh air is good for him."

"Yeah, Benzo was still asleep when I left. Julia and I had him out on the deck with us until the wee hours. He's beat." Rain chuckled. "And I'm not much better," she added easily as she fought to hold back a yawn with the back of her hand.

The three moved deeper into the library, and Rain flicked on the lights. "We need to talk to you about something, Marge, before we officially open for the day."

Julia set down the bag of books, then closed the door behind them and locked it. "Yeah, I'm going to keep patrons out until we tell her." She glanced at the clock before proceeding. "We have a few minutes, anyhow, and I didn't see any cars in the parking area on my way over."

"Tell me what?" Marge's brow furrowed as she set her purse down on the desk and gave them her full attention.

Rain handed her coworker the first edition of *Sparkling Cyanide* that she and Julia had discovered on the corner of the checkout desk the previous day. "Do you happen to know who left this here?"

Marge eyed the book carefully and shook her head. "No. Should I?"

"You didn't happen to see who left it there yesterday?" Julia persisted.

Marge looked to each of them, and confusion riddled her face before her gaze returned to the book. "No, I'm sorry, but this is the first time I'm seeing it."

"What do you make of it?" Rain asked.

"I'm guessing from your reaction, it's not one of our copies. Is it?" Marge looked up for confirmation and then dug into her purse to retrieve her reading glasses. She settled them in place and pushed them high on the bridge of her nose before turning over the copy in her hand. "It doesn't look familiar. Was it from your mother's original collection? I mean, does it have the library feather stamp inside?" Marge opened the book to search for the Lakeside Library stamp, and when she did so, Rain noticed something that they hadn't seen the night before. She wasn't the only one.

"Wait! What's that?" Julia's eyes lasered into the cover page. "Rain, we were so absorbed with the notes we found inside the book, and with trying to compare the handwriting to the Post-it Note, that we didn't even notice this!"

Marge pointed out the sticker and read aloud: *This book belongs to: Dennis Richardson.*

"Dennis Richardson? Where have I heard that name before?" Julia asked, drumming her fingers atop the desk.

Marge lifted her chin, "I know where you heard it." A smile formed on her lips, and she was quite obviously pleased with herself.

Both Rain and Julia did a double take before Rain blurted, "You do?"

"Yes. The night of the book club reenactment, someone mentioned that Dennis Richardson was the name of Lily's long-lost relative."

When Julia and Rain returned blank expressions, Marge continued, "Remember? Lily's family member, who lived up in Door County and recently passed away? Lily was in line to inherit his property on Lake Michigan. You can't possibly have forgotten that motive!" Marge smirked. She seemed to feel that being the one to bring it up was proof enough that she wasn't at all losing her memory. And she was sharper than a tack.

"Wow-za Ka-dow-za! She's right!" Julia exclaimed. "Nice one, Marge!"

"Thank you," Marge said proudly. Her grin widened.

"Do either of you remember which member of the book club mentioned Dennis's name that night? I can't put my finger on it," Rain pondered. She pushed a stack of books aside and took a seat on the corner of the desk, then bit at her thumbnail.

Julia recalled, "It was Naomi. Wasn't it? Because of her real estate connections, Lily had asked her if she would investigate the estate for her to see if the property was legit. And Lily planned to use Naomi as a resource to find another realtor up in Door County. Because Lily didn't believe she was even related to this man."

"Yes, that's right, Julia." Marge removed her glasses, folded them, and set them on the desk. "Good teamwork! See what happens when the three of us put our heads together?" Marge beamed. "We're unrelenting when it comes to solving a mystery."

Rain chewed at her lip and contemplated, "Yeah, but it still doesn't explain anything. How and why is a copy of Dennis's book inside our library? Who brought it here? And why are the notes inside in the same handwriting as the person who left the Post-it Note on the library's entrance? None of this makes sense."

"Are there any members of the book club you haven't gotten a handwriting sample from yet? I mean, did you verify *everyone* that was present that first night?" Marge asked.

Julia ticked off the members on her fingers. "So far we've checked the handwriting of Chelsea, Ruth, Naomi . . ." Her voice trailed off.

"And none of them matched?" Marge confirmed.

Rain shook her head. "Nope. Not a one. So, if you count us, and Kim, that's almost everyone. The Post-it Note could only have been written by someone who actually read *Sparkling Cyanide*. But we already know for a fact it wasn't Kim because she never read the book."

"Who's left then?" Marge prompted with a roll of her hand. "Because if you match the person's handwriting to the writing on the Post-it Note, then it'll confirm two things. One, that the person who wrote the note put it on the library door for a reason. And two, that the person is connected to Lily's relative somehow."

"She's right!" Rain said excitedly. "And we already confirmed that the notes found inside the book are a match to our Post-it Note. So, we have one down. We just don't know the reasoning behind it yet."

"But it wasn't Naomi—we checked that already," Julia said with a furrowed brow. "And she's the one the police are planning to arrest as soon as they build their case. If they haven't already." She then went on to explain to Marge that the alleged Laura Ingalls Wilder manuscripts were found inside Naomi's car.

"Shelby!" Rain blurted. "We didn't check Shelby's handwriting yet! Did we?"

Marge smiled wide and reached for her purse. "Well, that's not going to be a problem."

"Really, why?" Rain asked.

Marge removed several items from her purse and set them aside on the desk before plucking out a folded piece of paper. Then she handed Rain a recipe for cheesecake-stuffed strawberries and pointed out the handwriting. "The other day when Shelby was in the library, she said she was leaving here to go strawberry picking with a friend, and she mentioned this recipe. I told her I needed the recipe because it simply sounded like the perfect finger food. I have a church picnic coming up next Saturday, and I thought I'd bring it to the potluck. She copied the recipe from her friend's collection and dropped it off to me yesterday," Marge said. Her grin widened again, as if she'd just scratched a winning lottery ticket.

Julia scampered to the desk and hurried to retrieve the Post-it Note from the Wisconsin tourism book, then brought it over for the three to view. After reviewing and comparing the handwriting, clearly it wasn't a match.

The three sighed heavily.

"Well, that wasn't what I was expecting," Marge sighed, obviously disappointed.

"Now what?" Julia asked, rubbing her temples as if trying to ward off her headache that seemed to be building instead of getting better.

"Wait. There's only one other person—the woman who didn't come to the first book club meeting but participated in the second one. She took Kim's place during the reenactment because Kim didn't have a babysitter," Rain suggested.

"The nurse?" Marge asked.

"Yeah, Hannah." Rain slowly nodded.

Julia's gaze darted around the room, and it was evident the wheels in her mind were turning in real time.

"Looks like we need to go find Hannah," Rain said resolutely, "and verify her handwriting to see if she was the one who left that Post-it Note on our library door. And if so, how Dennis's book came to be in her possession and how it landed here. We need to find out if she's connected to all this somehow."

Julia held up an index finger. "There's one more thing."

"What's that?" Rain asked.

"How did Hannah land a job here? Where on earth did she come from? And what if *by chance* she knew Dennis before he died? That would be too coincidental."

"We don't believe in coincidences . . . do we, ladies?" Marge asked with a twinkle in her eye. "Seems to me we have a little more probing to do."

Chapter Thirty

Rain recalled overhearing a conversation between Hannah and Chelsea during the reenactment book club meeting, and a mention that Hannah frequented Brewin' Time. So, that afternoon, Julia texted Chelsea and asked for a heads-up the next time she saw Hannah enter the coffee shop. It took two days for the text to finally come through from the coffee shop manager, but when it did, they were ready. Marge covered the library while Rain and Julia hurried into town in search of answers.

Upon entering, Rain was surprised to notice that Hannah was not sitting alone. She found her seated in a back booth across from an older gentleman, who was dressed in a black suit. Formal attire was unusual for Lofty Pines, to say the least. And on a sultry Wisconsin summer day, almost unheard of. The lakeside town was usually dressed in T-shirts, cutoff shorts, and flip-flops. Even business owners in the community dressed casually, so the gentleman stood out like a mis-shelved book. A stack of paperwork, strewn atop the table between them, made it seem as if an official meeting was taking place.

"There she is—do you see her sitting with that guy over there?" Rain asked Julia finally, giving a nod discretely in the direction of the booth.

"Yeah. What now?" Julia whispered.

"Let's order some iced coffees and grab a table as close to them as possible. Try to act natural. Don't ignore her or anything—it'll seem weird otherwise." Rain waited for Hannah's attention and then sent a friendly wave from across the room.

Hannah replied with a faint smile and a return wave.

"See? We got this," Rain said, shoulder bumping her friend to add a little more convincing.

Chelsea greeted them on the wrong side of the counter, an oversized purse slung over her shoulder. Rain couldn't determine if the coffee shop manager was on her way in or leaving for the day.

"Hey, you two," Chelsea said with a crooked smile. "I'm glad I caught you before I left. I'm just heading out for a dental appointment. I broke a tooth, and I think it's going to require a root canal." She grimaced. "Not exactly looking forward to it."

"Oh, yuck," Rain said sympathetically. "That doesn't sound like a fun afternoon."

"Not at all," Chelsea grumbled. "But I have to know." She leaned in expectantly and whispered, "What are you two up to?"

"What do you mean?" Rain asked.

Chelsea turned to Julia and asked pointedly, "Why did you want me to let you know when Hannah stopped by? Something you two wanna share? Does this have anything to do with the investigation into Lily's murder? Is that why you wanted to talk to her?" She put a hand up on her cheek and held it there, nursing her toothache.

"Nah, we haven't heard much. We've decided to leave the heavy lifting to the police," Julia said dismissively with a casual wave of her hand, and then she looked to Rain for an agreeable nod before she continued. "Rain and I are just a little worried about Marge. She's been a bit forgetful lately, and since Hannah's a nurse, we wanted to run a few questions by her. You know, to see if she knows anything about Alzheimer's. I think she worked in hospice before moving to Lofty Pines, so we thought she might be a good resource. Rain tried to bring up Marge's forgetfulness one day, and let's just say, the conversation didn't go very well."

"Yeah," Rain added, "we're just wondering what signs we should look out for, moving forward. And how to best approach her about this again. She seemed to get pretty agitated, more so than normal, and I've heard that can be a sign of the disease too. Neither one of us has dealt with anything like this before, and we could use a little help." Rain lowered her voice. "But Marge doesn't know we're here to talk to Hannah about any of this, so . . . if you wouldn't mind keeping this just between us."

"Ahh, I totally understand," Chelsea said as she continued to rub at her cheek. "I hope you find the answers you're looking for. That can certainly be a tough one. Marge is such a sweet lady. I'd hate to hear she's getting that wretched disease."

"Indeed," Julia said, rocking on the balls of her feet. "We're just here looking out for a dear friend, hoping to find some answers. Perhaps there's something that can be done if it's caught in the early stages."

"Marge's lucky to have you two," Chelsea said, and then grimaced as the pain in her tooth seemed to remind her of where she was supposed to be. She turned on her heel. "I better get movin'. Don't want to keep the dentist waiting."

Rain stopped her with an outstretched hand. "Hey, before you take off, do you happen to know who Hannah's sitting with over there? I'd hate to interrupt them. Does that guy look familiar to you?"

Julia piped in. "Yeah, does he stop in here often?"

"Nope. Never seen him in here before. I'm guessing she's signing some paperwork since it all looks kinda official, doesn't it?" Chelsea said with a dismissive wave of her hand after regarding Hannah and her mystery guest in the corner booth.

"Oh." Rain sighed. "Maybe this is a bad time for her to chat with us."

"Never know until you try. Well, wish me luck! I'm off to the dreaded dentist," Chelsea repeated, turning and heading for the door.

"We wish you more than luck. We wish you a quick recovery," Rain said before the coffee shop manager slipped out the door.

Rain and Julia stepped in front of the glass countertop to order their food, then took the closest available booth near Hannah. Julia had added a donut to the mix and immediately dug into it the second she slipped into the booth. But Rain was too anxious to eat. They strained their ears to hear, but it was difficult at best because of the rumblings of multiple conversations reverberating in the room.

"It's too busy in here. I can't hear anything with this crowd," Julia said between bites.

"Me neither. I was just thinking the same thing."

"Maybe, on the way to the restroom, I should walk over to the table and introduce myself," Julia suggested after wiping chocolate crumbs from her mouth with a napkin. "Would that be rude?"

"I'm not sure." Rain chanced a look over her shoulder, and Hannah seemed deep in serious conversation. She toyed with her straw before taking a sip of the creamy iced coffee that tasted like liquid ice cream. It was deliciously refreshing on a hot summer day, but almost too rich to handle, as nerves were suddenly bubbling up in her stomach.

"You think I should wait until he leaves to go over there and talk to her?" Julia whispered. "I'm not sure I can hold it much longer. I need to pee," she confessed with a giggle.

"I hear you." Rain chuckled. "Coffee does that to me too."

"You have your phone with you?"

"Yeah, why?"

"I left mine in the car," Julia said, popping the remainder of the donut into her mouth. "You have the photo of the Post-it Note still on your cell. Right?"

Rain scrolled through her photos and shared her findings with Julia.

Her friend then swiped the phone from the table and stood up.

"Where are you going with my phone?" Rain murmured.

"I'm running to the bathroom, but I'll make a quick pitstop at their table, say hello, and see if I can shoot a photo of their paperwork, inconspicuously. Hopefully Hannah is signing legal documents or making notes of some kind, and I can get a snap of it. Then we'll see if Hannah's handwriting is a match."

Rain sat up straighter in her seat. "You think you can pull that off?"

"Dunno, but it's worth trying—right?" Julia said, and not waiting for an answer, she slipped out of the booth.

Rain wrung her hands in her lap. She wondered if they should've just shared all their findings with Jace instead of heading off on yet another wild goose chase. But she couldn't text him to ask him to join them now, especially with Julia holding onto her phone. If she turned to watch what Julia was doing, it would be too obvious, so she kept her gaze straight forward. It seemed like forever before her friend returned to their table.

"Well?"

Julia grinned and handed Rain the phone. The photo was a tad blurry, but they were able to expand it to read Hannah's signature on a formal document. And the signature was—finally—a match. It also looked oddly familiar to something else, but Rain couldn't yet place why.

With an outstretched finger, Julia asserted that it was indeed Hannah who'd left the notes in Dennis's book *and* had written the Post-it Note left on the library door. "See? I knew it!"

Rain sank back into the booth to ponder their discovery. Julia drummed her fingers atop the table. "So how are these two connected?"

"Dunno. Did you happen to get a closer look? What documents was she signing?" Rain asked.

Julia let out a long sigh. "I tried. But the answer is no. When I went over there, Hannah kinda tucked the paperwork toward herself, as if it were private. Neither one of them explained why they were meeting. And I didn't get an introduction to the mystery man sitting across from her either. Trust me, I was lucky enough to get her signature, to make a match. I barely got a hello before I felt the cold shoulder," she said with an eye roll.

"Lemme see the picture again." Rain reached for her cell and expanded the photo, then set the phone down between them. It was too blurry to reveal anything besides Hannah's signature. She looked up at Julia. "How'd you do it?"

"I told them I was answering a text from Nick! It's definitely a match, though, isn't it?" Julia asked, looking down at the photo where the telltale signature jumped out at them from the blurry papers.

"Uh-huh, nice."

Julia looked over to verify whether Hannah and the man were still in deep conversation, before she whispered, "The question then becomes: Why did Hannah leave a rhyme like that on the library door?"

"I think the question runs deeper than that," Rain replied, taking a sip of her iced coffee.

"What do you mean?"

"I mean, Hannah never admitted to knowing anything about Lily—or her death, for that matter. She basically showed up at the reenactment clueless and just filled Kim's seat at the table. Why didn't she say something? She clearly knows more."

"A helluva lot more," Julia said. "But that's not all." Her grin grew wide.

"What?"

Julia leaned across the table and whispered, "I inconspicuously knocked a business card off the table and then slid it over here carefully with my shoe. Don't look now, but if I handled the job correctly, there should be a business card of the mystery man she's sitting with, underneath our table."

"You naughty girl!" Rain said gleefully.

Julia shrugged and tried to suppress a laugh.

Rain peeked beneath the table. "It's there," she certified. "But I don't want anyone to see us pick it up."

Julia knocked a napkin off the table and, in one fell swoop, swiped both the napkin and the business card from the floor. It happened so fast Rain did a double take.

Julia's eyes doubled in size when both she and Rain read:

Jonas R Schulze, Esquire
111 4th Street
Sturgeon Bay, WI
Door County's Estate Planning Expert

Instantly, Rain recalled the envelope with the Door County address that had been left on the kitchen table at Lily's lakeside cottage, next to the two wineglasses. She realized the address was also a match. Things were oddly starting to come together, and not in Hannah's favor. How was she connected to this lawyer, and what was she signing? If anything, their trip to Brewin' Time had only added up to more questions.

Chapter
Thirty-One

Rain and Julia couldn't get back to the library fast enough to explain their findings to Marge. But instead of having the conversation where eager-eared patrons could overhear the latest gossip, they decided to wait and close shop a few minutes early to hold an emergency meeting out on the deck.

Jace was also summoned to the meeting and made an appearance in a white T-shirt and long swim trunks, which covered his knees. Rain couldn't help but notice his attire showed off his darkening tan. As soon as he was close enough, he tossed a family-size bag of Doritos on the table and took a seat to join them. Jace explained that since he had worked a double shift for Officer Bentley the day before, he was off for the remainder of the afternoon. Rain wished he was paying a visit under different circumstances. She longed to whisk him off on the pontoon boat, just the two of them, for a cruise around Pine Lake. But that would have to wait.

Julia stepped out of the cabin, with a cooler in tow, and handed each of them a bottle of cold water before taking her seat. This reminded Rain to refill Rex and Benzo's water bowls with fresh water from the hose before joining her friends. When they were all finally settled around the table, Jace finally asked, "So what's this all about?"

"Remember the Post-it Note we told you about that was left on the library door?" Julia asked.

"Yeah, the rhyme that talked about Lily's lack of a suicide attempt?" Rain prompted.

"Yeah. Why?"

"We think we figured out who wrote it," Rain said, removing the Wisconsin tourism book from her lap and opening it to reveal the note in question. She then pointed to the photo on her phone to show Jace that the handwriting on both matched. "It's Hannah."

Jace's brows came together in question. "And that proves what exactly?"

Julia cleared her throat. "It's our impression that the person who wrote that Post-it Note was trying to frame someone in our book club for Lily's murder. And we believe the person who wrote the note is Hannah."

"Yeah, and we know the person is attempting to frame one of us because the person is replicating the clues found in *Sparkling Cyanide* that we read in the book club. In that book, Rosemary's death is treated as a suicide until more clues come to light. We believe the same thing is happening here," Rain said.

Jace leaned back casually in the chair. "We already have our motive—I told you that. And that Post-it Note is correct—it *has* led us to someone from your library's book club. In fact, Naomi's in custody right now. We're holding her on a misdemeanor until we can solidify our case. Therefore, I'm not sure that this person, Hannah, writing the note is even relevant at this point."

Rain sat upright. "Misdemeanor? What's the charge?"

Jace uncapped his water bottle and took a gulp before he said, "Breaking and entering. Showing Lily's house when the house was under lockdown by our station."

"Wait—huh?" Julia asked.

Jace put his water bottle down, leaned forward, and clasped his hands on the table. "She wasn't supposed to take buyers through the house the night the lockbox went missing. The house was under our jurisdiction and considered part of a crime scene until we officially cleared it. The real estate broker's office knew that."

"And that's what you're holding her on?" Marge asked, stunned.

"We believe she's a flight risk. We're getting closer to building our case, and we don't want her to skedaddle," Jace said, popping open the bag of the Doritos and taking a handful.

Julia nudged her brother to hand over the bag, and she took a handful too.

Rain slipped the hardcover copy of *Sparkling Cyanide* in front of Jace and flipped open the cover.

"What's this?" Jace asked, licking the orange powder from his fingers.

"This book was found inside the Lakeside Library. It's not a copy of ours—we used paperback reprints for the book club. *This* book belonged to a man named Dennis Richardson. Lily was supposed to inherit his estate, wasn't she? I'm guessing you have the letter that was left at her cottage, in your evidence pile back at the station. But now that Lily's no longer with us, she won't be able to collect it. How do you explain that?"

Jace sat upright. "Wait. You're telling me no one saw the person who dropped off this book?"

"That's correct. And notes made in Hannah's handwriting were found inside that book." Julia said pointedly. "So now do you have doubts on Naomi's guilt? Isn't the job to prove that the defendant is guilty beyond all reasonable doubt? I personally don't think Naomi poisoned Lily," she said firmly.

"What's the connection between Hannah and Dennis?" Jace asked.

Rain twirled her ponytail between her fingers and admitted, "We're not entirely sure yet. We're working on building a connection."

"So, the paperwork left inside Lily's cottage. The letter that you wouldn't let us see the day we found her body . . . what was that?" Julia asked pointedly. "Did it say that Lily was going to inherit Dennis Richardson's estate or not?"

"No, not exactly," Jace replied. "It was a letter informing Lily that she had a relative named Dennis Richardson who was in hospice and wanted to discuss his estate with her."

"Ahh," Rain said.

"What's the motive to poison Lily? Jace asked.

"Dunno, but something fishy is going on. We just need a little more time and a few more pieces of the puzzle to figure this out," Julia said, reaching for more Doritos.

"Oh my!" Rain exclaimed. "I just realized something!"

All eyes shot in her direction.

"What's that, dear?" Marge asked, tapping her hand as a prompt to continue.

"Remember when we read *Sparkling Cyanide*? And the character Mark wasn't seated at the table when Rosemary was poisoned, yet he was the one, in the end, who was the killer! Hannah wasn't seated at our original table the night of book club either," Rain uttered. "But she's connected somehow . . . This is eerily the same."

"And the motive in Christie's book was that Mark wanted the estate. What if Hannah's motive is as old as the book?" Marge asked.

"Exactly!" Rain said eagerly. "Jace, did you realize that Hannah was meeting with the same attorney who had reached out to Lily in that letter left behind at her lakeside cottage?"

Julia took the prompt and reached into her pocket to share with Jace the lawyer's business card.

"What if Hannah was Dennis's nurse? Supposedly this Dennis guy was some long-lost relative that Lily wasn't even aware *existed*. What if Hannah was attempting to thwart Lily from receiving any payout from an insurance policy or estate?"

"That's all great in theory, but how do we prove it?" Jace asked.

Rain faced him squarely. "I don't know—but we will."

Chapter Thirty-Two

The next day, while Rain was unloading the books from the outdoor drop-off box and handing them off to Julia, she couldn't stop her musings about the case.

How will we find the missing pieces that link to Hannah, and what part, if any, did she play in Lily's murder?

"Hey, friend. You still with me?" Julia joked, knocking Rain softly on the head. "You're so quiet out here, it's making me nervous. It means you're thinking deeply. And inquiring minds want you to share. I'm guessing—" Julia stopped short, and her smile faded when Shelby stepped outside the library and headed in their direction.

It was obvious from the swiftness of Shelby's movements and the seriousness of her demeanor that their fellow book clubber wasn't happy. The last thing Rain had expected was Shelby to pay them a visit, when Hannah was the book club member at the forefront of her mind.

"Marge mentioned I might find you out here. Just the people I need to see," Shelby said evenly.

The tone of Shelby's voice was not at all welcoming, and Rain had no idea what was bothering her, but hoped a friendly greeting might turn her demeanor around. "Hey, Shelby, how are you doing this bright, sunny day? Marge help you find a few books in there?"

Shelby laced her arms across her chest and leaned back on her heels, tapping one foot angrily to the ground. "Not great, to be honest. Can we talk?"

Julia shifted the books she held in her arms and landed them over one hip. "Sounds serious. Should I give you two a moment?"

Shelby shook her head and reached out a hand to Julia. "Oh no. You're not getting off that easy." She chuckled. "I need to talk to you too." She glanced over both shoulders before adding, "Privately."

"Can you just give us a minute to drop these books off inside? How about Julia and I meet you out on the deck where we hold our book club meetings?" Rain suggested. "It's private out there, and we can discuss whatever's on your mind."

"Sure," Shelby said curtly, moving in the direction of the deck facing the lake.

"Would you like a cucumber lemon water? We can grab one from the library for you," Rain asked, before she walked away.

"Sounds great," Shelby said, and then turned her back completely away from them.

"I wonder what that's about?" Julia asked after Shelby had disappeared around the corner. "Geesh. Should we be afraid? She's about as ticked as I was when I had to wait an entire year for the next book in my favorite series to come out, and I was suffering that book hangover! Remember that?"

"I have no idea, but I'm bringing Benzo with me. Maybe he can help lighten her mood a bit." Rain opened the door and the two dropped the books off inside and let Marge know that they were being summoned to the deck for what seemed like a serious conversation. Rain moved on to the coffee bar and loaded a tray with three cucumber waters filled to the top with ice. Benzo was sprawled out next to the coffee bar and jumped to his feet as soon as Rain arrived. He stood smiling at her, his tongue lolling out.

"Come, my cute li'l puppers." Rain said, lifting the tray from the table and being extra careful not to spill.

Julia held the door for her and waved goodbye to Marge.

"We won't be long, Marge," Rain said as she balanced the tray of water in her hands. Benzo followed obediently, which some-what surprised her. She was half thinking he'd bolt down the cat-walk or knock the cups from her tray.

Marge looked over at them from above the rim of her reading glasses and smiled. "Not to worry, girls, I'll cover the library. Take all the time you need."

When they reached the outer deck, Benzo immediately moved to greet their guest enthusiastically, and Shelby patted him on the head. "Goodness. He really is gorgeous, Rain!"

"Isn't he, though?" Rain was pleased with her decision to bring her dog along, as Shelby's demeanor seemed to instantly mellow a few notches. Benzo sat obediently by Shelby's side as she scratched the top of his head. As soon as she stopped, he moved over to Julia, who willingly obliged with more attention.

Rain cranked the umbrella to shield them all from the hot afternoon sun before taking a seat at the table with the others.

Julia took a sip of the water and said, "This might be one of the best additions to the library that you've come up with, to date, Rainy." She raised her glass in a toast, and the three clinked glasses.

Rain hated confrontation but could see something was weighing heavy on Shelby's mind. "Okay. So, what brings you to the library today? Something's clearly bothering you. Did one of the books that you ordered not come in, or something?"

"Yeah, is this really library related, or something else?" Julia asked. "What did you need to talk with us privately about?"

Shelby looked at each of them squarely before blurting, "Why did you guys go over and look at Mick's boat? I'm sure it's not because one of you is *seriously* interested in purchasing it. That's a bold-faced lie, isn't it?"

The question caught Rain completely off guard. So much so that she had to shake her head to remove the cobwebs that had suddenly settled in her brain.

It caught Julia off guard too apparently, because her friend responded with "Huh?"

"Patrick needs to rest in peace. So I'll ask you both again. And I want a straight answer. What prompted you to go over and look at Mick's boat, and why are you two digging into the past?" Shelby crossed her arms and sat back in her seat, waiting for an acceptable answer. Rain wasn't sure either one of them could oblige.

"How did you hear we went over there?" Julia asked cautiously. "Did Mick tell you that?"

"No," Shelby replied curtly. "Jimmy called and told me. He said his dad is wondering why there's a sudden interest in the boat after all these years." Her eyes bore into them. "Which makes me wonder: Why the sudden interest from you two? Just because I brought up the accident at book club doesn't give you the right to play amateur detective. I already told you, but I guess I have to say it again. The accident had *nothing* to do with Lily's death."

"Ahh, I see," Rain said, breathing deep.

Julia however, cleared her throat, exchanged a look with Rain, and then took a sip of water before responding, "Look, Shelby. We know you were on the boat the night of Patrick's accident. You weren't home sick, as you claimed. I'm not going to tell you how we know—but we know. You were there. And Lily was trying to get you to 'fess up to what really happened that night, wasn't she?" Julia held Shelby's gaze with a direct return stare down.

Shelby's eyes doubled in size and her face turned ashen. When she finally regained her composure she said, *"What are you talking about?"*

Rain joined her friend and held Shelby's gaze in the stare-down. "Julia's not making this up. We know the truth. Lily had concrete proof that you were there and exactly what went on that night. Were you dating Jimmy, or did he come on to you a little too strong that night, and Patrick had to break it up? Or what?"

Shelby seemed stunned by the facts that had just rolled off Rain's tongue. She then seemed defeated as well. Her shoulders sank, and she rested her elbows on the table and put her head in her hands. "I can't believe this," she murmured.

"Were you in love with Jimmy?" Rain asked hesitantly.

"Yes," Shelby whispered. "I am." Her gaze shot up to meet theirs. "I mean—I was. I'm a happily married woman," she stated holding up her ring finger with a gold band. Then, as if trying to convince herself, she quickly recovered, "Dirk is everything to me."

It was then Rain realized Shelby might still have strong feelings for Jimmy, even after decades had passed. Young love was like that, and Rain knew this firsthand. Was that why Shelby was so adamant about protecting him?

"And Lily was mad the way he was coming on to you that night. Jimmy was getting too physical. Too handsy," Julia continued. "Was he a mean drunk? Is that it?"

"Uh-huh." Shelby's gaze turned to the lake, where a glittery path was met by the sun. The water was unusually calm, not unlike their conversation. It now seemed like they could hear a pin drop in the lull between them.

Benzo sauntered back to Shelby to soothe her, and this seemed to reawaken her from her faraway thoughts. "You have to understand, Jimmy's a good guy. I don't condone his behavior that night, but he only got physical when he drank, and I tried explaining that to Lily. It was an issue of alcoholism, not mean-spiritedness. But Lily was always so overprotective and expected everyone to behave perfectly. She was the mother hen over all of us."

"We think Lily was planning to pursue justice for Patrick," Rain said. "She had enough evidence to take it to the authorities. It was only a matter of time."

"We almost wondered if that's what got her killed," Julia added.

Shelby shook her head vehemently, denying that fact. "No. I don't believe you."

"It's true," Rain said.

Shelby sat upright in the chair. "But how? What proof do you have from that old boat that somehow told you all this? What exactly did Lily find? She was always digging into stuff that was none of her business. Lily wanted to be an investigative reporter, and she was the head of our high school's newspaper. Did she find an old spiral notebook or her cassette recorder in the bottom of a drawer or something when she was cleaning out her house and getting it ready for sale? Was that it? Her stupid notes won't prove a thing." Shelby folded her arms protectively over her chest as if desperately wanting to end the conversation.

Rain and Julia stole a look at each other before Rain said, "We're not going to tell you that. We'll leave that to the authorities to sift through."

Shelby planted her hands firmly on the table, leaned forward, and said. "You can't. You can't bring this to the police. You need to drop this right now! Nothing you do or say is going to bring

Patrick back. Don't you understand that?" Shelby clenched a fist and pounded it on the table. "It was a long time ago, and as I said to Lily before she died, it's a lost cause to drag everyone through that again. What good does it serve! Nothing! I mean, *nothing*! Nothing good can come of this."

"It's not really for you to decide, is it? Doesn't Patrick's family deserve to know what really happened the night he died? I think they have a right to get some answers," Julia stated matter-of-factly. "I would certainly want to know if it were my child or sibling who died out there on that lake." Julia flung her hand in the direction of Pine Lake, which was now so preternaturally calm it was hard to believe anything that horrific had ever happened out there.

A shiver shot down Rain's spine as she was reminded of the horror of it all.

"No. No. No!" Shelby shook her head. "This can't be happening."

"You yourself said Patrick's parents divorced over it. They need to know the truth," Rain said gently. "It might help them somehow."

"How is making Jimmy liable going to change anything? It's not! It's only going to drag him through the mud!" Shelby spewed. "It's not going to bring Patrick back from the grave! Don't you see that? Nothing you do or say will ever bring him back!"

Julia leaned in and patted Shelby gently on the hand to calm her, but her gesture, meant to be kind, instead backfired as Shelby recoiled like a snake poked with a stick.

"Look," Shelby said calmly, continuing to plead her case. "Jimmy has paid the price in full for that accident; I promise you that. His life—*our lives*—were never the same after that. No amount of jail time will compare to the life sentence he's already served."

"How so?" Rain asked gently.

"Jimmy started drinking heavily and doing drugs, and his life spiraled completely out of control after the accident. It was bad enough that we lost Patrick, but then we almost lost Jimmy too. But now he's clean and sober, and he has a serious girlfriend he met in rehab. I guess his girlfriend is a nurse, and she's been helping monitor his sobriety. And keeping him on the straight and narrow. He's finally happy again after all these years. Jimmy deserves all the happiness in the world."

Rain's heart skipped a beat. "Wait. Can you repeat that?"

"Repeat what?" Shelby spat.

"Did you say Jimmy is dating *a nurse*?"

"Yeah, why?"

"Is her name Hannah?" Julia asked.

"You know, I'm not really sure? Why do ask?" Shelby said, and then the wheels seemed to turn in her mind as well. "Oh, you mean the girl who joined us at book club. *That* Hannah? Is she from Door County? I did not put that together."

Rain waved a hand between her and Julia. "Neither did we. Until now."

Chapter
Thirty-Three

A fter reluctantly agreeing with Shelby to hold off on reporting their findings about Patrick's accident to the police until Lily's case was resolved, Shelby left them to ponder what steps to take next. The Lofty Pines Police Department was small by comparison to other departments throughout the state of Wisconsin. And as it was, the department was stretched to the max. The last thing they wanted to do was thwart their ongoing investigation into Lily's death by confusing matters until they themselves could make sense of it all.

Rain and Julia immediately closed the library and summoned Marge to join them in an emergency meeting out on the deck. Rain thought the three heads needed to come together again to figure out their next move. And with Naomi in custody, time was of the essence.

When they had explained to Marge everything that had transpired, she asked, "So, you absolutely think Naomi's arrest is wrong then? And you know with one hundred percent certainty that the Laura Ingalls Wilder manuscripts are not the motive for Lily's murder? Is that what you're telling me? You think the Lofty Pines Police Department is following the wrong leads?"

Rain stopped gnawing at her lip and said: "We don't know anything for sure, but we think Hannah might have something to do with Lily's death. We just need to put the puzzle pieces together and prove it."

"Yeah, Naomi and Hannah might be in on it together. We can't rule anything out at this point," Julia said.

"We need to sort this out and be *absolutely certain* before we share our findings with your brother, though. Right, Julia?"

"Rain is right," Marge said, clicking her fingernail to the table. "It's important to gather the evidence we need to prove our theory is indeed correct before muddying the waters down at the police department."

Rain couldn't agree more because the last thing she wanted was to lose Jace's trust—especially now. "Sounds like we have a lot of work to do."

Marge's expression morphed into one of worry, and she wrung her hands, then pinched her nose. "I suppose, I don't know," she said finally. "I just hate the thought of Naomi taking the heat if she wasn't the one in the kitchen. It seems so unfair."

The three chuckled at the older woman's kitchen reference. It helped ease tension that was building like storm clouds between them.

"We don't like it any better than you do, Marge," Rain said leaning into her. "But here's the thing. Like you said, we need more evidence before we go to the police. Besides, I don't want to jump to conclusions here. We could be totally off base with our theory, and, in that case Naomi might be the right person in custody. The only way this is going to work is if we have conclusive evidence to prove our findings."

"What is your theory of what happened to Lily? Specifically. What's the motive? Why would Hannah want Lily dead?" Marge asked.

"I believe Hannah was meeting with the attorney to see who would be next in line to inherit Dennis Richardson's property. As it was, Lily told Naomi she was surprised to learn about this relative in Door County. If there's no one left to leave it to, why not Hannah? What if she was Dennis's nurse? It's not out of the realm of possibility. She said she worked in hospice, and her patient recently died, which was the reason for her moving here," Rain suggested.

Marge's brows narrowed in question. "And the note? Why would she leave a Post-it Note on the library door? What was her motivation there?"

"We think someone knew we were investigating and wanted to mislead us with clues similar to those used in Agatha's novel," Julia said, drumming her fingers on the table.

"Ahh, good observation, Julia." Marge said. "Just like in the novel, this person is trying to frame one of us and lead us to believe someone in our group was responsible. And since Hannah wasn't at the first meeting, it would remove her from the suspect list."

"Then what about leaving Dennis's copy of *Sparkling Cyanide* in our library? Why would she do that? Especially since that was the only way we connected her to him. Would she be that absent-minded, you think?" Rain asked. "That one is really bothering me."

"Yeah, that's bothering me too. That part doesn't fit, in my opinion," Marge said.

"You know, it's not out of the question . . . Was Naomi involved with Hannah in this scheme or not? That's a big concern in my mind. They did meet at Lily's house on Sycamore Street. What if there was a sinister reason for their meeting that night?" Julia asked. "Lest we forget that connection."

"If that's the case, then Naomi is right where she needs to be at the moment," Marge said with a lift of her chin. "Apparently, we need to either exclude her or provide a way out for her. We need compelling physical evidence to move this investigation forward. Either way, I know exactly how we're going to do it."

Chapter
Thirty-Four

That evening, with a plan in place to seek out more concrete evidence to support their theory, Rain and Julia headed to the dog park with Benzo. Rain wanted to exhaust her dog before leaving him home alone for the entire evening. At Marge's suggestion, they had decided a visit to Alec Shield's residence might prove fruitful. Alec was the man Hannah was currently working for and apparently nursing back to health. And as luck would have it, Alec was Marge's longtime neighbor, merely a few doors down.

After leaving the dog park, Julia made a detour and turned onto the road where Kim's house was located.

"Where are we going?" Rain asked. "I thought we were headed home and dropping Benzo off before we all meet at Marge's. Why are you driving to Kim's house? I'm confused."

"I hope you don't mind a quick stop before we go home. Nick asked me to pick up a Weedwacker that Seth borrowed. Apparently Seth's was broken, and he finally bought a new one. Nick is anxious to have his back."

"Oh, okay. No problem, then," Rain said, scratching Benzo, whose head was planted between them.

Julia pulled into Kim's driveway and put the truck in park, then asked, "Do you want to wait in the truck? Or come with?"

"I'll crack the window and leave Benzo. We'll just be a minute, right?"

"Yeah, not to worry. I wouldn't leave him a second longer than we need to. And besides, we need to hurry and get over to Marge's house."

Rain cranked the window down and tucked Benzo in safely before exiting the truck. Before they could even ring the doorbell, Kim had already swung wide the front door and greeted them with a broad smile.

"Hey! How nice to see some friendly *adult* faces. Glad to see you two drop by my neck of the woods!" Kim exclaimed. "I feel like we need to catch up. It's been nuts around here. The kids get a little stir crazy when the weather doesn't cooperate."

"No kidding! With the recent stormy weather, the library has been busy too," Julia said. "We're just dropping in for a quick visit. What are you up to?"

But it was obvious what Kim was up to: she had her hands full. Rory was planted on one hip, and Ryder was hanging onto Kim's leg like cellophane. "We were just about to go outside and play for a few minutes. These two need one last run around the yard before bedtime. But please come on in." Kim held open the door and Rain and Julia slipped inside, careful to not let one of the twins escape.

As soon as Kim set Rory down on the floor, the twins took off running toward a heap of toys that had been abandoned in the middle of the living room.

"You want a cold one?" Kim asked, wiping her brow as if she herself could use one.

"Nah, we can't stay long. Benzo is in the truck, and despite the sun going down, it's still warm out there. We can't leave him long," Rain said. "But thanks, we'll take a raincheck."

"Oh, I heard you rescued a dog! Nick told us last time we saw him. That's awesome, Rain. I'm so happy for you. You're more than welcome to bring Benzo inside if you'd like," Kim offered. "I'm totally okay with that."

"Thanks, but I'm not sure how he is with kids yet, so I'd better wait on that. He can be a little hyper at times, and I don't want to rile up your kids before bedtime. But another time, for sure."

"Yeah, we'll definitely take a raincheck on that drink too, maybe next week," Julia suggested. "But for now, we're actually here to pick up the Weedwacker. You know how he freaks out if one of his babies is gone for a few days." She laughed.

"Oh! Sure, no problem. Please tell him we really appreciate him loaning it to us. Seth is out with his dad fishing right now, but I bet he left it in the garage," Kim said. "I'll pop open the garage door, and you can grab it on your way out. It should be hanging on a peg right next to the mower."

Suddenly, a bloodcurdling screech caught their attention, and the three looked to see Rory and Ryder physically fighting over a toy.

"Excuse me one moment." Kim moved to scold her children, causing Julia to lean in and whisper, "I'm so not ready for kids. I like my freedom too much. Is that bad?"

"No, it's honest," Rain said quietly. "But it might be something you ought to share with Nick . . . if that's how you really feel."

Kim returned with a handful of Silly Putty in her hand and held it up to them. "This." She shook her head in frustration. "This little gooey junk is what they're fighting about. Bedtime can't come fast enough." She sighed. "I should've sent them off fishing with Seth today. I really could use a break."

Julia reached over and plucked the Silly Putty from Kim's hand and held it preciously as if it were gold in the palm of her hand. This caused Kim to laugh aloud.

"What are you doing with that?" Rain asked.

"Kim, you mind if I borrow this?" Julia asked.

"Yeah, sure—why?" Kim's expression morphed to one of utter confusion. "You wanna babysit, Julia?" she asked as she waved a hand dramatically in the direction of her children. "Go for it! They're all yours!"

"No, but seriously. Do you mind if I take it?" Julia asked while rolling the Silly Putty between her fingers. "I'll buy them some new stuff to replace it. I promise."

Kim shrugged. "It's all yours. Keep it. It's doing nothing but giving me grief, as you can tell." She turned again to regard her now-cherubic children, who were giggling and getting along as if nothing had been amiss just moments before. As if they'd never fought a day in their life.

Rain was surprised Kim didn't press Julia to say what she wanted to use the putty for, and she herself was curious beyond measure.

"All right, we'll get out of your hair. Go take the boys for a marathon jog," Julia said jokingly, backing out the door. "And then put them to bed and pour yourself a cold one."

"Oh, you have no idea!" Kim's smile grew wide. "I'm totally on it!" She then leaned in and lowered her voice to a whisper. "Hey, by the way, any word on Lily's case? I mean, can you believe it? Naomi? The gossip wheel is turning fast in Lofty Pines, but I just can't believe it! She was one of the nicest people at the book club meeting. At least from what I can remember of that night after drinking a little too much." She giggled. "Anyhow, I'm shocked!"

"Yeah, we're just as surprised as you are," Julia said, clicking her tongue. "But I think the police are getting closer every day to solving this thing. It's just a matter of time."

Kim looked over both shoulders to make sure she was out of earshot, which she most clearly was, and then lowered her voice even more. "I shouldn't mention this, but one of the moms from the twin's playgroup—Candace—said she might have to testify. Can you believe that?" Her eyes widened. "Candace might have to take the stand!"

"Testify? To what, exactly?" Rain asked.

"She lives across the street from Lily's cottage, and her Ring camera caught Naomi's car leaving Lily's the night of the murder," Kim whispered.

"It did?" Julia asked.

Kim covered her mouth as if she shouldn't be sharing any of this, but then continued, "Yeah! Can you believe it?"

"Did Candace mention if she saw anyone else in Lily's driveway that night?" Rain asked.

"Yeah, so that's where it gets weird." Kim looked behind her, to see if the twins were still occupied with their toys, before adding, "Candace mentioned that she saw another car when she looked out her window, but for some dumb reason, the Ring didn't catch that. She lost internet, and it stopped working. But she swears she saw another car pull in. She just can't prove it. What do you think?" Kim asked, chewing nervously at her lower lip.

"I don't know what to think," Julia said in a faraway voice, as if she were taking all this information in like a sponge.

"Well, she's afraid to mention anything to the police about it because she doesn't want to get involved. Because she has no way to corroborate what she saw, so she's afraid to bring it up. It has me in a bit of a pickle because I don't know if I should say something. What should I do?"

"Go with your gut, I guess," Julia replied.

Kim's expression was worried. "But Candace told me not to say anything. She's afraid it'll drag her into a lengthy court case, and she'd have to find a babysitter. My gut says stay out of it." Kim turned then to look at her children, which seemed to solidify her belief that this decision would protect them.

"I guess that's what you should do, then," Julia said with a shrug.

Rain looped her arm through Julia's and retreated them both a step further from the stoop. "Well, I think we need to get going, with Benzo waiting in the hot truck. I'm sure the Lofty Pines PD has this all under control, and your friend Candace will be fine. See you soon!" Rain added before she and Julia headed in the direction of the garage.

After they had retrieved the tool and were backing out of Kim's driveway, Rain asked. "What was that about? Two people were in Lily's driveway the night of the murder? And what on earth do you plan to do with that Silly Putty?"

"You'll see," Julia grinned. "It's going to be epic."

Chapter
Thirty-Five

When Rain and Julia reached Marge's house, they were welcomed inside, and the scent of apples and cinnamon lured them to follow her into the galley-style kitchen.

"What are you making that smells so good?" Rain asked finally.

"Caramel apple pie. It's one of Alec's favorites. I remembered that from years ago when we used to get together for monthly neighborhood potlucks. We don't do much of that anymore," Marge admitted sadly. "The world is too busy these days. I miss the old times, when getting together with your neighborhood was a thing. And children played kickball in the streets and chased fireflies until long after dark. Ah, I'm aging myself, I guess. Kids today would rather be stuck inside with their noses in their cell phones or video games." She slipped on oversized oven mitts, reached into the oven, and plucked out the steaming pie, which filled the room with an even stronger alluring scent.

Julia stood next to the pie and waved the scent closer to her nose. "Marge, I think you've outdone yourself. Alec is one lucky man. Is he single? Because he might want to sweep you off your feet after a bite of this," she teased, licking her lips.

"Julia, have you gone mad? Yes, he's single, but my dating days have long disappeared. If you haven't noticed, I've got one foot in the grave, my dear. I'm not exactly dating material." Marge clucked.

"Don't talk like that, Marge," Julia corrected. "I thought it was you who always calls yourself"—she threw her fingers up in air quotes and made a face—"'a young chicken.'"

Marge immediately changed the mood in the room by saying, "Alec's not the only lucky one, though, to get a piece of homemade pie." She beamed. She reached back into the oven and plucked out a second pie.

Julie's eyes doubled in size. "Who's that pie-full-of-joy for?"

"Well, it's for us, my friends," Marge said with a twinkle in her eye. "Just as soon as we're done with our visit over at Alec's, this one should be cool enough for a slice. I bought vanilla ice cream too."

"Marge?" Rain asked.

"Yes, dear?" The older woman removed her mitt-gloved hands, dropped them to the countertop, and gave Rain her full attention.

"Have I told you lately how much I love you?" she asked, wrapping her arm around the older woman's shoulder and leaning into her.

Marge laughed gleefully. "You tell me all the time, my sweet. But I never tire of hearing it." She nuzzled Rain in return.

Julia, seemingly not wanting to miss out, wrapped her arms around both of them, brought them in close, and gave a tight squeeze—the three then shared a choking grunt and a laugh.

"Okay, enough of this love fest—what's our plan?" Julia asked after pulling away from them and leaning herself against the countertop. "'Cause I can't wait to dip my fork into that pie."

Marge carefully placed the first pie into a container made for delivery and handed it off to Rain before moving out of the kitchen, where they followed. As the older woman was slipping on a pair of tennis shoes that had been stashed neatly by the front door, she said, "Well, from what I gathered, Hannah is staying in the efficiency apartment in the basement of Alec's house. It used to be a mother-in-law suite, but unfortunately Ester died a few months ago. But it was time—goodness, Ester was in her late nineties! His mother sure led a full life. Anyhow, the apartment has been sitting empty until his nurse came, so they're taking advantage of the space. As you know, it's so hard to find temporary housing in Lofty Pines during the summer months. Those AirBnB lake properties are booked up years in advance."

"Nice job on the intel, Marge," Rain said, tapping her approvingly on the shoulder.

Marge looked up at her and smiled. "I know you two are worried about my forgetfulness, but I promise you, I'm not senile, nor am I suffering from Alzheimer's. It's normal to forget things at my age. I'm still on my game, as you can see," she stated firmly.

Rain wasn't sure she completely agreed with Marge, but only time would tell. They would keep their eyes and ears open and see if anything should progress before prompting her further to seek medical advice. She solidified this with an inconspicuous nod to Julia.

Julia plucked the Silly Putty from her pocket. "Hey, and just so you know, I've got the goods," she said with a sly smile.

"What the heck are you planning to do with that?" Rain asked. "Are you finally going to let us know?"

"I'm planning to get a print of Hannah's tires, to prove that her car was at Lily's cottage the night she was poisoned. We can match it to the picture you took on your phone the next day." Julia lowered her voice. "And yes, Rain, I did notice that you took a picture of the muddy tracks. I'm guessing the police already have a mold made of it, but they don't know whose tire they need to match it to." She held up a finger and smiled. "But we will find out!"

"Guess, I'm not the only brilliant one in the group. Nice work, Julia!" Marge said approvingly. She stood up and stretched, grimacing as if she'd just tweaked her back.

Julia looked at the older woman with concern and asked, "Are we walking over there, then? You look like you're in pain."

"Oh, it's nothing but my age talking again. I'll be fine," Marge groaned. "It's only a few doors down. Can you handle the pie, Rain?"

Rain lifted the container handle to demonstrate. "Yep, I got it."

Marge moved into the adjoining living room and returned lugging a tote full of books. She handed the bag to Julia. "And can you take this?" she asked. "My back is giving me trouble today; it's probably best I don't overdo it," she admitted finally.

"You betcha," Julia said with a wink.

The three walked down the wide sidewalk to a small white bungalow with blue trim, where Marge stopped abruptly and pointed out the house. "Here we are, ladies."

They took the shaded cobblestone path that wound around a large maple tree, to the front door, where Marge reached to ring the doorbell. The front door was ajar, allowing a breeze to blow through the screen door. Rain guessed the older home didn't have air conditioning, and wondered how anyone could survive, because the Northwoods humidity could beat out the hot temps of Florida occasionally. Especially since the home was located in town and didn't benefit from the cool lake breezes, which she'd gotten used to.

A man's voice bellowed from inside the bungalow. "Who's out there?"

Marge leaned into the screen and shouted, "Alec, it's me, Marge. I came to check in on you and bring you a caramel apple pie."

"Did I hear you say pie? Come on in, neighbor!"

Marge smiled at Rain and Julia before opening the door and holding it for them to follow. They traveled into a rather dark living room where an older man was sitting in a wheelchair. The windows were open, allowing the lace curtains to sway softly in the breeze. Rain was thankful the humidity was low and the temperature comfortable for him. But the lack of natural light meant she had to readjust her eyes before stepping farther into the room.

"How are you holding up, Alec? These are my friends from the library, Rain and Julia," Marge said, nudging Rain to take a step closer. "We came to drop off a few treats for you."

After Alec prompted her to do so, Rain set the pie down on a tray table near his wheelchair and then took a few steps backward.

"Marge, what a sight for sore eyes! I haven't had one of your caramel apple pies in years. If it took a surgery to get one, well I guess it was well worth it, wasn't it?" He grinned widely, showing a chipped tooth. He then let out a hearty laugh.

"I was just sharing with my friends how much I miss our neighborhood potlucks too," Marge agreed with a smile. "We also brought you some books from the Lakeside Library. I chose a few different genres because I wasn't sure what you'd like to read. And don't worry about returning them—you just give me a call, and I'll deliver them back and forth for you whenever you're ready."

Julia set the books down next to the tray table and smiled.

Alec leaned forward in the wheelchair and steepled his fingers. "You'd do that for me?"

"But of course!" Marge replied with a decisive nod.

"Mighty kind of you, Marge, I am grateful for it. I'm sure sorry it took all this for you to pay me a visit, but I appreciate you taking the time and your willingness to help me out." He looked down, reflecting on his predicament, and the glee on his face all but disappeared.

"It's no bother, really. I'm going that way anyway," Marge said encouragingly. "And anything else I can do, please reach out and ask. I'm just a phone call away."

Alec's white hair looked as if it hadn't been washed recently, and his clothes were a bit rumpled. Rain couldn't help but wonder where Hannah was.

"Where's your nurse?" Marge asked, and Rain was thankful the older woman had quite literally read her mind.

"Hannah went to run some errands for me."

Julia leaned in and whispered in Rain's ear, "So much for my Silly Putty idea."

Alec continued, "I told her I wanted fried chicken and mashed potatoes for supper. She's a good cook, that girl. I'm lucky to have her." He leaned back and tapped his stomach approvingly. "I'm not sure I ever want to recover because then she'll leave me for sure for that other man."

"Ahh," Marge said. "Other man?"

"Yeah, I warned her to not go off and marry that Jimmy fellow like she's been rambling on about. That young man seems like trouble to me," Alec said with a disapproving shake of his head. "Anyhow, I'm going to need her to stay right here, for at least the summer, and not run back to Door County. The likes of that happens, and for sure I'll never see her again." He scoffed. "She just better stick around till I'm back on my feet, like she's contracted to do."

Rain looked to Julia and realized her friend too, had taken the information in. His statement confirmed that Hannah was dating Jimmy.

Had she met Lily before the night she was poisoned?

Marge continued, "I was planning to offer to bring you some meals, but it sounds like I'm not needed. Sounds like your nurse is taking very good care of you."

"Well, now, I wouldn't take it that far. I'd never pass up a chance to have your potato salad again. No one makes potato salad like you do, Marge." He winked.

Marge clasped her hands in delight and rocked on the balls of her feet. "I haven't made that in years. We had such fun back in the day when the neighborhood got together, didn't we? Oh, how I wish those days never ended."

"We sure did," he said, tapping the arms of the wheelchair. "So, are you gonna just stand there? Or slice me up a piece of that pie?" he asked, smacking his gums.

Chapter
Thirty-Six

As soon as the words were out of Alec's mouth, Marge said, "I'd be delighted if you sampled a piece of pie. In fact, I'm sure it's still warm from the oven. If you lead me to your plates, Alec, I'd be happy to slice a hefty portion for you." She plucked the apple pie from the tray table and held it in her hands, awaiting further instruction.

Alec rolled his wheelchair along the wooden floorboards, past them to a hallway that led toward the back of the house. He called out in his wake, "I can hardly wait, Marge! Follow me, ladies."

When they arrived in the kitchen, Rain felt little airflow, even though the screen door on the back wall had been left wide open. The sliding glass door led to an adjoining back porch, shaded by a large oak, and a stretch of lawn beyond that. Her gaze returned to the interior of the kitchen, in search of a doorway that would lead to the basement.

Julia beat her to the punch. "So, Alec . . . you mentioned your nurse is living with you? Downstairs, in the in-law suite? Is that correct?"

"Yes, it's been so convenient to have Hannah close by. It's really been wonderful," he said, pointing to the high wooden cabinets that filled the back wall. "Marge, paper plates are up there, and cutlery in the drawer right below it. You mind grabbing them?"

"Who else wants pie?" Marge asked, turning to them.

When the others declined, Alec said, "You girls don't know what you're missing! But I'd be lying if I said I wasn't thinking that means more for me," he sang out happily.

Rain thought the man was so consumed by the idea of pie that Alec would agree to almost anything. She cleared her throat, "You know, Alec, I have a cousin who's looking for a place for the fall season. She's just looking for an efficiency, really. Any chance Julia and I can take a quick peek at your downstairs apartment, so when you're all healed up, and your nurse moves out, you could maybe rent it out to her? My cousin's a very good cook. In fact, I think fried chicken is her specialty." She dangled that add-on like a carrot, and Alec snatched it up like a rabbit.

"I don't see a reason why not." He flung a finger toward a wooden door located in the far corner of the room. "The entrance to the apartment is right there, at the bottom of the stairs. I'm sure Hannah wouldn't mind. You're right: I probably should line something up for the fall. I sure could use the extra money." He groaned in frustration. "Insurance hasn't even put a dent in my medical bills, which seem to be multiplying by the minute."

Marge gave each of them a slight push in the direction of the doorway before moving to plate the pie. "You two go on then and take a peek, but please hurry." Her eyes narrowed in on them, as if warning them to be careful. "We don't want to keep Alec from his rest time. Now, do we?"

"Oh, it's so nice to have the company, Marge—don't you worry about me. I'll let you know if I need to get some rest. Right now, I'm just anxious for a bite of that pie," he said, chomping at the bit. He reached his hands out to take the plate onto his lap, but instead Marge handed him a paper towel that she had plucked from its holder.

"Why don't I take it back to the living room for you," Marge said, not waiting for an answer and carrying the pie plate away from him. "It's much cooler in there with the nice breeze." She fanned a hand to her face to drive the point home. The man rolled behind her, desperate for his dessert.

As soon as the wheelchair had disappeared from the kitchen, Rain and Julia scampered down the stairway that led to the basement apartment. When they reached the carpeted bottom step, Julia flicked on the overhead light, illuminating the space. The smell of bacon hung in the air, as if a meal had been recently cooked, which caused Rain's stomach to respond in a rumble. A large cardboard box had been left on the bottom step, and Rain had to catch herself from tripping over it.

The room was surprisingly bright for a basement room with so few windows. On one wall, a tiny window close to the ceiling allowed afternoon sunlight to stream through, leaving a dusty shadow in its wake. The apartment was the very definition of efficiency. From where they stood at the bottom step, they could view it in its entirety. A few lower cabinets flanked a white stove, and a small matching refrigerator stood on one wall. A twin-sized bed with a bright yellow bedspread, on which a giant flower bloomed, was tucked against the other corner. It wouldn't take long for them to investigate such a tiny space. The carpet was so thick it left footprints in their wake the moment they left the stairs.

"Let's split up—you take that side," Rain directed as she flipped open the cardboard box that had nearly tripped her. Inside, she uncovered intricate hand-knit doilies, dried flower arrangements, and imitation fruit. Rain wondered if these were Ester's belongings that had been packed up to be donated. She tugged the box completely away from the staircase, pushed it aside, and then moved in the direction of the kitchen cabinets. She opened a few drawers to expose the usual kitchen utensils, as expected, but did a one-eighty when she heard an elated exclamation from her friend.

Julia had rushed toward a narrow bedside table under which a stack of papers had been tucked, almost hidden from view because the bedspread pooled on the plush carpet, nearly covering them. She lifted the yellow coverlet to expose her find to Rain, and then scurried over to show her the documents fanned out in her hand.

"Look!" Julia's eyes scanned the page before meeting Rain's gaze. "Jackpot! I just found Dennis's life insurance policy, and guess who's named as the beneficiary?" she said with a wide grin, as she held up the paperwork in triumph.

"What—?" Rain was just about to ask, but closed her lips when the sound of a utility door being flung open and the sight of Julia's jaw dropping caused her to turn her head.

"What the hell are you doing in my apartment?" Hannah stepped into the room, with fists clenched and eyes blazing, catching them completely off guard.

Both Rain and Julia were so dumbfounded at the accusation that neither responded. Instead, they stood like two kids caught with their hands in the cookie jar, awaiting a hand slap.

From across the room, Hannah's eyes bore into them. She stomped over, coming face to face within an inch of Rain's nose, leaned forward and, with a laser stare, studied each of them individually, looking for an answer.

Both remained mute.

"Give me that." Hannah ripped the documents from Julia's hands, causing a paper cut, which instantly drew blood.

"Owie!" Julia cried, and then popped the injured finger into her mouth.

"You deserve it," Hannah said flippantly. "You have no right to look at that. Or to even be in my apartment, in the first place. What exactly are you doing in here?"

Julia looked at Rain and then said with as much casualness that she could muster, "Alec said we could come down and take a look at your place so that when you decide to move out . . ." She stuttered, "D-did he mention, we might have someone who'd be willing to rent it? Or did you not see him on your way in?" She trailed off and then turned her head to avoid Hannah's penetrating stare. "I assumed Naomi was taking you house hunting anyway . . . so Alec's going to need someone to take over the rent, to pay his growing medical bills."

Rain wasn't sure if Hannah had ever mentioned her house hunt to Julia. She elbowed her in an effort to close her mouth. Had her friend just outed them for spying on Hannah while she and Naomi were touring the Sycamore Street property?

"Oh, is that so?"

"Yeah . . . so anyhoo . . ." Julia rocked on the balls of her feet while her gaze took in the room. "I love what you've done with the place. The decorating, I mean. It's nice and bright, and airy . . ." Julia seemed to paste on a smile in an effort to diffuse the situation, but it backfired.

Hannah shook the papers in front of her, and then waved them in front of Julia's face wildly. "That still doesn't explain why you were looking at my private papers, which have absolutely nothing to do with renting an apartment. Nice try, little Miss Nosy. Try again. What exactly are you up to?"

Rain swallowed. She couldn't remember being in the presence of someone who instantly, at the snap of a finger, changed like this and turned so agitated. It was as if Hannah was about to come completely unleashed in front of their very eyes. She was like a firework on the verge of exploding.

This was verified when Hannah shrilled, "Answer me!"

Her roaring voice caused both Rain and Julia to physically jump.

Nevertheless, Hannah's bite must've also ticked off her friend because Julia leveled her spine and, lacing her fingers firmly on her hips, said pointedly, "How is it that you're the sole beneficiary on Dennis Richardson's life insurance policy? Were you hoping for his entire estate too? You were his nurse, I assume?"

"That's right," Hannah said defiantly.

"Can you explain that to me?" Julia's tone was a little too accusatory in Rain's opinion, so she jumped in.

"I think it's wonderful news," Rain said with a weak smile. "Door County is such a lovely area. People come from all over the country to visit. Did you know they call it the Cape Cod of the Midwest?" she rambled on. "I'm sure it's well deserved after caring for Dennis until his last breath. That couldn't have been easy."

"You bet I deserved it!" Hanna's lips curved upward, and she jutted a thumb to her chest. "Not only that, but I also *earned* it!"

"And Lily?" Julia pressed. "What did she deserve? Did she deserve what she got too?"

"Dennis never even met Lily!" Hannah threw up her hands in frustration, shaking the documents again wildly. "I was the one who cared for him until he took his last breath! Why would he give his property away to someone he never met? He just felt guilty that his mother's sister abandoned her like she was trash. Like it was Dennis's fault Lily ended up in foster care." She scoffed. "That blood wasn't on his hands."

"No. But it is on yours," Julia stated firmly.

"She was dying from cancer anyway," Hannah defended. As if that made the action which had led to Lily's death acceptable. "Her days were numbered. No amount of chemo was going to turn that fate around."

There's no going back now, Rain thought inwardly. "So, it was a mercy killing then? Is that how you justify it to yourself? You decided to poison her instead of her slowly dying from chemo?"

"Yeah, I suppose you must feel like you saved Lily from a wretched death. How very thoughtful of you," Julia said, rolling her eyes and instigating Hannah further.

"What are you talking about?" Hannah shot back.

"I'm talking about that insurance policy. But that wasn't enough for you—you wanted the whole estate. Since Lily never had a chance to respond to the lawyer's letter, you tried to forge Dennis's signature! Didn't you? I bet if I compare Dennis's handwriting on the estate paperwork to the handwriting stamped inside his first edition of *Sparkling Cyanide*, they'll be a match! The handwriting was oddly familiar to the Post-it Note you left on the library door too, along with the notes left inside, and I've been trying to place it, and now I have." Rain finally declared. "A dead man can't leave notes behind—but you can. You've been practicing Dennis's handwriting, haven't you? So, you could sign over the legal documents in your favor."

"You're out of your mind! I never had to forge anything. The insurance policy was already signed over to me, and the will stated that his *entire* estate would go to me," Hannah said evenly. "I was to inherit everything from the very beginning. He only threatened to change it if he *found* Lily. But unfortunately, he died before the will was signed. I was only honoring his wishes and having the legal documents reflect *what he promised me.* I told the lawyer I had all the documents validated with two witness signatures and was ready to prove it."

"Oh, so with Lily out of the way it was pretty easy," Rain interrupted.

Hannah's expression grew cold as she continued with her rant, "Lily thought the paperwork was a hoax anyhow. She never even heard of Dennis!" she spewed. "Where did you find Dennis's book anyway? I've been looking for it everywhere!" Hannah scanned her tiny apartment in search of it, as if the first edition of *Sparkling Cyanide* would reappear at a moment's notice at her bidding.

Rain realized it wasn't Hannah who had mistakenly left the book behind; it had been someone innocent, offering them a clue. But it didn't change the obvious—Hannah had killed Lily. "Ah," she said, playing to Hannah's favor, "I stand corrected."

"So that's why you killed her," Julia stated. "You didn't want Lily to be found through the foster care system. You hoped the records on that would be sealed. And the money would go to you. And you were hoping Lily would think inheriting a Door County property was all a hoax or a way to get at her bank account numbers, and you could make it all go away. But then Naomi messed that up for you by telling Lily the property was legit. You needed to kill Lily before she had a chance to respond to that letter, so it would seem as if she'd never been found."

Hannah folded her arms tightly across her chest, tucking the paperwork beneath her armpit. "Really? Is that what you're going with? Naomi's already been arrested. So, no need to point fingers and poke the dragon at this point. I would say the police have this all under control. You two busybodies, who think you're smart enough to solve a whodunit, need to stick to your mystery novels and let it go. This is real life—it isn't fiction."

Lily's killer had officially hit Rain's hot button. "Yeah, you're right, Hannah, this isn't fiction, but you're wrong about something else—we *are* smart enough." She took a deep breath before making her accusation. "You planted the Laura Ingalls Wilder manuscript in Naomi's car the night you went to see Lily's house on Sycamore Street, didn't you? Naomi's realtor vanity plate led you to that opportunity," she said, putting the pieces together in her own mind, and then letting her conclusions roll off her tongue. "You were the one framing Naomi from the very beginning. When you found out the manuscript wasn't worth a hill of beans, and it wasn't in fact written by the famous author, you planned to return it to Lily's library. Because you found the manuscript at the lake cottage the night you killed her, didn't you? But you didn't want to leave the manuscript there. You thought you'd steal that too, until you found out it was worthless. And you had no way to return it because the police were all over the cottage, but Sycamore had been locked with a lockbox."

"Yeah!" Julia jumped in. "After all, you seem to be the handwriting expert at this point. It was easy for you to discover that the manuscripts were a fake. You're the one who left the Post-it Note trying to frame one of the book club members, and Naomi was your perfect alibi."

Hannah's eyes blazed, and she clenched one fist in a ball at her side while the other gripped the legal documents tightly. Rain though she might wind up and slug Julia in the mouth.

"Naomi didn't give you the opportunity to return the manuscripts back to Lily's library. She didn't leave you alone for a second in that house on Sycamore Street, did she? Because Naomi was on to you and your little scheme," Rain continued, in an attempt to take the heat off Julia. "She asked you to come and look at the house on Sycamore so she could confront you about how you knew Jimmy, because the investigation was coming together in her mind, and she wanted to verify whether she was right. It was then you decided to frame her instead."

"Prove it," Hannah said matter-of-factly.

"It's the oldest motive in the book—money and greed," Julia said, pointing a finger. "The proof is right there, in your own two hands."

Hannah looked at the stack of paperwork that she held in her hand and then frowned. Suddenly, it was like a light switch came on as a new sparkle shone in her eyes. "This is the only signed copy of the will, the one that leaves the entire estate to me. If it isn't *signed*, then they can't prove anything." she said in an unnerving tone, waving the paperwork in front of them. "For the first time ever, I'm glad Jimmy hasn't quit smoking yet," the corner of her lip curled upward. Hannah reached into her pocket and pulled out a Bic lighter, and lit the pages in her hand, which immediately erupted in flames.

"Highly unlikely that it's the only copy," Julia retorted. "I'm sure the attorney can print off another document in no time. Nice try, Hannah."

"True." Hannah smirked. "But it's the only copy with Dennis's forged signature on it, so you can't prove a thing," she said as she watched the pages burning in her hands, like some kind of pyromaniac.

"Doesn't matter. Your attorney is about to find out everything when the truth all comes out: that you were forging signatures on wills and that Lily was actually found. And I'm guessing those two witnesses who signed the will on your behalf are probably a forgery too." Rain said resoundingly. "You may as well just give up now."

"Not if I get to him first. Besides, he has just as much blood on his own hands. He was willing to do just about anything to make this all go through because I offered him a hefty bonus on the side. He'll never hear your side of the story." A wicked smile formed on Hannah's lips as she waved the burning pages in her hands, the embers dropping to the carpet, causing the fire to spread.

"What story? There is no story?" Julia spat. "Your attorney is going to find out that you killed Lily. And when he does, this little fit of panic and trying to cover your tracks will have been for nothing. If you could only hear how ridiculous you sound. Think about what you're doing. It's time to give it up, Hannah."

Rain checked the ceiling for a fire alarm, and then her eyes scanned the room in search of a fire extinguisher, but none could be found. She was surprised, however, that an alarm hadn't been installed, especially since Ester had previously lived in the down-stairs apartment. At this point, she couldn't understand why Alec wouldn't have installed one. She no longer had time to think about it, though, as, smoke began to curl toward the ceiling, like an eerie ghost.

"You're crazy!" Julia said, waving her hands in front of her face to avoid the plume of smoke that was quickly filling the room. "You'll never get away with this!"

"Hannah! Put the fire out before you burn the whole house down!" Rain screamed, as she lunged toward the nurse in an effort to squelch the flames.

Hannah turned on her heel away from them and headed in the direction of the sink, where it looked as if she might listen to Rain's plea and dump the burning pages beneath the faucet. Instead, the crazed woman tossed the legal documents to the floor, reached for the skillet of bacon grease that had been left on the electric stove, and dumped it onto the paperwork, causing it to instantly erupt in a blaze of uncontrollable fire.

Rain watched in horror as the grease fire traveled onto the plush carpet between them and along the bottom of the staircase. It quickly spewed flames traveling in all directions, like long sinister fingers, grasping at everything in its wake. The inferno then hit the cardboard box, filled with dried flower arrangements, and erupted into three-foot flames, blocking their exit up the stairs.

Chapter
Thirty-Seven

Because of the plush, shaggy carpet and the bacon grease, the room was immediately consumed with licking flames. The staircase had gone up like a tunnel ring of fire, and smoke saturated the room, leaving little air to breathe. Rain had seen on television how quickly fire could spread, but had never experienced it firsthand. The room had filled with smoke like a dark ominous cloud, so quickly it was astonishing. And it left little time to catch her bearings.

Julia was coughing and gasping for air.

Rain didn't know how they had become separated or how the flames had managed to come between them. Desperation sank in when she heard her friend croak, "Help me! Help me, please! I can't breathe!"

The licking orange flames and thick smoke were disorienting. Rain's arms thrashed around in search of her friend. "Julia! Julia!" she shrieked, and then she stumbled, tripping over a glider rocker and falling forward on one knee. She covered her mouth with the back of her arm, trying not to inhale the smoke, but to no avail. The fumes filled her nostrils and caused her to choke violently. Her eyes burned from the wretched smoke, and she blinked back

245

several times to attempt to see clearly, but it felt as if a cat had scratched and clawed her eyes out. The room grew eerily hot, as if she was entering hell itself.

"Good luck getting out of here!" Hannah hollered, "Maybe this will teach you to mind your own business next time!" And then Rain heard what she thought was a door slamming like a coffin.

Hannah's comment made the hairs stand up on Rain's neck and her stomach tighten. But she was interrupted by the sound of Marge's voice booming from the direction of the staircase. "Rain! Julia!"

"Marge, get Alec out of the house! *NOW!*" Rain screamed.

"Go out through the basement! It's too dangerous this way!" Marge cried, and then Rain heard a door slam.

The only exit that Rain was aware of was the stairs, which were now fully engulfed. And the utility door where Hannah had entered. She cast about frantically, looking for an escape, only to witness flames licking and swaying like hungry dragons.

If she and Julia didn't get to the utility door fast enough, she feared appliances with natural gas, such as a furnace or hot-water heater, would likely explode. She needed to get them out of there, or there would be zero chance of survival.

"Julia!" Rain hollered desperately. "Julia!"

"Over here!" Rain heard faintly, and turned in the direction of the voice.

Max, help me! Help me find Julia! Rain pleaded inwardly. *Be my guardian angel, Max, please!*

Max! I need you!

The smoke and fire were throwing Rain into a state of mental uncertainty. She flung her hands out wildly and caught the tip of Julia's fingers and then wove their hands tightly together. Little relief came over her, however, as she fought to think of a way out.

246

Her heart raced wildly as she struggled to think of an answer. Time. She was losing time.

Rain grabbed Julia by the wrist and dragged her in the direction where she'd thought she heard the door slam. Her hands scraped along the wall frantically until she found a doorknob, which was hot to the touch. She shook her hand from the burn and pushed forward, attempting to turn the knob again.

It was locked.

Rain screamed, *"Nooo!"* and banged on the door with both fists.

"She . . . locked us in here?" Julia sputtered as she coughed and choked while plumes of smoke, as thick as pea soup, made it almost impossible for them to see each other, despite them standing side by side.

"Your allergies!" Rain screamed, "Get on the floor, Julia, where the air is a little better!" With one strong arm she shoved her friend to the floor. Julia fell with a thud, and Rain heard her gasp and gulp for air.

Rain was frantic.

The small window was too small for either of them to crawl out of, and at this point, it was surrounded by flames anyway. She didn't know how she would get them out of there. Rain snatched the cell phone from her pocket and punched in 911. She was surprised to find she had one bar of service, considering where they were located, in the lower interior of the basement. Before she had a chance to tell the operator their predicament, the phone went dead.

"Ahh!" Rain screamed. But something else scared her more. Julia was no longer gasping for air or making sounds. She dropped to the floor and noticed her best friend was lying unmoving, her eyes closed.

"Julia!" she cried. "Julia! Wake up!" Rain shook her friend violently in a panic, and surprisingly, her friend came to momentarily as she wheezed for air. Rain held her in her arms. "Stay with me! Do you hear me! Stay with me, Julia!"

The next thing Rain saw was a pair of familiar work boots, moving quickly in their direction.

* * *

Rain tried to speak, but her mouth was as dry as the Sahara Desert. She moved her tongue around her mouth in search of enough moisture to inquire about Julia, but failed. Jace's solid arms firmly pulled her body, and she willed her legs to work as she stumbled outside into the sunshine. The sun was so bright, in fact, that Rain had to blink back several times to catch her bearings. It was like waking from a morbid sleep into heavenly light. Her eyes searched for Julia but came up empty. All she could blink into view were emergency vehicles off in the distance.

As soon as she was out on the lawn, far enough away from the burning bungalow, Jace tipped her head backward and filled her mouth with water. She spit most of it out on the ground. And then looked to him for more. "Julia!" she wheezed finally. Rain tried to swallow, tried to get the moisture in her mouth to work, and willed herself to speak.

"She's okay," Jace soothed as he smoothed her hair away from her eyes. "You're both okay."

Rain collapsed to the ground. Tears came then, heavy and strong. She curled her body in the fetal position and wept like the day she'd lost Max. Her body shook from the weight of it. The thought of losing her best friend had been almost too much to bear.

Jace fell to his knees and gathered her in his arms.

Rain crumpled into him and allowed his strength to be hers.

"I almost lost her! I can't live without Julia!" Rain wailed into him as they rocked back and forth.

"It's okay—*she's* okay. You're okay. Everything is going to be okay. I promise." Jace then held her steady until she heard her name being called out.

"Rainy!"

Rain looked to see Julia rushing in their direction. She stumbled to her friend, her arms open wide.

Julia ran to her and tackled her like she was a member of the Green Bay Packers.

"Oh, Julia! Oh, my sister," Rain cried, her wet tears sticking to the pink streaks of her friend's hair. "I thought I was going to lose you!"

"It's okay, we're okay," Julia soothed, just like her brother had moments before. "I told you before, and I'll say it again. You're never gonna lose me, Rain."

It was then it hit Rain like a moving train, "Marge!"

"She's in the ambulance getting checked over. She rushed to wheel Alec out of the house and threw her back out again. But she's going to be fine. I promise."

"And Hannah?"

Julia pointed to a police cruiser off in the distance. "She's in the back seat." Julia managed a weak smile.

Chapter
Thirty-Eight

Rain watched as Jace stood in front of a myriad of ingredients scattered across her kitchen island. His plan was to instruct her on how to make a Wisconsin brandy old-fashioned before the book clubbers' arrival, after which he would remain as bartender for the entire evening. After all, they were celebrating. The case of Lily Redlin's killer was officially closed. The mystery solved. And the perpetrator would be brought to justice.

"Do you want it sweet or on the sour side?" Jace asked, reaching for a glass. "You can go either way. If you want it sweet, you use 7-Up or Sprite. But if you want it on the sour side, you use Squirt or a grapefruit-based soda as your wash. It's really a personal preference. Which one would you like to try?"

Rain hemmed and hawed before saying, "I think I'll take it on the sweet side."

"Are you sure? Because I'm quite sure you're sweet enough," Jace razzed with a wink and a nudge.

"Touché."

"Alrighty then." Jace clapped his hands and rubbed them together enthusiastically before getting started. "First, you need to add the sugar cube and bitters before you muddle the fruit. You have to be careful not to muddle the rind, though, as it can get bitter," Jace warned as he took a muddler and smashed the orange slice and cherry expertly into the bottom of the glass. He then added the bitters and brandy before splashing it with Sprite and mixing it all together with a spoon.

"Do you leave all that fruit at the bottom?" Rain asked, looking into the glass. "Or do you take it out before you drink it?"

"It just stays down at the bottom of the glass, and you toss it when you're finished with your cocktail."

"Ah," Rain said as she watched him make another.

"I'll make a sour one so you can taste the difference and see which one you like better," he offered.

Rain leaned on her fist and watched as he worked. "Sounds good to me."

"Are you interested in a little history lesson, since you seem to be the only one born in the state of Wisconsin who has yet to try a brandy old-fashioned?" he cajoled. "Might you be interested in learning the history behind the cocktail?"

"Sure," Rain said with a smile, giving him her full attention. "I love history."

"In 1893, at the Chicago World's Fair, a company named Korbel—" He lowered his voice and said out the side of his mouth, "I'm pretty sure you're familiar with the name Korbel, and we'll get to that. Anyhow," he continued, "Korbel decided to introduce brandy instead of a whiskey, which up until that time, was typically the spirit used to make an old-fashioned. Many Wisconsinites who, as you know, originated from Germany, were already familiar with brandy and loved that it was being used for a new cocktail at the State Fair. Once they tried the combination, they were hooked and took the drink north, home with them. Did you know? To this day, Korbel sells more brandy in Wisconsin than anywhere else," Jace said, as if it was Wisconsin's only claim to fame, which clearly it was not.

Rain lifted a hand of defense. "Hang on a second. The brandy old-fashioned isn't all that our great state has to offer. What about the Green Bay Packers? The varieties of amazing cheese? The Northwoods lakes? The teal waters of Lake Michigan? The amazing, wooded trails, *and* the mouthwatering supper clubs?" Rain argued, "I could go on and on about our great state. The brandy old-fashioned is just *one* of many amazing contributions we can claim in Wisconsin."

"Yes," Jace defended, "which is why the brandy old-fashioned, has become the supper club cocktail of choice." He volleyed with a smile as he wiped his hands on a nearby dishrag.

"Well, aren't you just a wealth of knowledge!" Rain laughed, leaning on his shoulder, and taking in the scent of him. He smelled of aftershave and dryer sheets. And she couldn't get enough of him.

"I studied up on the history of it, from one of your library books," he said with a bashful grin. "I wanted you to see that I'm interested in stuff and that I'm not uncultured. I'm not just a pretty face, you know."

"Since we're on the subject—" Rain started, but then stopped herself short.

"Yes, continue . . ." He rolled his hand for her to do just that. "You think I have a pretty face?" he prompted, with a hip check.

"No, not that. We both know you're ruggedly handsome," Rain said honestly. "Of being interested in stuff. I heard you weren't much of a reader. True?" She studied him.

Jace's face reddened. "Who told you that?"

"Guess."

"She *didn't*." Jace narrowed his eyes. "Hey, come on now. I have a library card, and I've even checked out books. You've witnessed it!" he defended.

"Yes, but have you *read* them?" she asked playfully.

"Well . . . I read this one!" he said as he handed her a Brandy old-fashioned and took one in his own hand. "Cheers," he said, taking a sip and then intently watching for her reaction.

"It's good," Rain said, licking her lips. "You're right, though; it is pretty sweet." She puckered her face in jest.

"I warned you that you were sweet enough." He smiled and then pulled her in. "Here—try mine." They switched drinks before being interrupted by his sister opening the screen door.

"Hey, now! Drinking without me?" Julia asked accusingly when she met them at the kitchen island. "Where's mine?"

"Don't worry, he's making a Brandy old-fashioned for everyone tonight. The entire book club is coming, and I've convinced him to stay on as our bartender. Isn't that right?" Rain looked up at Jace, and he responded by taking another sip of his cocktail and grinning.

"So, I'll say it again, then. Where's mine at?" Julia whined.

"You're not getting one." Jace tapped his sister on the hand when she attempted to reach for a glass. "Nope, not after you outed me."

"Huh?" Julia asked. "'Bout what exactly?"

"About reading," Jace said flatly. He then bopped his sister on the nose.

"Oh, whatever." Julia chuckled. "Hey, Rain, I have a surprise for you outside," she said, changing the subject and ignoring her brother's accusatory glance.

Rain clutched her hands to her heart. "A surprise—for me? What is it?"

"You have to come outside and see for yourself."

"You can't bring it in here?"

"Nope, too big. Nick is carrying it over, and if we hurry, we might have time before the others arrive."

Rain looked to Jace, confused to see if he was aware of Julia's surprise, and he replied with a shrug. Then her eyes narrowed on her friend. "Carrying it over? Sounds mysterious."

Julia nudged. "Come on then. Bring your glass, if you must."

"I'll wait for the others to have my old-fashioned." Rain abandoned the drink on the island. She touched Jace gently on the arm before walking away. "Thanks again for making one for me, Jace. I really do appreciate the lesson."

"She doesn't like it, does she?" Jace asked, following them outside.

"Don't take it personal, bro. Rainy doesn't drink much," Julia said over her shoulder.

"She's right." Rain shrugged. "It's just not my thing. But I will have one tonight since we're celebrating. I promise."

"One more thing to love about you," Jace said behind her, and then when she turned to acknowledge his comment, Jace instantly blushed and retreated into the house.

"What was that about?" Rain asked. "He's not joining us for the big surprise?"

"He's afraid he'll scare you off by using the 'L' word." Julia grinned, tossing her arm around Rain's shoulder. "Stick with me, kid—you'll get to know my brother real fast."

Rain couldn't help but smile. "Aww," she said. But she'd already felt the love in her heart.

Julia held a finger to her lips, as if they were in cahoots. "Shh, that's our little secret."

Rain chuckled. "You know, your secrets are always safe with me. We will be besties for life," she held up her pinky for her friend to link in a pinky swear.

Julia then took Rain's hand and led her to the bottom of the deck staircase, where she said, "Close your eyes."

Rain did her bidding, and Julia guided her to where the two finally stopped short.

"Okay, you can open your eyes now."

Rain looked down to see two shiny new kayaks at her feet: one, lime green; and the other, a pretty shade of teal. "What's this?" she exclaimed.

"Remember how Lily said she wanted to move to her cottage on Pine Lake and enjoy coffee on the deck and then a kayak ride?" Julia asked, reaching for the lifejackets stacked on the teal kayak, and handing one to Rain.

"Yeah?"

"Well, seems to me we have the coffee thing down pat." Julia chuckled. "I thought we'd take up kayaking in Lily's memory. Whaddya think?" Julia snapped on her lifejacket and smiled.

"If we've learned anything, my friend, it's that life is short." Rain said, her tone thick with melancholy.

"True, dat." Julia nodded. "Up to you, Rain! What do you think? How do you feel about a kayak ride before dusk?"

"Julia, I think you're amazing, and I don't know what I'd do without you." Rain hugged her friend tight.

"Hey, come on. If we hurry, I think we can squeeze in a quick ride before the others get here. What do you say?" Julia asked eagerly. "Green or teal? Which one do you want to call yours?"

"I say you choose. Get in one, and I'll give you a push-off," Rain suggested, and Julia did just that.

Rain slipped off her flip-flops, stepped into the cool water, and climbed into her shiny new kayak. The friends shared a huge grin before they paddled away from shore and looked upward, where Rain was pretty sure Max had splattered the sky with hues of pink, purple, and orange. A picture-perfect painting and the ideal backdrop for their first ride on Pine Lake.

Chapter
Thirty-Nine

There were eight book club members from the Lakeside Library gathered around the table: Rain, Julia, Marge, Shelby, Ruth, Chelsea, Kim, and Naomi, settled in their original seats. Of course, Benzo and Rex were not far from the table either. Both were sprawled next to their respective owners and had received an acknowledging stroke to their fur as the evening wore on.

Dusk was upon them, Pine Lake officially too dark to view, but the sound of lapping waves to shore serenaded the group. Patio lights glowed below twinkling stars in the night sky. The moon shined a golden path across the water, adding another priceless addition to the ambience of their meeting.

"Thank you all for coming tonight. I know we've gathered much later than normal, but we decided it best to have our discussion at night, after the humidity dropped." Rain said.

As if on cue, a fresh breeze sent a wave of soothing air off the lake and across the deck.

Rain lifted her brandy old-fashioned. "Cheers, my fellow book clubbers!"

The others followed suit and lifted their glasses.

"To Lily!" Julia said.

"To Lily!" they all said in unison before taking a sip.

"Does this mean we're always going to meet later? I need my beauty sleep," Ruth bellowed, pushing the cocktail aside and reaching for the water bottle in front of her. And despite the cool breeze, she waved a hand to fan her face from an apparent hot flash.

"Oh, it works better for me to come after the twins are in bed," Kim said. "I'm totally up for changing the meeting time. Especially when drinks are involved." She grinned, taking a sip. And then when she noticed everyone's rolled-eyes reaction to her comment, she slumped sheepishly back in her seat.

Marge's eyes twinkled along with the overhead lights above. "Well, I hope you all have room in your bellies too. After we finish our cocktail, I brought a special treat to share. My famous caramel apple pie. Everyone who has ever tried it says it's the best they ever had," she said proudly.

"*Finally!* I get to try a piece of that pie!" Julia laughed. "It feels like I've been waiting forever for it."

"Where are you hiding it?" Rain asked, turning to Marge.

"It's in your oven now, and Jace is keeping track of the timer for me," Marge replied. "He said he'd handle spreading the caramel and plate it up for us as soon as it's ready."

"What a guy!" Rain beamed.

Marge's brows rippled in response, and she winked. "Indeed."

"This is way better than the last reenactment. Cocktails, pie, books by the lake—I'm feeling completely spoiled. Now that we know Lily can rest in peace, we can all get back to reading. I think that's what she would want," Shelby said, setting down her brandy. "By the way"—she lowered her voice to a whisper and leaned into the table—"don't tell my husband, Dirk, I said this, but our bartender-slash–pie deliverer tonight is a real hottie!"

Rain smiled inwardly.

Julia laughed aloud, catching Rain's attention. Then she covered her mouth to prevent herself from spitting out her drink. "Yes, but lest we forget, my brother's a cop. Anything you say to him can be used against you in a court of law," she teased, and then lifted up her glass.

"Speaking of that," Naomi said, turning to Julia, "I can't thank you and Rain enough for coming to my rescue. I knew you would solve Lily's murder . . . that's why I left you the clue. You were my only lifeline!"

"Naomi, you were the one who left Dennis's first-edition *Sparkling Cyanide* in the library for us to find," Rain confirmed. "Had you not done that, we never would've looked at Hannah as a suspect. Right, Julia?"

"It's true," Julia confirmed with a raise of her glass.

"Where'd you get her copy of the book anyway? I don't think you ever told us," Chelsea asked, turning to Naomi.

"After the reenactment book club meeting, I thought I'd pay a visit to the Door County property, to see if the estate could prove to be a potential motive for Lily's murder," Naomi explained, clicking her polished nails against her brandy glass. "I needed to know, and I thought maybe I could help."

Julia leaned into Marge and said out the side of her mouth, "See, we're not the only amateur sleuths around this table."

The group overheard Julia's comment, and laughter bubbled up around the table.

"That's not all that happened, though, is it? Can you clarify? You found the first-edition Agatha Christie book on your visit to Door County . . . then what?" Chelsea asked, with a roll of her hand, to prompt Naomi to continue.

"Yes. And I also saw a photo of the homeowner of the estate in this case—Dennis—sitting next to Hannah. At first, I couldn't place her. When I realized where I had seen her before, and that she had sat in Kim's chair the night of the reenactment . . ." Naomi pointed to Kim, and the mother of twins responded by raising her glass.

"Anyway," Naomi continued, "I got uncomfortable when I realized Hannah had acted like she and Lily had never met . . . and here she is in a photograph with the man whose estate Lily was set to inherit?" Her eyes widened. "Well, let's just say . . . it made me very nervous. So, I took the book and kept it in my purse, hoping I could share my findings with the police."

"Why did you leave it at the library that night? When you asked Rain and I who was about to be arrested?" Julia interrupted. "Why didn't you just give it to the police and explain?"

"I didn't think anyone would believe that I had nothing to do with Lily's murder. I knew the police had the Laura Ingalls Wilder manuscript in their evidence pile. And I knew it was only a matter of time before they came for me. They asked to search my car, and knowing I was innocent, I never thought anything of it. Never in a million years did I think they'd find something to hold against me," she defended.

"I think that's what surprised me the most too. That you didn't trust me or Julia to have your back. And you didn't share what you knew with us. I understand why you would want to hide the original Agatha Christie book from the police—I do. But why us?" Rain reached out a hand to show she wasn't asking out of malice, but mere curiosity.

"I thought I needed more time to solidify my findings. So I asked Hannah to come to Sycamore Street to show her the house, hoping I could get her to slip up, so I could get a tape recording of it. admitting that she knew Dennis, but the whole thing back-fired." Naomi sighed.

"You thought you needed more leverage?" Marge asked.

"Exactly." Naomi nodded.

"What then?" Kim asked, setting her glass down and leaning forward intently.

"Before I knew it, Hannah had framed me. It became like a snowball effect. I didn't want to make it a 'he said–she said,' thing," Naomi said, throwing her polished fingers up in air quotes.

"Or in this case, a 'she said–she said' case," Julia's grin widened .

"Right!" Naomi mirrored Julia's smile, showing her perfectly white teeth.

"Wow," Ruth said loudly. "That's a lot to take in, but I bet I'm not the only one with lingering questions. Am I?" She looked around the table, seeking corroboration.

Julia turned her attention to the woman seated beside her, "I have one for you, Marge: Any word from Alec after losing his house to the fire? I hope he's doing okay."

All eyes turned to Marge, waiting.

"Yes, he's on his way to Arkansas. His sister is taking him in until he's fully recovered, and then he'll return to Lofty Pines to rebuild his house. He's not quite ready to trust another nurse, especially a live-in one," Marge said quietly.

"I can imagine that shook him up quite a bit," Rain murmured.

Shelby turned to Julia. "Do you think your brother would step away from his bar duties, and fill in the blanks? Like Ruth said, we still have a few lingering mystery questions." She turned to Ruth then to confirm, and the older woman agreed eagerly with a vigorous nod of her head.

"I don't see why not," Julia replied, waving Jace over from across the deck to join them at the table.

As soon as Jace arrived, he stood by Rain's shoulder and asked, "Ready for round two, ladies?"

The group erupted in giggles before Kim handed him her glass and said, "I'll take another if you're making more."

"Anyone else?" Jace turned on his heel to retrieve Kim's glass for a refill before Rain stopped him with a light touch to his arm.

"The members of the book club would like to ask you a few questions before you mix up any more cocktails. Are you okay to step into the hot seat?" Rain asked.

"By hot seat, do you mean you want me to join the book club? I'm not much of a reader," he admitted finally. "Though I do have an interest in history." He then explained proudly with the group, the origin of the Wisconsin old-fashioned, once again. When he had finished, Julia interrupted with a dismissive wave of her hand.

"Don't worry, bro—we're not asking you to join our book club. I think there are a few lingering questions about Lily's death that some of us would like answers about." Julia cleared her throat. "If you don't mind."

Nods of agreement went around the table.

Jace placed his hands on his hips and asked, "Like what?"

"Like Candace's Ring camera!" Kim said. "She mentioned that she saw *two* people in Lily's driveway that night. But she couldn't prove it 'cause her internet went down."

"Anything that happens on a Ring device is saved to the cloud. Technology allowed us to collect enough evidence *before* the internet was interrupted, to show Hannah's car in Lily's driveway the night in question," Jace confirmed.

"Ahh!" Rain said approvingly.

"We also had a tire cast made from the mud prints found on the side of the driveway. We were able to match one of them to Hannah's vehicle too."

"And you made a match to mine?" Naomi said, turning her attention to the officer. "Because, yes, I was there that night. Lily asked me to stop by to look at the estate letter she had received in the mail from Dennis, to see if I thought it was legit. I'm no lawyer or anything, but she couldn't wait to have an answer on the property. Either way, I'm glad I'm no longer a suspect." She said this in a light tone, but Rain could feel the undercurrent of Naomi's frustration. And could hardly blame her after she had been wrongfully accused.

"Had Hannah ever met Lily before the night she was killed?" Ruth asked.

"We don't think so," Rain said. "But why wouldn't Lily open the door to someone dressed in hospital scrubs, who probably introduced herself as Dennis's nurse. The nurse of the man whose estate she was due to inherit. Hannah probably seemed safe to her."

Nods of agreement again circulated around the table.

Marge turned their attention back to Jace. "So, you have enough evidence against Hannah, right, Jace?"

"Yeah, we have more than enough for a conviction. We tested the DNA on the wineglasses, and we can put Hannah directly at the scene of the crime. Not to mention the neighbor's corroboration that another car had been in the driveway, along with the cast of the tire treads, as we discussed. We have the motive, from the attorney's office. I'd say it's a tight case, thanks to you all," he said, and then sent a look of approval to Rain.

"When did Hannah decide to use Visine to poison Lily? She wasn't in attendance for the first book club meeting, so how did she know about our conversation? Did you ever learn if maybe she watched that episode of *Dateline* too?" Rain asked.

"Yeah! Good question," Shelby nodded.

"Lily told her," Jace said. Met with shocked expressions, he continued, "When Hannah went to meet with her that night, to see what she knew about Dennis's estate, they discussed the book club. It was then she decided she needed to act fast. Hannah could easily point the finger and frame one of you to create the perfect alibi. She used what was left of the Visine in her purse, and the rest she collected from Lily's bathroom vanity and spiked her glass of wine."

Words of surprise and "Poor Lily" reverberated around the table.

"Anyone find out any information on the forgery of the Laura Ingalls Wilder manuscripts? Did anybody learn more?" Chelsea asked. "I'm still wondering about that."

Ruth held up a hand and spoke in her usual bellowing voice: "Naomi asked me to investigate it since I love to dig into the history of authors' lives. Anyhow, between Naomi's real estate searches and my digging into Lofty Pines history, we found a family who had been a second cousin to the author and had lived there during the depression. We believe they forged the manuscripts and left them inside the hidden room of Lily's Sycamore house so that their grandchildren might benefit after their death. They were in danger of losing the house during the Depression and were afraid the continued recession would never end."

"That's so interesting!" Chelsea said. "They're for sure a forgery?"

"Absolutely they are. I talked to Irene over at Waters Edge Library, and through the proper channels they were able to figure it out and confirm it." Marge said. "A handwriting expert verified it, right, Jace?"

He nodded his assent.

"Who knew handwriting would be the key to everything!" Rain exclaimed.

"What about Jimmy?" Shelby asked Jace tentatively. "Is he in trouble now too?"

"We're reopening the case from Patrick's accident. We don't think he had anything to do with Lily's death, though. From our understanding, Hannah was told that Jimmy's alcoholism was a direct result of the accident, and she took it upon herself to silence Lily. So, technically Hannah had two motives in this case: greed for the estate, and preventing Lily from bringing up anything against her boyfriend regarding the boat accident," Jace replied.

Julia turned to Shelby. "Have you talked to Jimmy?"

Shelby's eyes turned down to the table, and she shook her head sadly. "No, and I doubt I ever will. I don't want anything to do with him at this point. This whole thing . . . well, it's been awful. It seems our original friend group from back in the day has completely disintegrated."

"Hey, no one ever explained to us how Lily had the cassette tape in her possession in the first place," Julia pondered. "Or why anyone had a tape of those events that unfolded that night."

Shelby lifted a hand. "I think I can explain that one. Lily was on the newspaper committee in high school, and she brought that little tape recorder with her everywhere. She was collecting stories that summer and was planning to do an article, during fall kick-off, on how everyone spent the summer in Lofty Pines. My guess is that she was reminiscing and going through old tapes recently and came across it when she was preparing the big purge before her move."

"That makes sense." Rain said.

A lull came over the group before Jace's cell phone erupted in his pocket. "Excuse me, ladies—I need to take this," he said, walking away from the table. Benzo left Rain's feet and immediately followed.

"It's weird, isn't it, how life imitates art?" Chelsea stated matter-of-factly. "Turns out Lily's death was just like the Agatha Christie book that we read in book club. In *Sparkling Cyanide*, the person who *didn't* sit around the table when Rosemary died turns out to be her killer. Which is exactly the case for Lily Redlin. The person who missed our first book club meeting did the deed. And the motive was the same: greed."

"So, Rain . . . what are we reading next?" Marge asked.

Rain searched for Jace from across the deck. Their eyes met as he continued to talk on his cell phone while stroking Benzo's head.

"Romance," she said with a smile.

Recipes

Authentic Wisconsin Old-Fashioned Cocktail

Found in supper clubs across the great state of Wisconsin

Note: This cocktail can be made with either whiskey or brandy.

Also, it can be made "sweet" (with 7-Up or Sprite) or "sour" (with Squirt soda or a grapefruit-based soda)—thus, the sweet and sour variations, to taste.

The brandy old-fashioned, aka the Wisconsin old-fashioned, is practically the state's official alcoholic beverage, found in supper clubs and bars across my great state. In addition to brandy, or whiskey, the *old-fashioned*, calls for muddled fruit and a topper of lemon-lime soda.

Ingredients
3 dashes Angostura bitters
2 orange slices
2 brandied or maraschino cherries
1 sugar cube
2 ounces brandy

7-Up, Sprite (for sweet), or Squirt and club soda, chilled (for sour), to top

Garnish: brandied or maraschino cherry and orange slice

Instructions

Add the bitters, 2 orange slices, 2 cherries, and sugar cube to an old-fashioned glass, and muddle to combine.

Add ice to fill the glass, then add the brandy.

Top with the 7-Up, Sprite, or club soda, and stir to chill.

Garnish with a skewered cherry and an orange slice.

Leave the fruit in the bottom of the glass, and toss when finished.

Cheers! 😊 And be sure to share with all your book club friends. Ps. Author Holly Danvers has not yet sampled this cocktail but plans to . . . on the release day of this book!

Marge's Salted Caramel Apple Pie

The Crust

Using both butter and shortening, allows for a perfect flaky crust

Ingredients

2½ cups all-purpose flour

1 tsp salt

6 T unsalted butter, chilled and cubed

⅔ cup shortening, chilled

½ cup ice water

Instructions

Mix the flour and salt together in a large bowl. Add the butter and shortening.

Using a pastry cutter or two forks, cut the butter and shortening into the mixture until it resembles coarse meal (pea-sized bits with a few larger bits of fat is okay). A pastry cutter makes this step very easy and quick.

Measure ½ cup of water. Add ice and stir. From that, measure ½ cup since the ice has melted a bit. Drizzle the cold water in, 1 tablespoon at a time, and stir with a rubber spatula or wooden spoon after every tablespoon added. Stop adding water when the dough begins to form large clumps. Do not add any more water than you need.

Transfer the pie dough to a floured work surface. The dough should come together easily and should not feel overly sticky. Using floured hands, fold the dough into itself until the flour is fully incorporated into the fats. Form it into a ball. Cut dough in half. Flatten each half into 1-inch-thick discs, using your hands.

Wrap each tightly in plastic wrap. Refrigerate for at least 2 hours and up to 5 days.

When rolling out the chilled pie dough discs, always use gentle force with your rolling pin. Start from the center of the disc and work your way out in all directions, turning the dough with your hands as you go. Visible specks of butter and fat in the dough are perfectly normal and expected!

Proceed with the pie recipe below.

The Homemade Caramel Sauce

Ingredients

1 c granulated pure cane sugar

6 T salted butter, room temperature, cut up into 6 pieces

½ c heavy cream, room temperature

1 tsp salt

Instructions

Heat granulated sugar in a medium, heavy-duty saucepan over medium heat, stirring constantly with a rubber spatula or wooden spoon. Sugar will form clumps and eventually melt into a thick, amber-colored liquid as you continue to stir. Continue to stir, being mindful not to allow it to burn.

Once sugar is completely melted, immediately stir in the butter until it, too, is melted and combined. Be careful in this step because the caramel will bubble rapidly when the butter is added. If you notice the butter separating or if the sugar clumps up, remove from heat and vigorously whisk to combine again. If you're nervous about splatter, wear kitchen gloves. Keep whisking until it comes back together, even if it takes 3–4 minutes. Return to heat when it's combined again.

After the butter has melted and been combined with the caramelized sugar, stir constantly as you very slowly pour in the heavy cream. Since the heavy cream is colder than the hot caramel, the mixture will rapidly bubble. After all the heavy cream has been added, stop stirring and allow to boil for 1 minute. It will rise in the pan as it boils.

Remove from heat, and stir in the salt. Allow to slightly cool down before using. Caramel thickens as it cools.

Cover tightly and store for up to 1 month in the refrigerator. Caramel solidifies in the refrigerator. Reheat in the microwave or on the stove to desired consistency.

The Apple Pie Assembled

Ingredients

Homemade pie crust

Homemade salted caramel

6–7 large apples, cored, peeled, and sliced into ¼-inch slices (11–12 cups total)

½ c granulated white sugar

2 T lemon juice

¼ cup all-purpose flour

¼ teaspoon ground cloves

¼ teaspoon ground nutmeg

1½ tsp ground cinnamon

Egg wash: 1 large egg beaten with 1 T milk

Optional: coarse sugar for sprinkling on crust

Instructions

Preheat oven to 400ºF.

Make the apple filling while the dough is still chilling in the refrigerator: Place apple slices into a large bowl. Add sugar, lemon juice, flour, cloves, nutmeg, and cinnamon. Gently toss to combine. Set aside.

Roll out the chilled pie dough: On a floured work surface, roll out one of the discs of chilled dough (keep the other one in the refrigerator). Turn the dough about a quarter turn after every few rolls until you have a circle 12 inches in diameter. Carefully place the dough into a 9 × 2–inch pie dish. Tuck it in with your fingers, making sure it is smooth. With a small, sharp knife, trim the extra overhang of crust and discard.

Fill the pie crust with the apples. Pile them tightly and very high. Drizzle with ½ cup of the salted caramel, reserving the rest for topping.

Make the lattice crust: Remove the other disc of chilled pie dough from the refrigerator. Roll the dough out, 12 inches diameter. Using a pastry wheel, sharp knife, or pizza cutter, cut 16 strips ½ inch wide. Carefully weave the strips over and under one another, pulling back strips as necessary. Using a small, sharp knife, trim the extra overhang. Crimp the edges of the dough with a fork or your fingers.

Lightly brush the lattice top with the egg wash. Sprinkle with coarse sugar.

Place the pie onto a large baking sheet, and bake for 20 minutes. Keeping the pie in the oven, turn the temperature down to 375°F, and bake for an additional 40–50 minutes. If the top of your pie is getting too brown, cover loosely with aluminum foil. The pie will be done when the caramel begins to bubble up. A small knife inserted inside should come out relatively clean.

Cool pie before serving. Drizzle the pie with the extra caramel sauce to serve. This apple pie is best served on the same day, but it can be covered tightly and stored in the refrigerator for up to 3 days.

Acknowledgments

My deepest gratitude to Faith, who pushed for this book to be written. And who so completely trusts me to follow my nose and allows me the gift of writing off the seat of my pants but is also willing to trudge through the weeds to expose a finished masterpiece. Thanks also to Sandy, who continues to cheer me on from the sidelines and encourages my growth as a writer. I'm so humbled to have these two extraordinary women in my corner. To all those at Crooked Lane Books who work behind the scenes: Rebecca, Madeline, Dulce, I'm eternally grateful. To the wonderful cover artist, Jesse Reisch, thanks for another beautiful cover for the Lakeside series! I feel blessed to have been given the opportunity to write and publish these mysteries for the cozy fans, who continue to be *the best reader fans out there*. And it's only because of the personal champions on my behalf— the bloggers who consistently shout out my work: Dru Ann Love, Lori Caswell, Meg Gustafson, Karen Stallman, Debra Jo Burnette, Lisa Kelley, Linda Langford, Ileana Munoz-Renfroe. And of course, the cozy groups: Save our Cozies, Cozy Mystery Village, Get Cozy with a Cozy Mystery, Cozy Mystery Lovers, Denise Swanson's Mysteries, Romances, and More. Thank YOU!!! A shout out to my author

Acknowledgments

friends *you know who you are* whom I depend on dearly when I need a break from the writing cave. And keep me sane in this roller-coaster business. Sending hugs your way!

All writers depend on the expertise of others to share the "unknowns" of their fields. Here are just a few of them that I owe utmost respect and gratitude:

Al Klimek, retired Brown County Medical Examiner, thank you for your firsthand expertise; any misinterpretation of the facts is clearly my own. Yes, I still owe you that beer!

Renetta, thanks for all things real estate and for finally landing us in our dream home. Although it's your fault the views do distract me from my work from time to time! Ha!

Julie Burkard, thanks for the first beta read while facing the shores of Green Bay. Thanks for helping me explore "the holes" and talking me off the fence. You know exactly what I'm referring to. Wink!

Thanks to my lake friends, who tirelessly cheer on from the sidelines—you know exactly who you are and yes, we'll celebrate over barbecue together. Cheers, to you!!

Mark, I don't know what else to say. *Thank you* seems so inadequate for the support you've kindly and consistently given. So, I say it again: you really are a gem! Without you, I would've tossed in the towel a long time ago and these books would've been nothing but a wish. Only because of you, I'm still writing . . . eleven books later.